RELIC

DEATH WAVE CHRONICLES BOOK 1

ANDRE JONES

ALIEN PRESS

ISBN: 978-0-6489105-6-5 (paperback)
ISBN: 978-0-6489105-7-2 (ebook)

A catalogue record for this
book is available from the
National Library of Australia

DEATH WAVE CHRONICLES

To save humanity, civilisation must be destroyed.

Nature is brutally harsh. She plays no favourites, and she rarely gives a second chance. Humanity had its opportunity …

Now it's her turn.

The Death Wave Chronicles is a blend of mythology, 'weird science', fringe science and pseudoscience. Throughout the storyline — moreso in some novels than others — I will touch on subjects such as Gaia myth, Earth chakras, the power of crystals, ley lines / earth energy grid, druidism, UFO's, aliens ... even Atlantis.

I hope you enjoy the read.

THE MESSAGE

"I bring a message on behalf of Earth. You may call it Mother Nature,
and you may call it Gaia — which is not entirely correct but will
suffice for now due to your lack of comprehension of the natural forces
which surround us all.

"The world has succumbed to a plague.
Mankind's ingenuity, believed to separate it from 'animals', enabled it
to inhabit every niche of land, thereby spreading infection across the
globe.

"Mankind has also developed a lust for wealth and power to the extent
that the pollution and desecration are now global, threatening the very
fabric of the world.
Just as a microbe cannot fathom the complex world in which it lives,
Mankind is also incapable of fathoming the complexity of the world.
Every living thing on the earth has a role and is connected — or was.
Mankind alone has lost its connections, believing itself separate from
everything else.

"A messenger will arrive — Mankind's one chance to survive.
Those who have lost their connection, who cannot bring themselves to

attune, to live in harmony with the earth and the forces around them, will perish.

"Resonating with all that is, she is Nature incarnate. It would be foolish to thwart her, for Gaia's wrath is never subtle, always fatal. Treat her well.
Mankind's continued existence relies on its ability to learn respect for the world.
Adapt or die."

Vitor Magalhães Xaschoal
Wai-wai shaman – 2046

PROLOGUE

"Why is it mosquitoes never bite you?" Ken looked to his daughter as he swatted away yet another unrelenting bloodsucker. Given the humidity, she was still only in her shorts and singlet, not that the weather ever caused her discomfort.

"My good genes and their poor taste, I guess." Rhyllien shrugged. "How much longer to Oriximiná?" Rhyll watched the darkening rainforest pass slowly. The boat, more a barge really, drifted with the sluggish current, requiring only the occasional polling to move it away from a potential grounding on the rocks, fallen trees or mud banks.

"It was going to be tomorrow, but with that old motor out of commission, add another day, maybe two." Ken sat his wiry frame beside her, dangling his feet in the water as well. The water was nice and cool, in contrast with the hot, clammy night air.

"Watch out for the piranhas." Rhyll pointed.

"Where?" Ken exclaimed, pulling his feet out immediately.

Rhyll burst out laughing. "They're close by but won't bother us."

"Picking on your old man now?" He grinned, repositioning himself.

She splashed water at him. "There's nothing old about you … except your jokes. How have you and Mum survived in jungles all your life falling for tricks like that?"

"Perhaps you're smarter than the both of us? Speaking of your mum, when we get to Oriximiná, remind me to radio back to camp to keep her updated. She'll worry about the delay otherwise."

"You want me to call? You know she'll give you an earful about the motor."

"I'll have you know, young lady"—her dad sat up, all dignified—"I am quite capable of handling verbal abuse from your mother."

"Yeah, especially when she's a hundred kilometres away, living with a tribe the rest of the world knows nothing about." Her teeth shone in the moonlight with her wide grin.

Ken nodded. "That does help," he conceded. "She's quite a formidable woman."

"I can't wait until we are all back on the *Aurora*," she said, and sighed.

"Yes, the *Aurora*'s a grand boat but no good for these waters. We were lucky to get this."

"Lucky?" Rhyll shook her head. "I believe we recently discussed your bargaining prowess?"

He patted the deck. "Well, yes. She has a few leaks … a small cabin to keep the rain off us."

"You call that a cabin?"

"Lean-to, then."

"And a dodgy motor—"

"Okay. All true, but given the situation with the university, we had no time to delay. They want these artefacts urgently."

"I hope it's worth it."

"I'm sure they're a game changer. If I'm right, it will set historians spinning. You won't find these in your studies."

"Wouldn't the Smithsonian have paid more for never-before-seen relics?" Rhyll asked.

"Undoubtedly. They do have deeper pockets, and these are

priceless to some collectors, but the relics belong here, to these people. Better for them to decide what they do with their heritage. It's not our decision to make. And it isn't about the money."

"You wouldn't be you if it was." Rhyll had always been proud of the ethics of her parents. It was how she was raised — caring for the indigenous populations, their cultures, and the environment. Regardless of what continent they were on.

They watched as their shadows, cast by the lantern hooked over the cabin rail behind them, undulated on the water's surface.

"That's *Aedes aegypti*." Rhyll pointed to the mosquito currently resting on her arm.

Her dad glanced over. "I'm still glad we got those booster shots. They can carry—"

"Yellow fever, dengue, chikungunya, and Zika virus. Wasted on me though, since they don't bite me … like the piranhas." She grinned.

"You've been keeping up with your studies, then."

"I wouldn't have it any other way, and I much rather this life than sitting in a stuffy classroom." She cringed. "Fancy getting an education out of books alone. Out here is the best place for me, and I love every part of it. Besides, I'm 'one with Nature', after all. The village shaman said so."

"He did take a keen interest in you. I think he was trying to marry you off to his son."

"Really?" Rhyll looked genuinely surprised.

"Oh yes." He nodded.

"Considering your skills with bartering, I'd be interested to hear what you said."

"Three goats and a working motor and she's yours."

"Dad!" she smacked his shoulder.

"Mind you, they did admire your red hair and green eyes. There's the blood of Celtic kings running through your veins you know."

"King Ellis? Doesn't sound very Celtic."

"Kenric Elisedd — an old Welsh name."

"Ah well, royal blood must make me worth ten goats at least!"

"It's plain to see I'm not too good at haggling." He chuckled. "Perhaps I'll leave the bartering to you and your mother."

Rhyll looked up. "Can you hear that?"

Ken turned his head slightly and waited. "No … What is it?"

"I thought I heard another motor."

"Sweetheart, apart from the twenty-year-old generator back at the dig, this bunged-up motor is the only mechanical device in a hundred kilometres."

"It sounded like it was coming from downstream." Rhyll remained silent for a few more minutes, listening for the elusive noise. Even with the full moon, upriver was still dark, especially in the shadows of the vast Amazon jungle.

Ken stood up, careful not to slip on the deck with his wet feet. "Time to find a place to moor, I guess. Can't be drifting all night now, otherwise we'll capsize in the rapids." He picked up the long pole and pushed towards the bank.

"It's shallow enough here," Rhyll said, once they brushed up against the reeds. "I'll do it. Otherwise, you'll be picking more of those *haementeria ghilianii* off all night." Rhyll pointed to the two leeches already attached to his calves. "Leeches never seem to be interested in my blood either."

"Bugger. They are relentless."

"That's nature for you. She never gives up and doesn't play favourites."

"Whose side are you on?" he asked, as he removed the leeches by sliding his fingernail along his skin to the mouth and pushing sideways.

"Let me think … Who was going to barter me for a few goats?"

"They were very fine goats."

She laughed as she slipped up to her hips into the dark waters. Feet sinking into the ankle-deep mud, manoeuvring the barge to shore was easy enough. Rhyll then waded up the side, grabbed the mooring line, and stepped through the maze of tall reeds to find something firm to tie it to. She stopped to take a closer look at the reeds in the bright moonlight. Touching them, feeling their texture ... the flow of energy. An introduced species, she decided. The effects of human habitation even extended this far.

A gunshot shocked her to stop momentarily. A motor burst into the silence of the night. Rhyll turned, but the river and barge were hidden by the mass of reeds. Pulling on the rope, she started moving back through the morass. The motor died down. Only the sound of a boat wallowing in its wake remained.

"Wasn't there another with him?" She heard a gruff male voice. The tall reeds swayed as the boat's wake swelled through them.

"That daughter. Maybe she's hiding in the cabin," a second, rougher voice said.

There were sounds of boots on wood. Two men? It would only take them a moment to search the cabin.

Terrified of what she'd see, Rhyll edged closer. She hadn't heard her father speak or call out since the gunshot. Through the growth, Rhyll saw the low bow of the barge a metre or so away. The other boat was unseen, obscured by the bulk of the cabin. Ducking lower in the water, she moved to the barge and slowly pulled herself along the side. Then she saw her father, his body half hanging over the side, his right arm dangling in the water, leaving a darker trail.

Tears welled up, but Rhyll stifled her cry. As she neared him, she saw blood running down his arm. It moved! She hoped he was only dazed or unconscious. As Rhyll edged closer, she realised it was simply the eddy of the water. Her father was dead.

She reached out to hold his hand one last time, but felt the cold, hard surface of his gun. Rhyll hated guns, as did her mum, but she understood that with the life they led, some sort of weapon became a necessity. Her dad insisted they learn how to use it, and every few months he would give them a refresher, along with some martial arts training whenever they could find an instructor. She released the gun from her father's grip, carefully, to avoid splashing.

An unseen arm reached out of the darkness, and Rhyll gasped at the intense pain as she was hauled out of the water by her wet locks and dragged onto the barge.

"Look what we have here," the man with the gruff voice said.

"Good," his partner replied. "We got what we come for." He held up the box containing the relics. "Let's go, John. Remember, no loose ends."

"Seems such a waste." The one called John leered at the wet singlet clinging to her body.

"Sure is. No arguments from me. But our orders are 'no witnesses'. You going to do her or you want me?"

Before he was able to respond, Rhyll raised her father's gun and pulled the trigger.

The grip on her hair stopped immediately, as John stared stupidly at the small hole in his chest.

Rhyll twisted and fired several rounds at the other man diving for his boat before John collapsed on top of her, pinning her down. By the time she struggled out from under his dead weight, the boat was speeding away. She dropped the gun and crawled the short distance to her father, rolling him out of the water and cradling his head. "Dad, Dad, Dad ...." Tears flowed freely as she wept, her whole body wracked with sobs. In her grief, she failed to notice the motor of the other boat had stopped. Pain exploded in her side, pitching her sideways and knocking the breath out of her.

As she lay there in agony, weak and barely able to move, she heard the boat approaching again. Feebly, she groped for the gun, every move torture. The deck was slick with the blood of her father, of John, and now her own. She felt the boat bump when it came alongside. Boots approached.

"Ah, shit. I think John's gone."

"Make sure the girl's dead, and let's get the hell out of here," a third voice said.

"Don't have to tell me twice."

Rhyll's heart pounded. *They are really going to kill me!* She heard the rifle click behind her head. She let out a gasp.

"Bugger it."

"What's the matter now?"

"Bloody empty."

"Shit, Harry. Reload and get it done!"

"Yeah, yeah." Harry fumbled at his belt for another round.

It was a struggle to turn, but she wanted to face the bastard who'd murdered her father. Overhead, a flash of lightning lit up some of his features: bearded, close-cropped hair, and a hook nose. The silhouette of the man stood there. He was sliding the round into the chamber when he noticed her staring at him.

"Sorry, darlin'. I've no choice." He cocked the weapon and pointed it directly at her.

A gun barrel looks immense when pointed at your head. "Everyone has a choice." Rhyll refused to close her eyes. Her body was getting numb. "Even morons like you." She felt the blood soaking into her shirt and sticking to her skin.

The shot didn't come. As if in slow motion, Harry dropped to his knees and slumped forward, forcing her to the floor with his bulk on top of her. The rifle went off, but the bullet ricocheted off the deck.

She struggled to get out from under Harry. That was when she saw the blow-dart protruding from his neck.

It was only the slickness of the blood that enabled her to finally pull her arms free. She then rolled Harry off her and pushed him over the side with her muddy feet. Wearily looking towards the idling boat drifting nearby, she noticed another figure collapsed over the wheel, not moving. Rhyll turned her attention to the dark shoreline and the reeds. Nothing. Not that she expected to see anyone if her saviours didn't want to be seen.

In her stupor, she crawled back to her father. With his murder, their perfect life was ruined. She turned to John's body. Did his hand twitch?

"You still alive, John?" she muttered. "One way to find out." Blinking through the tears and grief, Rhyll crawled over and pushed him to the water, eventually rolling him over the side with a splash. It felt like it took ages, and her breathing laboured, but it was done. She coughed. When she wiped her lips, she saw blood on her hands.

John drifted in the dark waters with Harry's body, pockets of air in their shirts keeping them both afloat. He suddenly sputtered, flopping over. The coughing went on for a full minute before he struggled to his feet in the shallow water.

Frantically, Rhyll reached for the rifle, aimed and fired. Nothing. *Damn it!* In his haste to kill her, she realised, Harry had fired the one and only round. And missed.

Weakly, John managed to get close enough to the barge and gripped the low edge with his one good hand.

There was no time to search for her dad's pistol in the dark. Rhyll crawled to the edge, awkwardly swinging the rifle at him like a club, nearly dropping it in the process.

John ducked, the butt glancing off his head. "That hurt, bitch," he said, holding his head where blood was trickling down from a gash. "I reckon I can wait it out." He was breathing heavily.

Rhyll knew the truth of it; her energy ebbed minute by minute; second by second. Only anger had kept her going until now. More lightning flashed. *That's funny,* she thought, *not a cloud in the sky.* A cool breeze caressed her face, in startling contrast to the humidity that had beset them for weeks.

You are one with nature. The village shaman's voice echoed in her head.

"Now my minds going," she mumbled. The blood seeped down her back and side.

… One with nature …

"Nothing ever bites you …" she heard her father's voice say.

She smiled at the memory and her dad's funny reaction. "Watch out for the piranhas," Rhyll muttered in reply.

… one with nature …

"Oh, I'm not worried about fish." John's voice broke her from her reverie.

"Not worried about piranhas?" Rhyll thought hard about them. "You should be," she forced the words out. She wished deeply. *Piranhas. Piranhas.* "They haven't feasted for a long time."

Collari ... you are one with nature ...

Her body started trembling. Going into shock, a part of her mind thought. Rhyll slumped to the side. Piranhas ... piranhas ... piranhas ...

She slowly fell sideways, unmoving beside her father's body, oblivious to the screaming coming from the frenzied water.

CHAPTER ONE

*V*AGUE *IMAGES OF MANY NATIVES, CAMPFIRES AND DRUMS SWIRLED around her head. Rhyll thought she recognised the old shaman, but it was hard to make any sense out of anything as she was led into the group. There were no women present, but a newborn baby was introduced to her. They took her hand, placed it on the babe's hand, and there was a tingling and a flash—*

Rhyll's dream was disrupted by violent shaking, and the images dispersed like mist in the wind. The sense of tranquillity was still there, but not as intense.

Her eyes flickered open. It was dark, dank, and cool. Not night but something else. She was on her back, lying on something hard. She sat up with a jolt, and dust and grit fell off her. She was naked, on some sort of large, circular formation.

Her hands weren't covered in blood. Where was the barge? Where was her father's body or that of the murderers?

Rhyll wiped the grit from her face. The area around her had a faint luminance, some areas lighter than others, but there was still a lot of darkness. The damp, musty smell reminded her of when she was caving with her parents. *Oh, Dad...*

So many questions tumbled through her head: *Dad's dead. But why did they kill him? And why did they bring me here? Who brought me here? Where is here? And why?*

More powerful shaking and thunder impinged on her consciousness, and a loud cracking made her realise she wasn't safe.

Gingerly edging to the side, she swung her legs over and slowly lowered herself, tentatively feeling for the floor. Rhyll stood, testing her weight and gaining her balance. Now that she was upright, some feeling came back to her legs.

In the dim glow, she made out shapes. Tall, straight columns surrounded her. They weren't stalagmites or stalactites, but those in the immediate area had a faint, subtle glimmer. Some were thicker than others, many were at weird angles, and a couple had fallen and broken. They weren't glowing as much now.

"Hello?" Her voice was soft and flat, lost in the vastness of the dark spaces. Looking down, she saw the ground was level and dusty, except for a few fragments of fallen column. As she took a tentative step, there was another muffled detonation. Through her bare feet, she felt the ground shake, but it was not as intense as before. Rhyll held onto the stone bench for support until it diminished.

Another crack was followed by a loud splintering noise, this time close behind her.

Instinctively, she ducked and hugged the side of the bench for cover as a column crashed onto the far end of the raised surface, showering the area with grit and razor-sharp shards. She felt stings along her forehead and cheek before the column rolled to the floor.

Blinking through the dust and glare, Rhyll waited for the air to clear. She touched her face, feeling the wetness of the blood that oozed from the cuts. She spied her backpack and boots on the floor nearby and grabbed them, relieved at finding something familiar.

Checking to see nothing else was going to fall on her, Rhyll stood and searched through the pack to find basic toiletries, her penknife, clothes and underwear, some notebooks, and her tablet and stylus. Absently dabbing at her cuts with a handkerchief, she placed the pack on the bench and examined the immediate area again.

Moving closer to one of the columns, she ran her fingers along its surface. Cool, hard, and very smooth, the columns were huge crystal formations, and as her hands ran lightly across this one, the glow intensified slightly. Stepping away, she noticed a glowing.

"That's so weird."

When her parents were granted permission, they took her on a visit to the giant crystal cave in Naica, Mexico. Those crystals were huge and spectacular but haphazard; many of these were even more impressive in size, and the area was less chaotic.

Taking a few steps around the area to get a better perspective, she realised the bench itself was formed from a crystal column that had been cut perfectly level, with a body-shaped depression in the centre. It was about two metres in diameter and one metre from the ground. Other than the scuffing where she'd slid off, there was a thick layer of dust and grit outlining where she had lain.

A line of crystals was spaced down the centre of the bed. At one end was a larger, multifaceted crystal bigger than her fist. Seven smaller ones were embedded within the depression contoured for her body. Each crystal was a different colour, and she recalled many cultures used them to heal the body and spirit. They came out easily. Each had eight sides, was roughly the size of a golf ball, and felt warm to the touch, glowing when she handled them.

Only marginally experienced with her mother's gemmology work, these crystals seemed very clear. The larger crystal looked off-kilter, rocking marginally when she touched it, but tentatively placing both hands on it and twisting a tiny bit was enough to set it correctly. There was a click, and she stepped back in surprise when the benchtop began to vibrate, pulsating with a purple iridescence.

A tingling sensation coursed through her body when she touched it. Looking down, the light source appeared to come from very deep within the crystal.

The glow of the pulsating crystal was reflected by hundreds of crystals in the surrounding walls.

"Where the hell am I?" she whispered in frustration and wonder. "What *is* this place?"

She sat on a fallen column and contemplated her situation. Other than elusive dreams, the last thing she recalled was ... *dying* — or she thought she had — on a barge next to her father's body after thieves shot them and stole the most valuable anthropological finds of the century.

"I was shot!" She felt no pulling of the scarred tissue, but there was evidence of an injury just below her ribcage where the skin puckered slightly.

Rhyll had no memories of this cavern — how long she had been here, how she arrived here, or even where 'here' was. If the amount of dust outlining where she lay was any indication, she had been here for a long time. Idly rubbing her thumb over one of the crystals, she found comfort in feeling its warm surface. Her thumb stopped when it felt a roughness. Looking closer at the green crystal, she found an indentation on one of the facets. It was shaped into something like a rune ... or a glyph similar to some Incan ones she'd seen.

Checking the other crystals revealed similar indentations, but each engraving was a different glyph. Turning back to the bench, it was evident each specific crystal fit snugly within its individual niche and not in any other.

She pulled out her tablet. Not surprisingly, it had a flat battery. Placing it back inside her pack, she made notes in her notebook, detailing which crystal fitted into which niche, drawing the bed and the body outline.

Rhyll was contemplating what to do next when the ground vibrated again — not as strong as before but more persistent.

Realising the possibility of another column falling any moment made finding a way out prudent.

She pulled out some clothes and wiped herself down with the shirt, gave it a quick shake, then dressed in her hiking clothes: khaki cargo pants, olive long-sleeve shirt, and her sturdy boots.

Popping the green crystal into one of her voluminous thigh pockets, then wrapping the remaining ones carefully in her underwear, she stowed them in her backpack. Rhyll took a long look at the cavern. It was one of the eeriest, yet most beautiful sights she had seen, and she wasn't sure if or when she'd be returning.

Distant sounds of machinery encroached on her thoughts. Machinery meant people. With a tinge of regret, Rhyll donned her pack and made her way cautiously towards the sound. Without knowing exactly how, she always sensed directions; this time she was travelling east. Carefully climbing over fallen columns that were at odd angles, she eventually worked her way to the end of the huge cavern and paused to regain her breath.

Part of her wanted to scream it was all impossible, yet the practical part told her she was here, so that was obviously not the case. Looking back, she noted the large crystal that had been her 'bed' was still pulsating with purple iridescence. The columns, which had glowed as she passed, now gradually faded as she put more distance between them. Those in front began their glow.

As Rhyll continued towards the sound, the walls began closing in, creating a narrow fissure. There was no telling how far it extended or even if it simply stopped after a few paces. The columns didn't extend this far, the surroundings now becoming rock. On a whim, she pulled the green crystal from her pocket. Apart from providing reassurance, the dim glow extended a couple of metres — sufficient to ensure she wouldn't step into a rift. Her progress slowed, and the path began angling up.

The noises she had been following stopped. She waited for it to recommence, but the silence continued. Only a distant drip reached her ears, which reminded her that she didn't know how long it had been since she'd had a drink of water. Or food …

She guessed it was twenty minutes of wriggling and climbing — she had no way to tell the time — before she felt the movement of warm air. Though not strong enough to be called a breeze, it was still a sure indicator that the surface was closer.

There was a slight curve in the fissure. A shaft of light.

Rhyll pocketed the crystal and shuffled faster as the ground rose sharply.

Breathing in the fresh but dusty air, she emerged into the heat, closing her eyes at the blinding glare of the sun. Once she regained her composure, she kept her eyes down until they adjusted to the bright light. As she slowly raised her head, she looked around, still using her hands to shade her eyes.

"No!"

The sight of the devastation traumatised her. She was at the bottom of a very deep man-made chasm. Only barren, broken land was visible. Several large trucks were winding their way up a long, spiral road along the wall, and bulldozers were scattered here and there.

All her life had been sailing oceans and hiking through swamps and rainforests. Rhyll had seen pictures and heard sad stories of this sort of devastation — and that was traumatic enough. She had refused to contemplate what being in that sort of place would be like. It was so abhorrent and would bring her to tears.

She took a few unsteady steps, feeling ill. She was surrounded by it. Broken land. Broken earth. Mining in its worst form. Open-cut, indiscriminate rape and pillage of the land. Rhyll stumbled a few feet before dropping to her knees, throwing up. She beat the dirt with her fists. "Why? Why? Why?" Rhyll wept.

Eventually, as if in a trance, she got to her feet and staggered away from the split in the cliff wall. There was no escaping the nightmare; the devastation surrounded her. Still in total shock, she quivered with rage and despair at the wanton destruction, causing her to stumble and trip.

"Hey, you!" a voice called out.

Blearily, Rhyll looked up. About forty metres away, a man in dirty clothes and a hardhat climbed down from his excavator. She hadn't heard him, so lost was she in her anguish.

"You okay?" the man called out again as he approached.

Coughing up dust, Rhyll turned to face him.

"Hey there. You know you're trespassing?" Seeing that it was a girl, his attitude changed to a less belligerent tone.

"Where am I?"

"Where?" He removed his hardhat and scratched his sweaty hair. "Miss, this is Erdany property — all fifteen thousand acres of it."

Rhyll wiped her eyes. She hadn't heard of them, but she took no interest in corporation names. Turning around and scanning the horizon, she didn't see anything she recognised. "But *where* is it?"

"Well, let's see." He took his hardhat off and wiped the sweat from his brow, pushing his wiry hair back. "Do you know Oriximiná?

Rhyll nodded. The *Aurora* was berthed there. And the university that had helped sponsor her dad's last dig.

"We're 'bout a hundred and sixty miles north."

"But ... everything north is protected rainforests!"

"Where you from, girl? You one of them greenies?"

"This is the land of the Wai-wai and Katuena peoples. Where are they now?"

The man's radio squawked, and she heard a faint, tinny voice.

He held it to his ear and listened. "Yeah. There's some girl here ... No, not native. Red hair. American, I think, or maybe English ... No, she's white. How the hell would I know how she got out here?" As he spoke, he turned, looking up. A drone had appeared from the south and was hovering nearby. "Yeah, yeah. Okay." He gave a thumbs-up to the drone. "Better come with me. Gotta take you up to the road. It's dangerous here, and the boss definitely wants to speak with you."

Numb, she walked slowly to the excavator, remotely aware the drone followed. Once by the huge machine, she climbed the ladder he pointed to and entered the cabin. As she climbed, she noticed he was watching her backside but trying not to look obvious. The cabin was dusty, as expected, but it seemed in good repair. There were two bucket seats. Rhyll unclipped her backpack and sat down.

"Can you drive this?" he asked, replacing his hardhat.

She looked at him as if he were mad. "No."

"Then that's my seat."

Silently, she changed positions.

"Better buckle up too." He sat down and started to reach across to grab her harness, the back of his hand brushing against her breast.

"I can manage, thanks." She pushed his hand away and placed her pack on her lap.

"Fine." He put the machine into gear, and using a joystick, he moved them off with a lurch.

The electronics on the dash blinked on and off intermittently, though the excavator didn't appear affected.

"Damn thing." He smacked the console.

They weren't moving fast, but Rhyll fumbled for the seatbelt before she was thrown out of the chair with the rough terrain. Through the window, the dead ground jarred every one of her senses.

"… not much longer." The driver was talking to her. "There'll be a jeep coming for you by the access road."

She didn't respond. Staring outside, she watched other excavators loading trucks with dirt as theirs climbed the spiral track out of the massive pit. It looked like a scar on the world.

At the crest, the excavator slowed to a stop. There was a black jeep waiting. "Here we are. Better move it. The boss isn't happy with you hippy trespassers." The driver climbed out.

"I'm not too happy either." Rhyll climbed down after him,

slinging her pack loosely over her shoulder. The excavator driver opened the car door and started coughing. "Damn dust." He closed it when she sat down, then strolled back to his excavator.

"Hey, girl. Where you from?" the jeep driver asked.

"Everywhere," she answered, again putting her pack on her lap.

The engine died. Cursing, the driver had trouble with the ignition. Once it fired, he accelerated away in a spray of gravel, his eyes watching her in the rear-view mirror. "How'd you get way out here? Any more of you?"

"Are you the boss?" Her despair was turning into anger.

"Who? Me? Ha! No way—"

"Then shut the hell up and drive." Rhyll's mind churned. Her father murdered. The traditional lands of the Wai-wai desecrated! They had lived in harmony with the land for thousands of years without any white man ruining their lives with trinkets and disease …

CHAPTER TWO

The rattling of the keys echoed off the begrimed concrete walls.

"The acoustics in this dump suck."

"Dobson. You've been bailed, asshole," the guard's whiney voice grated.

Dan rolled over, the squeaky bunk protesting with the shift of his weight. "And I was getting used to the stench. It has a quality even the Middle East can't compare."

"Too bad. Out."

Dan rubbed his eyes, sat up, and turned. His feet slapped onto the cold concrete floor as he stood and stretched. "Can I book the same room for next week?"

The stolid face of the cop remained fixed. He pointed to the exit.

"Ah well. I'll probably be back in Oz if I'm lucky," he said as he exited the cells. A barred window in the corridor opened.

"Sign here. Grab your things," the cop behind the counter said.

Dan signed and collected his belongings: blue hoodie — blood stains included — cell phone, and wallet. He deliberately checked the contents of his wallet.

"Wow. It's all there this time." Shaking his head, he looked at the cop behind the counter and then back to the cop who'd opened his cell. "You guys related? At first, I thought it was the voice, but now I see similarities with the ears, flat noses ... no neck." Turning, he strolled towards the foyer, seeing his Uncle Phillip waiting impatiently.

"About time. What took you so long?" his uncle growled, making an effort to rise from the plastic bench in the foyer. "I haven't time to come and bail you out whenever you cross the line."

"Yet here you are. Thanks."

"This is the last time," Phillip said.

"I've heard it before."

"Your father's serious this time. I've done all I can to keep you employed, but even family will only stand for so much. He has a task for you. Stuff it up, and you'll be freelancing 'til retirement."

Dan stopped on the pavement. "I hope it's somewhere out of Miami." He threw his hoodie on, seeing the black clouds overhead.

"Brazil."

"You're kidding. What's in Brazil this time? How about Madrid? There's an anti-GMO rally—"

"You're not endearing yourself to the one person who's trying to help. You fail to realise your choice in this is extremely limited." A soft rain had started, making the drab Miami skyline even more dismal. "Look at it this way: at least the rain is warmer." His uncle stopped by the car, fishing for keys from his pocket.

"What's in Brazil?"

"Your redemption?"

"What?"

"A story no one else wants to cover. Something about ancient burial grounds being destroyed by mining. The villagers are revolting."

"Is that a personal opinion?" Dan countered.

"What?" His uncle looked puzzled.

"Forget it."

"For once in your life, take this seriously! This is your last and ONLY chance to get back into your father's good graces. I've never seen him so pissed off."

"OK, OK. Got the ticket?"

"Here." Phil pulled an envelope with the Brazilian Airlines logo from his coat pocket.

"Not Qantas?" Dan looked dubiously at the envelope as if it was going to give him leprosy. "I'd even condescend to fly United."

"Hardly anyone's flying to where you're going." Phillip opened the car boot.

"Where is that, exactly?" Dan ripped the envelope to read the tickets. "Manaus?"

"Yep. Back to your old flame on the Amazon. Maybe she's forgotten you. Here, you'll be wanting this." His uncle handed him his backpack, then walked to the driver's door. "There's a briefing on the story — what little there is on it — some local currency, and we've transferred funds to your credchip. I've taken the liberty of getting some of your gear from your flat. Your flight leaves in three hours. Don't miss it. Otherwise, you'll have to wait a week for the next one, but by then you'll be unemployed." He seated himself, starting the engine. "If you stuff up again, best not to come back," Phil called through the window.

As Dan walked around to the passenger side, rummaging through the backpack, his uncle drove away.

"Thanks, arsehole." He stood on the roadside as the rain began in earnest.

With minutes to spare, Dan raced through the check-in desk at Miami International and squelched into his cramped seat on the plane, bumping fellow passengers in his haste. He wondered if they were more annoyed about being jostled or being dripped on.

Once they were in the air and the seat belt lights went out, Dan grabbed his pack and headed for the toilets, desperate to get out of his damp clothes. In the pack was a fresh shirt and trousers. He quickly stripped, realising there was no spare underwear.

He changed, banging his elbow and head numerous times in the confined space. When the door rattled, he stuffed his wet gear into the pack and made his way back to his seat.

He checked his watch. Four hours, forty minutes to Manaus, then a seven-hour coach journey to Caroebe.

"Just great," he muttered, and sighed in frustration, wondering if cancelling the coach and getting a local flight was possible.

The jeep continued for another twenty minutes while her mind seethed. Subconsciously, her hand went to her pocket. Rhyll touched the crystal, surprised it was warmer. Holding it gave her a sense of calm. Nowhere in their journey was there any reprieve from the destroyed earth. She felt an ache — as if the broken land was a wound in her side.

When the car came to a stop, Rhyll had to control herself, her body shaking with anger and frustration. She wanted to scream but didn't want to be thought of as a "stupid girl". She let go of the crystal.

As the cloud of dust settled, a thin man opened the door. "This way, Miss." He almost dragged her out of the car.

"Get your hands off me!" she yelled, slapping him away.

In his surprise at the sudden outburst, the man let go.

"You're in enough trouble. Don't make things harder for yourself." He turned to the driver. "Joe, head over to the garage and get the Merc ready. The boss will be heading into town later."

As he led the way into the building, she heard the driver coughing behind her as he drove away. The fluorescent lights of the ground floor main office flickered as they walked through. Despite the air-conditioning, the place still reeked of sweat. Tables covered in charts held down by rock samples were everywhere. Maps were tacked on the wall, with coloured pins here and there. All the occupants she saw were white males — some young, some old; not a local amongst them. Everyone fell silent when she came in, as if they'd never seen a girl before.

She ignored their ogling, following the thin man upstairs.

"Here she is, Mr Lewis." He ignored the bald thug-looking guy standing by the doorway.

A short man behind a desk looked up. "Thank you, Grant. That will be all."

The office was sparsely furnished, with a few bookshelves on the wall to her left and a large map pinned to the wall beside it. To her right was a cabinet and a bar fridge, and there were a couple of chairs near Mr Lewis's desk. The floor was covered in carpet tiles; some of the edges were curled up, some taped down.

"I'd offer you a drink, but I suspect you're underage for whiskey. Water, perhaps?"

She nodded, not trusting herself. Still shaking and seething. His accent was American, as were the accents of those of who had spoken to her so far.

"Please, have a seat." Lewis pointed to the beefy man by the door. "My apologies. This is Burgess."

Rhyll took the offered seat, spending a moment to study Mr Lewis while she put the backpack on the floor. He was shorter than she, and appeared to be in his late forties, his hairline receding. His slightly worn and dishevelled suit hung off him as though it were designed for a larger body, and he reminded her of pictures she'd seen of jockeys. His red sneakers looked out of place.

"I have bad arches." Lewis saw her look. He opened the bar

fridge and pulled out a bottle, pouring the contents into a frosted glass. He stepped over and offered it to her.

Despite it coming from a plastic bottle, Rhyll accepted the cool water.

"You're trembling. Are you cold? Injured?" he asked.

She shook her head, finishing the glass in one go. *I'm very pissed-off!*

"Ah. I see. No need to be afraid. You're safe for now — as long as you behave." He paused, but Rhyll still remained silent. "So … Care to explain what you're doing out here? Any friends nearby? If they're trespassing and get injured from the mining activities, we can't and won't be held responsible. I'm sick and tired of you protesters coming onto the site. I thought you learnt the lesson last time. I reckon Burgess and the men need to revisit your camp."

"I think it's you who should be explaining yourself." She stood and walked over to the map on the wall. Having studied her father's maps, she thought she recognised the area but obviously had it wrong. A huge area between the Rio Nhamunda and the Rio Mapuera was circled.

"You've got it all wrong … ah … What do I call you?" Lewis asked.

"Rhyllien."

"Well then … Rhyllien. You're the one trespassing. The Erdany Mining Co-op has been mining here for over two decades—"

"Where are the indigenous? The Wai-wai and the Katuena? What did you do to them? They were one of the last tribes in Pará State to have had no contact with civilisation. You take away their forest, you take away their spirit, their means of living … you kill them."

"Natives? I believe there were savages here years ago. What was left of their ramshackle huts were pulled down. Way before my time, though. Such a messy business dealing with ignorant natives. They'll be much better off now. A new community was constructed. Now they have sanitation, water, and electricity. Everything to make their lives more bearable, I'm sure."

Rhyll's legs felt weak. She barely stopped herself from collapsing, leaning against the bookshelf.

Lewis continued: "I've called the authorities, and they're on their way. How many of you are there? Where are your friends hiding?"

"There's no one left." She turned to him. "Everyone I knew is either dead or gone. And you did this!"

In the distance, she heard a low rumble of thunder.

"Who's dead?" Lewis turned to Burgess. "Where was she found, exactly?"

"Near section 32. Bob reported her."

"Get him in here, and send a team out to 32; she says her friends are dead. Keep this quiet. We can't afford any media hassles with multiple protestors dead, even if they were trespassing."

Burgess pivoted and strode out the room without closing the door.

Rhyll felt heat in her pocket. Reaching down to touch the crystal, she felt subtle energy run up her arm and through her. She sat heavily in the chair, somewhat calmer. This was all too confusing.

"We'll search the area for the others and get to the reason for your presence." Lewis brought her mind back to her current situation. "I should caution you. My man, Burgess … Let's say he has a zeal for his work. He's had run-ins with you protestors before. It didn't go so well for them last time; medical facilities out here are pretty low-tech."

Burgess returned and closed the door.

Lewis continued. "So, Rhyllien, tell us how you got way up here undetected. How many friends are with you, and what are the plans for the next protest?"

"I don't know what you mean. I'm not—"

The slap from Burgess rocked her head back. She felt heat in her left cheek immediately. Tears sprung to her eyes, and she tasted blood.

Undisturbed by Burgess's methods, Lewis repeated the questioning. "It's many miles of rough terrain from the protest camp. How did you get up here undetected? Did you have inside help? How many of you are there? Are you planning on attempting to sabotage equipment again?"

Being in no position to argue, Rhyll needed to think quickly. She didn't believe how she got here, so how could she expect them to? The bodyguard would happily keep beating her — she was certain by the gleam in his eye.

"I'm alone. Too many of us would attract attention. I'm scouting the area to see what we need," she lied.

"That's more like it." Lewis reached for her backpack. "Were you in contact with anyone? Any pictures? Radio?" He rummaged through. Finding the old tablet he chuckled, seeing the battery was flat. "No pictures or vids, then?" He pulled out her clothes, seeing only underwear at the bottom. He tossed the pack to the floor.

"Did you search her, Burgess? Maybe she has a communicator on her."

Burgess ran his hands all over her. "Perks of the job," he leered. His hand stopped on her thigh pocket. He pulled out the crystal. "What've we got here?"

"Where did you get this?" Lewis asked, accepting the item from Burgess and glancing over it.

"It's an heirloom," Rhyll stated.

"Really?" he chuckled. "Before I became manager here, I had a bit of a background as a gemmologist. That's a small reason why I'm here — never know what will turn up in the digs. I still like to think I have a bit of skill in the field." Lewis quickly fished through his drawer, pulling out a small, ornate wooden box.

"My grandfather's loupe," he explained, putting on a pair of white cotton gloves. "He was also a gemmologist." Handling the crystal with utmost care, he brought it under the desk lamp, studying it intensely, the magnifier held in place by his squint. "Fascinating …" He then reached for a worn book on the side of the desk and flipped through the pages with one hand. Every now and then he'd pause, look closely at the crystal, then flick a few more pages. He repeated the process in silence until finished.

"Where did you say you got this?"

Rhyll didn't answer straight away. His interest was real enough, but she didn't trust him at all. "Seriously, it's an heirloom, probably a cheap trinket. Something my grandmother left me," she lied.

"Do you know what it is?" He looked up briefly. "This green gemstone, if I'm not mistaken, is a diamond." His hands were shaking. "Do you have any idea what it's worth?"

"From your sweat and the sound of your voice, more than a few dollars. I thought it was just a crystal, not a gemstone."

"Gemstones can be crystalline in form, some aren't; it really depends. If it has beauty or intrinsic value, it can be categorised as a gemstone." Lewis sat back in his chair, thinking. "And this is definitely of intrinsic value, not only for its clarity and colour but its size! Why would you be hauling this *heirloom* over the countryside?"

"What, and leave it in my tent with all those protestors? I'd rather keep it close."

"Ah. But not in a bank … because it's a mere trinket?"

"Exactly. Only of value to me, as all my family … has passed away."

"I'm sorry to hear that. But I'm still not convinced you acted alone. We're over forty miles from the Nhamunda River, and São Lucas is twice that. You didn't fly in, you aren't sunburnt, nor do you look remotely like you've been hiking, so how did you get here?"

Rhyll remained silent, unable to think of a plausible reason for her presence.

"Understand this. You're a girl in a foreign land and in no position to argue. Tell me what I want to know, and we can come to an arrangement. Perhaps I'd be less inclined to press charges on you and whoever else is out there." He waved at the window. "Erdany takes this sort of thing very seriously." He waited for her to say something. "And if you are alone as you say … Well, that puts you in an even more tenuous situation."

"How much worse can it be?" she asked.

"For a girl who acts so independent, you aren't too wise to the real world, are you? Put it this way: there are a lot of men here who have been isolated for several weeks, if not months, and then there is you. Quite attractive, too — not that some of the men care about that. And nowhere to go, and apparently, no one to rescue you." He waited for some response.

She wasn't stupid and knew exactly what he was referring to, having had the excavator driver leering at her as she went up the ladder, and his feeble attempt at groping, then Joe, the jeep driver, watching her through the mirror. Men!

Many of the native girls she met on her travels were already married and having children at her age. She recalled her father joking about the shaman wanting to marry her off to his son … All gone!

The air was warmer, still humid, but fresher than the air-conditioned muck. Natural. Her head cleared. She needed to focus. The camp was on a hill. From the second-floor office, she could see a long way, and none of it was pleasing. "The forest … All destroyed …" She wept at what she saw. A scar on the land, all the way to the cloudless horizon.

… One with nature …

"What was that?" he asked.

"You've destroyed all the forests … You've destroyed the people!"

"No. We relocated them—"

"Mere shells of what they once were. You don't know them like I do. The moment you killed the forest, you killed them." Rhyll seethed. *Murderers.* She heard the rumble of thunder through the window, louder now.

… One with nature … She heard in her head.

"Oh, that again?" Lewis scoffed. "People have their own worries. No one gives a shit about the natives. There's still plenty of forest for everyone. Now, tell me where you got this. Are there any more?"

"There's just the one—"

"Ahh!" Lewis dropped the gemstone onto the carpet.

Rhyll turned at his yell. He pulled off his slightly charred glove and blew onto his hand.

"It burnt me," he whimpered in surprise.

"Maybe it knows who its rightful owner is."

"Is this some kind of trick?" he gasped.

"No." She watched him. "No trick. I don't understand it either. Any of this … everything that's happening is real … somehow. Too real."

He started coughing.

… One with nature …

"Burgess. Take Miss Ellis to the old storeroom. I believe she needs to have a quiet place to contemplate the trouble she is in." Lewis wiped spittle from his mouth.

"What? You're not taking me anywhere!" Rhyll yelled.

"Guess again, honey." Burgess dragged her to her feet by her hair.

Rhyll yelped at the pain. She turned and lashed out with her foot, scoring a kick to his knee.

Burgess grunted but came back with a punch to her stomach.

Rhyll folded over and dropped to the floor, wheezing and feeling nauseous.

"Was that necessary?" Lewis shook his head.

"Oh yeah."

Rhyll lay on the floor, getting her breath back.

"Think about your situation, Miss Ellis. Consider my words." Lewis nursed his hand. "The authorities should be here in several hours. If you don't tell me the full story, you won't see daylight for a long time. I'll make sure of it."

Burgess reached for her. She felt his meaty hands firmly on

her shoulder and hair, dragging her off the floor. "You don't want any more trouble, miss."

"You mean *you* don't want any trouble!" Rhyll retorted, trying to disengage from the man. His fingers were ruthlessly gouging into her shoulder.

"Nope. I kinda like trouble." He stopped and slapped her hard on the side of the head, causing her ear to ring.

Rhyll grunted in shock, pain, and surprise. Unbidden tears erupted. "What was that for?"

"That's for nothin'." The smug grin on his face proved Burgess was the sort of person who enjoyed bullying. "Imagine what'll happen if you really piss me off."

Without another word, he resumed hauling her down the stairs and past the staring, silent office staff. Not one of them protested. At the end of a musty hallway, he opened a scuffed door.

"I might bring you somethin' to eat later." Burgess pushed her in roughly into a dim room, firmly closing the door behind him.

Stumbling, Rhyll tripped and struck her head on a metal bookcase. She fell to the floor, unconscious.

CHAPTER THREE

"Boss, you might want to look at this."

"What is it, Williams? I'm busy." Tyrone Stradjek adjusted his cybo-visor. He was having the best round of golf.

"Remember that Lewis clown down in Brazil? We installed cams because we thought he was fiddling the books?"

"I do. Yes, have we finally something recorded to nail the bastard? That Erdany shithole has become a pain in the ass. I'm beginning to think it's done its job and we move on."

"You should definitely take a look," Williams suggested.

"Ok, patch it through." He sighed, putting his five-iron away and moving to his chair. Placing his goggles on his uncluttered desk, the monitor slid up from the oak top with the click of a button. Despite the glitches and flickering, he watched the vid at fast speed first before he stopped, skipped back, and turned up the volume.

Lewis was talking to a redhead. It wasn't until she turned that Tyrone realised she was a teenager, not a woman. He zoomed in and froze the vid.

"Shit." Lewis was examining a massive green jewel. "Did he just say green diamond?" Tyrone muttered. The audio was crackly, barely decipherable.

He reached into his safe, opened a file, and carefully sifted through the dog-eared pages until he found what he was looking for. It was a detailed sketch of ancient relics from various surveys of what was believed to be Incan ruins.

The colouring may have been off slightly, but he found what he was looking for: the octahedron shape looked very similar to what Lewis held in his grubby hands. This particular sketch was left in his father's personal belongings. It was one of the items he was searching for before he died in the Amazon.

As a boy, Tyrone followed in his father's footsteps and became interested in ancient artefacts — especially very lucrative ones. He cared little for intrinsic value or cultures; his interest was purely monetary. If the stories he'd overheard from some of his father's colleagues were anywhere near the truth, there were supposed to be seven gemstones created for some epic world cataclysm. But, like the Mayan end-of-world scenarios and many other doomsday conspiracies, it all came to nothing. The rumours died, as did belief in these stones. Until now. His father had died for these; Tyrone assured himself that they would be *his*.

Checking the latest market analysis on green diamonds, he found they were almost as rare as red diamonds and were going for a cool million a carat. They were so rare that it was twenty years since the last one had appeared for sale. Assuming Lewis was correct, that this was in fact a rare diamond, he wondered how this girl got her hands on it, and if there were others. He also wondered if she had a gold disc, the item his father had been searching for before he died. A red-haired girl, the daughter of Ken Ellis, had gone missing at the same time.

"Williams, is this time on the screen local or what?"

"Central Brazilian local time. They're an hour ahead of us."

"Do we know who the girl is? Where she came from and what she's doing way out in the Amazon?"

"Facial recognition is going through the database, boss."

"Good. Let me know as soon as it comes up with something. I'm thinking we need to grab that stone — maybe the girl too. If it is what I think it is, we will do extremely well. Lewis has already helped himself enough on behalf of the business. No way is he going to keep this. Who have we got down there?"

"Grant Richards," Williams responded after a pause. "He's a moron. Basically, an ass-licker, and he will do whatever he can to be bumped up the ladder."

"Good. Brown-noses generally follow orders. Call him. Grab the girl and the stone and get them up here before those cops arrive; if they get their hands on it, we'll never see it again. Emphasise that I don't care how it's done, as long as it's done. Organise a hoverpod ASAP to pick them up. Get them to the Miramar warehouse."

The humidity hit him immediately. Dan wasn't a fan of it, his shirt clinging wetly to him. The flight from Miami was forty minutes late. The coach he had been booked on had already departed and the next wasn't until tomorrow, so unless he wanted to hang around overnight he needed to seek an alternate means of travel. The only good fortune was the reimbursement of the ticket cost due to the tardy flight, but it would take several days for it to appear in his account.

To quell his frustration, Dan sat in a diner and ordered coffee and breakfast while he considered his options. Checking the map on his tablet, he saw that Caroebe was another five hundred and fifty kilometres by road, and that wasn't even his final destination. Nala Xaschoal, his 'old flame' as his uncle put it, was manager of a protestor camp based near the Erdany mine. It was another couple of hundred kilometres beyond, and if memory served him well, the road was bone-jarring.

Their separation wasn't on the best of terms ... hence his reticence for a reunion. While they got on fine, a life in the Brazilian jungle, surrounded by strangers speaking a language he didn't understand, already had taken him out of his comfort zone. Nala was born to it, surrounded by friends and family; she knew the language, and she had her studies. Fun and pleasant times were had, but these were short-lived as neither was prepared to leave their own world. And then there was his own career.

Nala buried herself in her work, and Dan finished what he was sent to do: interview the locals and report on the tenth anniversary of the camp.

A generous benefactor had started the camp two decades earlier to bring attention to the devastation wrought by the mine. It worked for a while, even going to court regarding trespass by the protestors. What was swept under the carpet by the well-paid but unscrupulous legal team was the then-illegal deforestation and wiping out of the indigenous natives — some whom had never set eyes on white man.

Corporate greed prevailed and the protestors lost, thereby strengthening Erdany's hold on the land. There was suspicion money changed hands because shortly after the local environmental laws were weakened, the deforestation increased, and the open-cut mine expanded.

To the corporate mind-set, creating a new village and rehousing was a good thing, but they completely failed to understand the connection those natives had for their land. The indigenous continued to eke out a subsistence living, but slowly died off with the introduction of viruses and diseases, for which they had little immunity.

Nala returned to the scene with her education and skills, and turned things around for the better, bringing what aid she could to the natives.

When he left, Dan had no idea he'd ever be back. His one regret was not calling her, and then the continued delay exacerbated the dilemma — and a decade rolled by.

A group of noisy miners came into the terminal, disturbing his contemplations. He thought nothing of it, other than the irritation of their blatant disregard for noise levels. Then a thought came to him: *FIFO.*

Fly In Fly Out. They flew back and forth to mines all over the country. If he swallowed his self-respect, he could at least ask if they were heading anywhere near Caroebe.

Dan turned and closed his eyes at the dust cloud from the departing hoverpod. There were a couple of extra seats and since it was on the company tab, it was free. Their vulgar banter was definitely an eye-opener, and he surmised that, regardless of education standards — or social class — once they were indoctrinated into a particular career path, their language and ideology conformed to what was acceptable in that industry.

He couldn't complain about being dropped off at Rorainópolis. While it was several hundred kilometres from where he wanted to be, it was still seven hours north of where he had been.

Dan donned his backpack, grabbed his bag and strolled to the small building serving as a terminal, hoping to find a bus or coach. It didn't look like the paint or décor had changed at all since his last visit. Some of the memories came back; he found his way to the bus terminal north of the exit and checked the timetable.

With his limited language skills, and assuming he was reading it correctly through the scratched perspex screen, the faded timetable indicated a local coach would be departing at 12:30pm. It wasn't ideal, but São João da Baliza was as far as he could go before the bus turned south to Nova Carolina to complete the roughly triangular circuit back to Rorainópolis.

Dan checked his watch. He had a couple of hours to spare. Time for lunch and a shower. He wasn't expecting any lounge area at such a small airstrip, but for a handful of coins he could have a shower and change into fresh clothes. He then recalled his 'fresh clothes' were still damp from the rain in Miami. A nearby market stall provided clothing, though the only shirt to fit was one of the kinds you'd wear after losing a bet, and he cringed at the cost. Still, he felt refreshed after the wash and once the food was in his belly, all would be right with the world.

. . .

Several hours later, sweltering in the clammy hinterland of the north Brazilian rainforest, Dan watched the departing bus turn at the intersection, feeling like his spine had been crushed.

The road condition had gradually deteriorated. It was a relief to stand, stretch and move around, but he knew the road was only going to get worse from here. He noted the definite signs of a mechanics' at the intersection by the wrecks surrounding the fence. Grabbing his gear, Dan ventured over to the local store to grab some snacks, toilet paper and cigarettes. He didn't smoke, but discovered years ago it was best currency for bartering when in remote locations.

Thirty minutes later he was dodging the worst of the potholes as he ambled along on a motorbike. It was rusty, the brakes squealed, it blew smoke and had an old milk crate as a seat, but considering the only other options of walking or a mule, this was the preferred choice. It only had to get him a couple of hundred kilometres, and for the cost of the cigarettes and a bottle of cheap whisky it was all his.

Over a hundred kilometres later, the bitumen stopped and the rest of the trip was on dirt.

The protest camp was where he'd last seen it, opposite the turn-off to the Erdany mine. Some of the tents had been renewed and it was slightly larger than he remembered, but it had changed little in a decade. Dan puttered to the side of the road and killed the motor.

"Hey, mate. You lost?" a tall, tanned protestor called from under the faded shade-cloth.

Dan noted the familiar accent straight away as he rested the bike on the kick-stand. "Nah, mate. I came to see Nala Xaschoal." He vaguely remembered this guy, though his hair and beard were longer.

The guy examined him, scratching his beard. "Hey, aren't you that reporter dude?"

"Dan Dobson," he introduced himself.

"Bruno. Nala was so pissed at you, man."

Dan blanched. "Is she around?"

"Nah. She's gone walkabout visiting her family in the village. Should be back in a coupla days." Bruno lifted a can out of a bucket of water where it was keeping cool. "Wanna beer?"

"Sure." Dan accepted the drink as he considered his next move.

"I guess you can crash here until she comes back. A couple of blokes left last month, so we got an extra bunk or two."

"Great. Thanks. How are things going with the mine?"

"Pretty shit, I reckon. Much quieter than when you were here last. Reckon things are winding down."

"What makes you say that?"

"Each year more miners leave than return. Can't see much going out these days."

Dan looked down the road to the mine. "That can't be a bad thing."

"Give it another year or so and we'll have to find honest work."

"That soon?"

Bruno shrugged and drank more of his beer.

"Remind me where the loo is." Dan dug into his pack and brought out the box of toilet paper. "I do remember the important details." He grinned.

Bruno wiped his mouth, pointing. "You gonna leave that here?"

"It's what I brought it for."

"Excellent."

Dan strode to the back of the row of large tents, nodding to the others he saw. Some were doing minor chores around the place; others were tending the small plot of vegetables.

As he made his way to the toilet, he decided a quick visit to check out the mine was in order. While seeing Nala would be nice, his main task was to report on the destruction of ancient burial grounds. *No time like the present.*

"I'll see what Erdany is up to, take a few pics and then get the real story from Nala and the villagers," he muttered, as he stacked the rolls in the cupboard. It turned out they were using torn sheets of old newspapers and brochures.

He gave himself a quick wash and headed back to the motorbike.

"Heard anything about ancient burial sites?"

Bruno shook his head. "Maybe Nala has those details. I've not heard anything."

"I should be back in a couple of hours. See you then." Since the ignition was shot on the bike, he had to push it along the road to get some speed before he could jump-start it. Once it fired up, he waved over his shoulder.

Before long, the vegetation along the roadside dwindled to small patches of scrub and weeds, then to almost nothing. Beyond the fence line, the ground was bare. Bulldozed, flattened here, churned up there with piles of tailings all around. After reporting and exposing previous mines, he expected it to be bad, but this destruction was maniacal.

"And this is only the perimeter." He scowled.

Dan stopped when the security booth came into sight. He lay the bike against an embankment, donned his pack and continued stealthily on foot, already snapping pics of the barren terrain.

As he neared the compound, he heard the buzzing of a drone. Too late, he realised it was moving towards his location. He quickly stowed his camera as he started running back to the bike.

Sliding down the embankment, he reached the bike but a work truck with the security logo on the side drove up before he could jump start it. A burly guy got out and dragged him to the truck, slamming him against the panel. After his hands were zip-tied, he was picked up and dumped in the back of the truck.

No one had asked a question or uttered a word.

· · ·

Ten minutes later in a dilapidated upstairs office, the questions started.

Who was he and why was he trespassing? Was he working with the other protesters? It didn't seem to matter what he said, the burly guy seemed to enjoy punching him; the little guy in glasses and ill-fitting clothes asked the questions.

"You know, with your obvious PR expertise, you could be a cop," he said to the henchman called Burgess.

"They're just stupid pigs."

"Exactly. You'd fit right in. Swift promotion for your type." He ought to learn to keep his mouth shut. Burgess didn't have a sense of humour. *Yep. Just like a cop.*

CHAPTER FOUR

Rhyll regained consciousness and looked around in confusion, still coming to terms with her predicament, the devastation around her, and the loss of the local tribes. She had little idea what to do about it.

Tentatively she felt her cheek, unable to detect any swelling, but it throbbed and was sure to be bruised — maybe a black eye. Her knees were sore from her stumble, and her head had a lump where she struck the cupboard. She felt dampness in her hair, and her fingers came away with a trace of blood. The drumming noise in her head resolved into torrential rain on the tin roof.

She had little idea how long she'd been unconscious, but the realisation of her backpack still being in Lewis' office made her seriously consider escaping. She didn't want anyone rifling through her belongings and finding the other crystals. After she recovered her composure, Rhyll stood to pace the room, thinking of escape.

She stopped in shock.

There was a man lying on the floor in front of the door. She stepped closer. He had blood from cuts on his cheek and above his eyes. From the amount of blood pooled on the concrete floor, he had been there for a while.

Rhyll looked around, but there was nothing to clean the wounds with. She checked for a pulse.

"At least you're breathing," she sighed with relief. He didn't look like one of the mine people. Sunburnt, not tanned; dressed in jeans and a shirt with one of the crappiest designs she had ever seen.

"Hey, mister." She shook him a few times, but when he didn't respond she checked for a pulse again. Satisfied he was only unconscious, Rhyll stood to pace the room, thinking of escape.

The floor area between the shelving was three paces wide and five long. The storeroom had a long narrow window near the ceiling. It was frosted but allowed a small amount of light in. There were some boxes in one corner full of papers, and an empty, metal bookcase below the window.

"Not too bright, any of you," she chuckled as she tested her weight on the shelves. They bent slightly, but when she moved closer to the sides, she found they gave greater support. As long as she was careful, the shelves shouldn't topple or buckle.

Placing her feet near a support, Rhyll was able to reach the window when she was a few shelves from the top. The latch moved easily, but the window had been painted over so many times it wouldn't budge. The window wasn't frosted as she'd first thought, but covered in built-up grime and dust on the outside. Either way, visibility was still nil, and she had no idea who or what was on the other side. She'd have to break it to escape and considered the best way to do so was to use her boot.

If the man came to, maybe they could both climb out.

"If they didn't damage him too much," she considered.

Climbing to the top of the bookcase, she lay on her side to bring her leg up to reach the zipper on the side of her boot. It was precarious, as the shelf wasn't that deep, but the little bit of extra room with the windowsill helped.

Carefully turning to face the window again, she firmly tapped the glass with her heel. It was enough to make a spider web of cracks. Putting her hand into the boot, she pushed, hoping the glass would gently splinter instead of smashing all over the place. She pressed against it firmly. With a snap that sounded very loud in the confined space, the glass gave way. Her hand went through, and the boot dropped to the mud outside.

A quick glance outside showed no one in the vicinity. It was wet and overcast, but the longer shadows indicated she'd been unconscious for several hours at the least. She removed her other boot and used it to remove the jagged edges, brushing the shards to the side. Cautiously, she put her head through to check the area fully. She guessed she was on the east side of the building, towards the northern end. It was over a two-metre drop to the ground. The rain lessened as the front of the storm passed.

She heard coughing. A man she recognised from the office stumbled around the corner. He leant heavily on the side of the building, threw up, then staggered off towards the accommodation units. He didn't look back or seem to care about the teeming rain.

Looking up, she found the only thing she could hang onto was the window frame, and that didn't look like it would hold her weight as it was so weathered and buckled.

The other option, besides falling, was to go feet first on her stomach and use the inside edge of the bookcase to hang on to before dropping. Regardless of how she decided to get out, there were still a few shards embedded in the rock-hard putty that would slice her belly to ribbons. Although it would take extra time, she could see no option but to climb back down and retrieve the cardboard from the boxes to use as a lining to slide over the sharp edges.

Back on the floor, Rhyll noticed the man sitting up.

"Nice to see you're awake. You okay?" she asked.

"Which one of you is talking to me?" he asked, tentatively touching his swollen eyes.

"There's just me. I'm Rhyllien, or Rhyll for short."

"Rhyllien?" He looked up. "What's that, Scottish? Or are you clearing your throat?"

"Welsh, I'm told. It has a *hy* in it. Sort of guttural."

"I'm Dan. Anyway, thanks for getting me into this mess."

"What? How did I do it? I only just got here myself."

"You got caught, so they increased their surveillance and found me."

"And that's my fault?"

"Glad you agree."

Rhyll shook her head, failing to understand his logic, and continued with her original plan. This Dan was an idiot and could worry about himself. She quickly strode to the stack of boxes.

"What are you doing?" Dan was standing now, leaning against the wall and looking at the broken window.

"What's it look like I'm doing?" She emptied a box and then flattened it.

"Looks like you're going to get me another beating when they see us scuttling around outside."

"Us? You're assuming you were invited."

They both heard rapid footsteps approaching in the corridor. Before they could think or do anything, the door swung open.

To her surprise, it was Grant, not Burgess, in the doorway.

He pointed the gun at Rhyll. "You and I are going for a ride. Get a move on," he said earnestly. He was white and shaken, blood dripping from his nose onto his shirt.

"What's going on?" she asked.

"Everyone's sick. I'm leaving before I get it. I'm to take you with me."

"Why's everyone sick? Where are we going? You're already bleeding." Rhyll pointed.

"What!" Grant wiped his nose, alarmed at the blood he saw. "We can talk on the way. Let's go."

"I'm not going anywhere, with you or any— Ow!"

Grant had reached in and grabbed her long hair, pulling her roughly into the corridor.

"No time to argue."

Dan limped forward. Grant waved the gun at him. "Don't be a hero. You want to die quick or slow?"

"I'd rather die old."

"Slow it is then." Grant kicked the door closed and locked it.

"You can't leave him!" she exclaimed. "Let go of the hair. I'll be glad to be out of here."

Grant let her go, shoving her toward the main office.

"I'll need my backpack." Rhyll went to the stairs.

"We don't have time."

"You go then. I'll stay, thanks. I've never been sick."

"We're both going, I said." Grant pushed her through the door into the main office.

"And I said *not without my backpack!*" Rhyll shrugged his weakening grip off and kicked him in the shins.

Grant grimaced with pain, trying to backhand her, but she easily avoided it. He was slow and too preoccupied with rubbing his leg.

She noticed quite a few of the men were absent from the office. Those remaining were either vomiting into their bins or leaning on the tables with heads in hands. Some were coughing, and others seemed more delirious, muttering to themselves. She guessed the others, like the man she'd seen earlier, had returned to their rooms.

"What's going on?" she asked.

"Listen, girl." Grant made to grab for her, but she dodged. He started coughing again. "We haven't time to argue," he rasped.

"Exactly." Rhyll ducked his skinny, outstretched arm and took the stairs two at a time. She heard yelling and banging from the back room. Continuing up the stairs, she quickly entered Lewis' office, almost tripping over Burgess; a bullet to the side of the head had made him a gruesome, bloody mess.

The room also smelt of bile. Lewis was slumped in his chair. His desk and the area around him showed evidence of projectile vomiting.

"What's happening to everyone?" she cried, looking at him in bewilderment. His breathing was very shallow, and he was unconscious and covered in reddish spots. *Measles?*

She hated him and what he did, and for his threats, yet she

took pity all the same. Rhyll loosened his collar before fetching the water and a glass. She tried to get him to drink, but he didn't respond. The water dribbled down his chin to his soiled shirt.

Rhyll could hear Grant gasping downstairs, and Dan was banging on the door. She collected her pack. Her green crystal was nowhere in sight. A rummage in the drawers proved futile.

"Any idea where my grandmother's heirloom is?" she asked from the top of the stairs.

"It's safe," Grant replied.

"Can I have it? It means a lot to me." Rhyll came down the stairs.

"I don't think so"—he coughed—"It means more to others. Let's go." He bent over with another coughing fit.

"Are you okay?" Rhyll stepped closer.

"Does it sound like it?" he wheezed. "We're going! Or you can damn well stay. Right now, I don't give a shit." Using the wall as support, Grant lurched to the front door. He stumbled, landing awkwardly on his knee. He went down with a cry of pain, and the gun went off. The bullet hit the floor and ricocheted into a wall.

While he was kneeling and whining, Rhyll took the opportunity to race to the storeroom and unlock the door. She ducked as Dan lurched through, fists first, running into the opposite wall.

"You came back." He sounded surprised when he turned.

"I'll probably regret it." She ran back along the corridor.

Grant was up, sweating heavily, leaning against the doorframe. He waved the gun. "He can't come."

"Can you walk?" she asked him.

Grant hobbled a few feet.

"I'll take that as a no. You're too heavy for me, so you'll need Dan's help."

"Why would I?" Dan asked.

"'Cos if you don't, I'm as good as dead." Grant's breath was laboured. "I may as well shoot you both now." He cleared his throat. "And I've got the codes for our flight."

"Sounds fair." Dan grabbed Grant's arm and put it over his shoulder to help take the weight off his bad leg. Outside, they staggered through the light drizzle to the end of the building and the carport where the jeep was parked. Grant stumbled a few times, but the trio finally reached the car. Rhyll opened the back door, and Grant more or less fell into the back seat. "I hope you can drive," she said to Dan.

Dan ran around to the driver's seat.

"I need my boot." Rhyll splashed her way around the building, spying it in the mud below the broken window. Avoiding the broken glass, she shook it in case shards had fallen inside, before putting it on.

The jeep came sliding around the corner and skidded to a halt next to her. Dan flung the door open.

She jumped in. "Where's the landing strip?"

Dan answered by planting his foot and heading to the exit gate of the compound.

Rhyll was thrown back in the chair, her boot half on. She glared at him. "Can you drive?"

The car crashed through the boom gate as they whizzed past the guard shelter.

"There's a landing field just down here."

"How did you know?"

"I passed it when they brought me in."

She looked at the dead landscape: dirt and rock, with only weeds now replacing the once magnificent forests, water torrenting along the ditches on the sides of the road.

Dan swerved, turning towards the airstrip, crashing through the gate. It flung open, one side springing back and clipping the tail. The car lurched as the road dipped suddenly. The airstrip was in a long depression between mounds of overburden.

"Where's the plane?" he asked as he slowed the jeep.

"Hoverpod on way," Grant wheezed, leaning against the window, leaving mist and red flecks of spittle.

"Is that it?" Rhyll pointed.

A sleek, white hoverpod approached from the north.

Grant nodded, pulling the door handle. He half fell, half staggered out.

"I've never seen one before." She marvelled at it.

"No?" Dan wondered. "Even down here they're fairly common — generally AI-controlled." As he walked around the car, he noticed the flat tyre, and a piece of metal poking out of the grill; water dripped underneath.

"AI?" Rhyll asked.

"Where have you been, girl?" Dan looked at her. "Artificial Intelligence. It's fully programmed and automatic. Voice recognition mostly." Dan pointed to Grant. "Must be something important to send one. This model's fairly upmarket. Or it could be the cheaper version with a remote pilot only."

The hoverpod gracefully descended, squelching on the hardpacked surface.

Rhyll noticed an oval-shaped icon depicting Earth on the side.

"Let's move!" Grant hobbled closer and touched a panel on its sleek side with his palm. A door swung up and as the steps folded out he staggered inside.

Rhyll and Dan walked closer, looking in as Grant collapsed into a chair. He fumbled with a water bottle, dropping a tube to the floor, tablets tumbling out.

Climbing in and wiping the rain off her face, Rhyll was amazed at the interior with its smooth, cushioned panels. It looked nothing like the interior of any aircraft she'd seen before. After she placed her backpack on the carpeted floor, she sat in the soft seat, noting there were only two. "Where's Dan sitting?"

"He's not coming." Grant shuffled through the contents of a first-aid box.

"What do you mean? He helped you."

"The boss only wants you and the diamo—"

"Why me?"

Grant didn't answer. "Door close," he commanded.

"Hey!" Dan jumped on the top step, the stair servos whining in protest at the sudden weight increase.

Grant pointed the gun, his hand shaking, and fired.

Dan lost his grip, falling hard onto the landing strip.

"No!" Rhyll shrieked. She reached down, grabbing the closest thing. The hard case of the first-aid kit smashed against Grant's face, bloodying his nose more. He yelped in pain, dropping the pistol.

Releasing the case so she could pull herself out of the chair, Rhyll scampered outside to assist Dan.

"Dan?" she cried. Seeing him lying there, eyes closed, she checked his pulse. His shoulder was bleeding, but he was alive. Kneeling in the mud, Rhyll started to tear open the shirt.

"Hey, this is an expensive shirt," he complained, coming to.

"You actually paid money for it?" Rhyll resorted to undoing the buttons. "Roll onto your side. I need to see if it went through." She peeled the shirt over his shoulder and upper arm. "Good. It's just a graze. You were lucky." She heard a whimper of pain from the pod.

"Stay there." Spurred into action, Rhyll went back to grab the first-aid kit and her backpack. On a whim, she went through Grant's pockets, quickly finding what she was looking for. Grabbing her crystal and the medkit, she kicked the gun out the door and raced down the steps after it.

"What's that arsehole doing?" Dan gasped.

"Bleeding like you." Opening the medkit and shielding it from the rain with her body, she rummaged through its contents. One of the things her parents had taught her was basic first-aid. They had spent their lives in the jungle or some other exotic location, miles away from civilisation. Among the sundry packets of bandages, there was a spray bottle of antiseptic.

"This'll probably sting."

From the face-pulling he made, it did. After liberally spraying the area, she wrapped the wound with a firm bandage. "Hurt anywhere else?"

"Only if you prod it." He winced. "I think I banged my head, too."

She felt the bump. Her fingers were damp with rainwater and blood.

"Yeah. You'll live. Take these," she said, handing him a couple of tablets.

"Any water?"

"Nope. Just chew and stop being a sook." Rhyll used one of the larger bandages to make a sling. "As for Grant, I hit him with this case," she added to his previous question. "I think I knocked him out."

"Way to go, girl." As he spoke, they saw the roof of a speeding car on the other side of the embankment separating the landing strip from the road. The vehicle drove straight towards the compound.

"Lewis said the authorities would be here in a few hours. I guess it's about that time."

"The jeep's cactus, but we can lie low out of this rain and wait for them to leave. I doubt they'll come down here; no reason to." He sat up, trying to stand. "Want to help?"

She pulled Dan to his feet and supported him as they staggered to the car.

He half fell, half slumped into the back seat. "At least we're out of the rain." Dan winced as he reclined.

"Actually, I like it—"

The pod started buzzing, and the steps retracted.

"I think Grant's recovered." She turned and shielded her eyes to watch the pod rise.

"Or maybe it's programmed to return automatically," Dan suggested.

The pod rotated to the north, then zipped away.

CHAPTER FIVE

"MR WILLIAMS, YOU BETTER COME LOOK," THE OPERATOR CALLED through the door of the darkened room.

"What is it, Simmons?" Williams strode from his office to the controller's desk. On the monitor, he saw the interior of the hoverpod. Richards was alone. He was bleeding and coughing blood.

"Richards?" William called over the radio. "What the hell's going on?"

They saw Grant fumble for the headset. "Here," he croaked, "boss."

"What's going on?" Williams repeated. "Where's the girl?"

"No girl." He coughed again, wiping his mouth and smearing red spittle across his face and the back of his hand.

"What's wrong with you, man? You're sick."

"Everyone's dead."

"What?" Williams looked incredulous. "You're not making sense. You killed everyone?"

The sad figure shook his head. "Sickness. All dead. In only ... hours."

Williams muted the coms, speaking to Simmons. "Turn back and scan the area."

"Sure thing." The pilot used his joystick and flipped a toggle. A view from the underside of the pod appeared on the side monitor. The pod curved to the west, showing the mining area from a few hundred feet. All but one of the machines in view were stationary. It was near the top of the dig, heading more or less towards the compound but no longer on the road. It simply ploughed over the top of the mounds of overburden.

"What the hell's going on?" Simmons muttered.

The compound came into view as the pod finished its turn. Several bodies lay in the dirt. Most were closer to the accommodation units to the northeast and a couple nearer the main office.

There was a white, banged-up police car in front of the office.

"Lewis' Merc is still there," Simmons noted.

Williams picked up the phone and dialled. There was a ringtone. After a few rings, a male answered over a static line.

"Olá?"

"Olá. Você pode falar inglês?"

"Si, I can speak Engleesh. Who ees dis?"

"I'm after the manager, Mr Lewis. Mr Trevor Lewis. Is he there?"

"Não. Everybodee is deed."

"Dead? You sure?"

"Yees. All deed."

William slammed the phone down. "Damn. It's true. They're all dead!" He flicked the hoverpod coms back on.

"Richards. What the hell happened? Did someone hit a gas bubble? Toxic fumes?"

"Sickness ... not gas ..."

"Where's the girl?" Williams probed. He looked to Simmons, who was tapping his arm, pointing. On-screen, a police officer in a dishevelled uniform came outside, looking at the drone and waving for it to land. Williams shook his head to Simmons. "Where's the girl, Richards?" he repeated.

"Escaped ..." They heard his rasping voice.

"Tell me you got the diamond?"

"Got …" Grant tapped his pocket. Then his other pocket. They watched him frantically searching all his clothes, then trying to look at the floor. "Gone …" he whimpered.

"Has the girl still got it?"

"Must've …"

"We're sending you back. Get the diamond." Williams pointed.

Simmons complied. The pod curved back towards the strip.

"Too … sick," Grant mumbled pathetically.

"Listen, you useless piece of shit, if you don't get that gem, there's no point coming back."

In a short time, the pod was back over the strip, where they could see from the forward camera a lone figure sitting in the front seat of a jeep. "Land right next to the car. May as well help that fool out."

***

"Shit. Why's the pod turning?" Dan watched as it curved over the compound. "It's coming straight to us."

"If Grant needed help to move, surely he's too sick to fly."

"Must be remotely piloted. Damn it."

In a spray of muddy water, the hoverpod landed beside them. The door opened, and Grant emerged like a broken man. He fell down the steps to the sodden ground.

"What's he trying to do?" Dan looked stupefied. "He can barely crawl, let alone walk."

Grant leaned up on an elbow, making a vague, pitiful attempt to wave them over.

"Should we help?" Rhyll looked on, helpless.

"Are you kidding? I don't give a shit about him. He shot me! I don't know what's going on, but after seeing the others, I don't think there's anything we can do. There's definitely some sickness here. We're probably—" He stopped, hearing a car. "Damn it," he hissed. The local police car drove over the rise and steered towards them.

It slid to a halt in the mud. The cop came out, looking at the pod, then Grant, then the jeep. Hand on his holster. *"Venha aqui,"* he called out over the pod's buzzing.

"He wants us to come over."

"You understand Spanish?"

"Portuguese."

The cop waved them closer.

"It's not like we're in a position to argue. Your wound needs a doctor." She climbed out. *"Nós estamos vindo,"* she called back. "Let's go." She reached in to help Dan to his feet.

"How do you know Portuguese?" He walked towards the cop.

"My parents taught me, and I've been in and around Brazil for years." She watched Grant, but he wasn't moving.

Seeing a wounded male and a girl, the cop took his hand from his holster, encouraging them to come to get in his car. Dan slumped against it while Rhyll opened the door for him to slide in.

Again, the pod whirred and lifted off, hovering about fifty feet up; it turned to them and remained motionless. Waiting.

The cop went over to check Grant, coming back in moments.

"Is he dead?" Dan asked.

"Yees. Deed. All deed." The cop pointed to the back seat. "Een," he said to Rhyll.

The cop turned and drove towards the gate. The car coughed as the electrics flickered on and off. The hoverpod raced to block the road, only leaving access back to the compound. The car slowed. The cop reached out, waving for it to move.

The pod swivelled side to side.

"I think that's a 'no'." Rhyll tapped the cop on the shoulder. *"Banheiro.* I need to pee anyway."

Cursing and banging the steering wheel, the cop spun the tyres in a hasty U-turn and drove back to the office. The pod followed, hovering above them when they pulled up.

Donning her pack, Rhyll helped Dan out as he slid across the back seat. They moved inside, and he sat down in a chair — the farthest from any bodies.

"I'll be back in a minute." She went in search of the toilet as the phone rang.

The officer stomped his boots to rid the mud and answered the phone. "Olá." The cop's eyes followed her out the room as he listened to the voice on the phone. Replying *si* mostly and nodding.

Giving the corpses a wide berth, Dan searched for another first-aid kit. When he found one, he sat and rummaged through it. It was mostly empty, and what was left was out of date. Leaving it, he looked for the kitchen where he dampened a cloth and wiped his face. He noticed the stairs at the kitchen's side door.

"I'm going to get my backpack ... mochila." Dan pointed up the stairs.

"Pare. Volte!" the cop called, waving him back, clearly irritated about everyone wandering off.

"Yeah, yeah," Dan muttered, continuing.

Though the sink was grotty, Rhyll washed her face. Nothing was right about any of this. Now with a few moments to herself, the improbable situation came to the forefront of her mind. How could she be asleep for so long? What was she doing in that cave? How was she alive, and where was her father's body? How did she get here? Why wasn't she more horrified by all these deaths? Had she become inhumane during her 'sleep'?

"How callous can one be?" she cried. Rhyll shook her head to clear it, but the feeling of dread and despair remained. "I need to find who killed my father. Where my mother is ..."

Digging into her pocket, she found the crystal was warm, and there was the slightest tingling.

"What are you?" She sniffed, holding it up to the light for closer study, pocketing it minutes later, none-the-wiser. She filled the basin, feeling the cold, refreshing water when she stuck her face in, but it didn't alleviate her despondency.

Water dripped onto her already damp shirt as she wiped her face with her hands. The sound in the back of her mind was real and had been getting louder, but she couldn't see anything from the dirty window.

Rhyll made her way back to the front office, noticing a backpack on the floor at the base of the stairs.

"That's new." She bent down to retrieve it.

It was heavy. Looking inside, she saw a camera case, lenses, notepads, and some electronic device, similar to a tablet but nothing close to anything she'd seen before.

Dan's, she guessed, slinging it over her shoulder as she entered the main office. Dan was no longer there. Neither was the cop.

"Dan?" she called, walking through. She stepped outside into the glare of the low sun as the clouds were breaking up. Suddenly, she was turned around and pushed hard against the wall. "Ow. What?"

"*Nós vamos agora*," the cop said, zip-tying her wrists.

"What are you doing? Where's Dan? *Onde está, Dan?*"

The background noise of the excavator intensified as it loomed over the last mound. They both turned. Rhyll recognised the driver she'd first met — the one Lewis had ordered to return to the office — slumped in his seat.

The excavator pivoted, crashing to the ground and heading towards the garage where Lewis' Merc was parked. The machine's clanking track grazed a large boulder, skewing the large vehicle to the left, now guiding it towards the cop car and the front office.

The cop swore, dragging her out of the way.

"Dan!" Rhyll screamed in warning, seeing him gagged in the back seat of the police car, hands behind his back. She struggled to free herself from the cop's grasp.

Dan twisted at the scream, seeing the look on both their faces. Glancing over his shoulder, he too saw the massive excavator coming at him. He awkwardly wriggled across the seat, struggling to open the far door with tied wrists and wounded shoulder.

Rhyll screamed again as the bucket at the front end of the large earthmover pushed the car into the building before driving over the left-hand side, crushing metal and shattering glass. Barely slowing, it then ploughed into the office, destroying the side wall. Lewis' office came crashing down, and breaking wood and smashing glass could be heard as the excavator continued.

"Watch out!" Rhyll yelled. The radio tower, attached to the side of the building, toppled towards them. They both scuttled out of the way.

Unable to use her hands, Rhyll tumbled to the mud, landing hard on her knees, then falling over to her side. It was a struggle to get up, especially with the two backpacks.

The cop hauled her to her feet. He tried to remove the packs, but her arms were through the straps. He swore and went to check on his car. He reached inside through the shattered window to try the radio, but it was dead.

Rhyll limped beside him, fearing the worst as she glanced in. No Dan! She sighed in relief, then staggered to the other side.

"There you are." He was several paces away, lying on the ground, covered in mud.

"Hmmp fffdt." Dan shrugged.

"Oi! A bit of help here?" she called to the cop.

He came over muttering and roughly pulled Dan to his feet.

"Your shoulder's bleeding again," she observed.

There was more crashing from the excavator as it cleared the building, dragging debris behind. Now it was heading towards two large, white metal containers.

"Gahh!" Dan pointed with his head frantically, eyes wide. "Gahh!"

Rhyll pulled his gag out. "What?"

"Gas! It'll explode." Dan turned to the cop. "Boom! Understand that?"

"Merda!" The cop looked back to his car.

"Lewis' Merc!" Rhyll shouted, dragging Dan towards the garage. His pack slipped off her shoulder and swung awkwardly from her arm, hindering movement.

Despite his excess weight, the cop ran ahead and opened the front and back doors, then jumped into the driver's seat looking for the keys.

"It's push-button!" Dan yelled, realising they hadn't moved.

"É um botão!" Rhyll repeated.

Seconds later the silver Merc SUV roared to life and churned out the garage and away from the gas cylinders. The excavator crashed into one, knocking it off its mount and into its partner. There was then a spark, followed by an almighty boom.

Fire and shrapnel flew in all directions.

Rhyll ducked instinctively when something struck the car. The SUV raced through the gate, sliding precariously as the cop gunned it down the road.

Breathing deeply, they began to relax. Rhyll was looking out the back window, watching the plume of smoke rising. She glimpsed the hoverpod high overhead and following.

"That was close," Dan said, noting the sharp metal protruding through his door. He turned his back to it and wriggled closer, hoping the car didn't lurch too much.

"The hoverpod is following us," Rhyll pointed out.

"That's weird." Dan grimaced. "Maybe it wasn't Grant that was so important. I did hear him say something about you and a diamond." He used his head to indicate the cop. "I wonder who was on the phone? As soon as he finished, he tied me up."

"The diamond maybe, but why me?" Rhyll shrugged, wondering why he was sitting with his back to the door, facing her. "That can't be comfortable. Why are you sitting like that?"

"What diamond?" He shook his head, making 'shushing' motions with his lips.

"It's not like I can show you right now." She indicated her tied hands.

Suddenly, Dan shifted positions, his hands now free as he removed the cut zip-ties from his bloodied wrists.

Rhyll then saw the metal fragment sticking through the door he had used to cut the bonds. "Lucky you."

"Turn around," he said. He then picked at the buckles of his backpack to undo the strapping.

"That's a relief," she said, rolling her shoulders. "Thanks."

Dan wiped his muddy hands on his thighs before rummaging through his pack. In one of the many pockets, he pulled out his penknife. He then carefully cut her ties.

"Even better." She rubbed her wrists, noticing the cop looking at the mirror.

"Ei o que está acontecendo?" the cop said.

"Apenas ficando confortável," she replied. "He wanted to know what we were doing. I told him we were getting comfortable," she explained to Dan.

The cop started swearing, banging the steering wheel.

Rhyll examined Dan's shoulder. "Got anything else in your pack?"

"Not for this, no. Getting shot wasn't on my itinerary."

"What *was*? Why were you snooping around here in the first place?"

"Journalism is *not* snooping."

"I thought you were a journalist from what I saw in your pack."

He leaned back, resting his eyes. "A group started here twenty years ago, protesting about the destruction of the forest and the removal of the indigenous tribes—"

"Yes, the Wai-wai." She nodded.

"I was here ten years ago to cover their ten-year anniversary. You know about the Wai-wai?"

She nodded. "My parents were working on a dig with them."

"When? Where? This place has been a ruin far longer than you've been around."

Looking to the front, she saw a shantytown. What's that?" She turned to the side window as they slowed.

Placard bearers ran to the roadside waving signs as the car approached.

Dan looked. "That's the protester camp."

Rhyll started winding down her window. The cop yelled at her and then turned his attention to the protesters as they started throwing rocks at the car.

Blaring his horn, he swore and sped off, regardless of how close they were to the car.

———

Nala returned to camp the next day before lunch. As she passed the tents, she saw a few people with bandages on their heads and limbs.

"Hey, boss." Miguel waved. "Good visit? How are the indigs doing?"

Nala went a few days a fortnight, doing her rounds of the more remote indigenous natives.

"They're restless about something, but they'll survive. And that will be the last time I hear you calling them that. I would have thought by now you'd show more respect to the first nation peoples." She dropped her pack and sat, accepting a cup of water from Miguel. "What the hell happened here?"

"Lewis came past last night – except it wasn't Lewis. Looked like the fat cop that drove in earlier."

"You're not making sense. What fat cop? You mean Rodriguez? Why was he in Lewis' SUV?"

"Yep. Dunno about the why, but there were some problems at the mine late yesterday. We heard an explosion. There was a fire with lots of smoke. Me and the others were going for a look. Thought we'd wait for you."

Nala sighed. She'd been born in the area, left for her studies, and then returned to take up the position here over fifteen years ago. The generous monthly stipend from the university helped. She'd forgotten how many times her group had had a run-in with Lewis and his mob from Erdany.

"Hey, you remember that reporter that came here for the tenth-year anniversary?"

"How would you know about it? You weren't here."

"I saw it on the TV, and that old chieftain with his message of doom."

"He was a shaman, not a chieftain."

"Was he? Well anyway, it's what inspired me to come here and help. It was an exposé on the atrocities this mining scum were committing."

"OK. Sure. I remember him." *Too well.* "What's that got to do with it?"

"He was here yesterday. He asked for you, but as you were away, he went in there instead. Shannon says she reckons she saw him in the back seat of the Merc when it left."

"Does she?"

"Yeah, with some redhead chick—"

"What redhead girl?" Nala's heart skipped a beat.

"I only caught a glimpse. Some teen." Miguel shrugged. "Rodriguez arrived in his car. About an hour later, there was an explosion, and Rodriguez raced out in the SUV, nearly hitting us and then speeding off."

"Did anyone see how this girl arrived? Was she with Rodriguez when he first got here?"

"Nah. He was alone in his old cop car, and no one's been on the road for days. One of those hoverpods was following the car."

"Following the cop car?" Nala looked at him in confusion.

"Nah. The Merc when they left. Why would it be following Rodriguez?"

She ignored his question. "And it was heading to São Lucas?"

Miguel nodded.

"Okay. Tell the boys we'll go in for a look at the mine after I have a quick wash and some food."

"Righto, boss." Miguel sauntered over to the others around the fire to tell them the news.

CHAPTER SIX

A NOISE WOKE RHYLL FROM A BAD DREAM. THEY WERE ALL BAD dreams lately — dreams of smoke and chanting. Touching a baby. She felt no more refreshed than when she'd lain down, exhausted, the night before. In fact, now she was awake, the memory of the devastation she'd witnessed gnawed at her again.

Rodriguez had driven until late at night. They'd arrived here, and two other officers had come out of the station and taken them to these cells. Side by side, a bunk and a bucket each. There was no searching or any processing. She'd overheard Rodriguez tell them to lock them up and wait for further instructions. That was the last she'd seen of him.

Dan was on his bunk, drooling in his sleep. His shoulder hadn't been seen to, and she was worried it would become septic.

While there were no distractions, she quickly made use of the bucket.

More coughing came from the front office of the police cells — the same noise that woke her. She had heard it on and off since their arrival late last night. It was getting worse. Lightning flashed through the high windows.

"Olá, posso pegar um pouco de água, por favor?" she called out after hearing another bout of coughing.

A chair scraped, then an officer trudged in. Like Rodriguez, this cop wasn't looking in good shape either. He passed a bottle of water through the bars.

"Obrigado." She thanked him. "Do you speak English?"

"Americano?" He nodded. "Bit."

"Why are we here? When can we go? My friend needs a doctor." She pointed to Dan, indicating his arm. "Médico."

He nodded, understanding. "Rodriguez says you stay. Gringo come to take you."

"What gringo?"

"Americanos. Muito dinheiro."

"Lots of money? Americans? Why?" she asked. "Por quê?"

He shrugged, started coughing, and then turned away, staggering back to the front office.

Rhyll went back to her bunk, opened the bottle, and dribbled a bit on her hands to wash them.

"What did he say about rich Americans?" Dan mumbled, waking up.

"Sorry to wake you." She wiped her hands on her shirt and passed him the bottle. "It doesn't make sense. Why would Americans want me? And why 'much money'?"

"Maybe because of this diamond?" He took a drink from the bottle. "Are you famous? Are they after a ransom?"

"You're the journalist. You tell me. Does *Rhyllien Ellis* ring a bell?"

He shook his head. "Okay. I've got a bunch of questions. Why were you at the mine? How did you get here? You're not from the protest camp. And you haven't explained to me about this diamond. Interesting you have parents who taught you Portuguese and know the Wai-wai. Where is this dig they are on?"

"You won't believe a word I say anyway."

"Let's start with this diamond then. I'll believe what I can see and touch."

Rhyll considered it, thinking about what happened with Lewis. She unbuttoned her top pocket and pulled it out. As always, the crystal was warm and vibrating. She was no closer to determining how it worked or what it did, but she sensed it had something to with what was going on. She just wanted to know how so she could stop it.

"Hello? Earth to Mars …"

Rhyll looked up, broken from her thoughts. "Sorry." She handed it to him. "Be careful."

Dan put his hand out, surprised at the size of it. "That's one big rock," he said as he admired the deep-green, multifaceted crystal. "Eight sides."

"Lewis called it an octahedron and says it's a diamond." She waited. "It doesn't burn you or vibrate?"

"No … but it's warm and feels … comfortable. If it is a diamond, it's incredible. I can understand why someone would be after it. Where on earth did you get it?"

"That's where it starts getting unbelievable. Even I think I'm going crazy. I was shot here." She lifted her shirt to expose her ribs near her armpit.

Dan looked away. "As a journalist, I'll find out how unbelievable it is … once I get internet."

She dropped the shirt and began telling her story. It even sounded ludicrous to her. "At least you didn't laugh," she said afterwards. "It has to be a weird, horrible dream. It's all impossible."

"When was this?" He handed the jewel back.

"When? June 2021. Why?"

"My shit-o-meter is cranking up."

"Shit-o-meter?" Rhyll laughed. "I did say it was hard to believe. I can't understand how this mine has been going for so long without my parents knowing about it. I've never heard of it."

"You said your parents were on a dig with the natives. I gather they are archaeologists?"

"And very good ones," Rhyll nodded. "Father was killed …

murdered in a robbery after some relics." She wiped her eyes quickly. "I saw a map at the mine, but it can't be the area I thought it was. There are Wai-wai tribes scattered through the northern Amazon area. Many had none or very little contact with non-natives."

"Where did you think you were?"

"On the border of Para and Amazonia states, near Roraima in the Trombetas National Park."

"You are. Or were. We're in São Lucas, farther north in the State of Roraima."

"But it's a tiny village, barely even on the maps. Rorainópolis is the nearest large town. But how could they be mining in a preserved national park for twenty years?"

They heard another fit of coughing from the front of the station, then the noise of someone throwing up. A chair scraped, followed by the sound of someone hitting the floor.

"Hello? Olá?" Rhyll went quickly to the bars. "Are you okay?" Through the partially opened doorway, she could see the corner of a desk and the edge of a window, but that was it.

Silence was the only response. Rhyll called out several more times, with no result.

"Why is everyone getting sick? Tell me that, Mr Journalist."

"I want to know why *we* aren't." He lay down in pain.

"You're looking feverish," she observed.

"Maybe I spoke too soon, and I *am* getting sick ..."

"No ... No, this is different. You don't ... *feel* the same ..."

He turned to her. "What?"

"I can't explain ... Those that are coughing – like Grant, and those back at the mine, or Rodriguez, and now this one – they felt *different*. You just feel feverish, not like them."

"Ah well ... As long as a fever is better." Dan sighed, lay back, and remained silent.

After a few minutes, Rhyll heard him snoring again. She lay down in her bunk, not for the first or last time wondering what the hell was going on.

From the light across the wall, it was mid-morning when Rhyll woke to the sounds of trucks. She was thirsty; one bottle of water between the two of them wasn't going to last, and Dan needed it more than she did.

They neither heard nor saw from the cop in the front office again, though she called many times for more water or food.

"Dan, wake up." Her fellow cellmate was still in a fever-induced sleep. She got off her bunk and wandered over. "Dan," she whispered, shaking his foot.

"Wha—"

"There are people outside," she whispered.

Dan rubbed his face with his good hand and took a breath. "Who? These *Americanos*?" His whisper rasped with his dry throat. He picked up the water bottle before realising it was empty and dropping it to the floor. "Why are we whispering?"

"I'm not sure. Something doesn't feel right."

The sound of more trucks came through the barred windows. After a few minutes, they could hear muffled voices outside. In the background, the droning sound of hoverpods could be heard.

"Some are speaking English." She shrugged. "I wonder if it's the CDC or WHO?"

"I doubt it's either of them. They don't exist — at least not in any recognisable form."

"What do you mean? Who else is there?"

"Who else? I can't think of the complete list ... but there's Global Infection Franchise, Global Health Organisation — they're the two largest in this region — Global Organisation for Disease Eradication, Department of Infection Control—"

"What happened to the CDC and WHO?"

"Well, with the turmoil after the 2019-2021 pandemic—"

"I heard about that."

"Since then, big pharma really got into the vaccine game. We knew they were all for profit, but the pandemic – and fear –

really paved the way for vaccine patents; that's where the big money lay. When nations were fighting over religion, borders, or politics, the bigger pharmaceutical organisations were gearing up for the next outbreak. Several organisations got in on it early, vying over who had the rights for the patents, then they became militarised.

"Rumours spread — conspiracy theories about how some of these corporations engineered a virus just to make more dollars by then selling a vaccine. With some of the major governments going down, they had bigger and better resources. Soon, there was a franchise on plagues ... on sickness." He got up and stretched a bit.

"But they help people, right?"

"Oh yeah. Those that can pay."

"And if you can't pay?"

"If you want to live, there's always one way or another to pay; work, work the land ... dying people will do many things to save themselves or their loved ones."

"That's terrible!"

"Welcome to 2056. Where have you been?"

"When?" Rhyll's face went pale. "I thought you said 2056?"

"I did." Dan sat on his bunk, looking at her. "17th October 2056. When did you think it was? Maybe it's you who's feverish."

"But my father was killed in 2021. I turned 16 in 2021 ... I was born in 2005 ..."

The silence between them grew as the noises outside continued.

Dan reached through, holding her on the arm. "Maybe a lie-down. I think you need a drink."

"I would if there was any." Rhyll lay back, but her eyes remained open, deep in thought. How could she possibly have been *asleep* for thirty-five years? *What's happening?*

• • •

The shafts of sunlight had changed dramatically when she sat up. She must have dozed off.

"There she is," Dan greeted her.

"This is all real, isn't it?" She turned to him, a haunted look in her eyes.

"I don't know what to say ... but yes. Everything I said is the truth."

Rhyll nodded. "It does make sense, given what I've heard ... I even sense it's true, but I don't understand any of it; the hoverpod, the mine going for twenty years. Why I didn't die from being shot."

"And nobody wants to be a 53-year-old teenager."

"Lucky you're a journalist; you're not funny at all. You mentioned major governments going down? I assume America had to help some nation find their freedom?"

"So young, yet so cynical." Dan chuckled. "Sorry, no. In this case, America had its own troubles. The north and south got back into it, trying to relive the first civil war, no doubt fed by right-wing nut-jobs flogging their conspiracy theories over the internet and the dark web. So, now America is three major territories: the Democratic Allied States, the Central Commonwealth States, and the Western Union. Most people who didn't want to be involved either headed north to Canada or south to Mexico."

"Americans crossed into Mexico?"

"Ironic or what? And no wall to stop them."

"What about Europe?" she asked after a while, trying to take it all in.

"Basically, east and west. Russia, China and North Vietnam formed a pact against the old EU and the rest of the world."

Rhyll looked appalled.

"I guess overall it's much better, now that the territories have been sorted out and are semi-permanent. Life continues, though there are always skirmishes along the borders, but those are mainly over trade."

"Not politics or religion?" she asked.

"Politics has always been about money — moreso these days. It's become far more corporatised — you get what you pay for. Poor countries get swallowed overnight with a coup; richer countries — or those with rich or strong allies — fight tooth and nail to remain independent."

Outside, the vehicle noises finally stopped, replaced by orders being given and the sound of many footsteps on the gravel.

Dan sat up more and leant against the wall, tucking his pillow behind for comfort. "It's been what, three days now since the mine? News reports of mysterious deaths are the sort of thing they live for. My guess? It's the GHO," Dan suggested. "Or the GIF. Those two organisations have been working in South American regions for a while. I've seen some of their work before. They compete with each other, but we'll be fine." He sat up. "They'll comb house by house, business by business in a pattern," Dan reassured Rhyll. "They will get to us at some stage."

"I'd rather they got to us sooner, considering your fever and our lack of water." She dragged her bunk to the wall with the barred window up near the ceiling. "Hey, you. Olá. We're in here and need help!" she called out several times.

Within minutes they heard voices in the front office, boots on the floor, and the sound of a chair scraping. Three figures in military-style EV suits walked slowly into the cell area. One had his weapon ready and another had some device from which he quoted numbers, which his colleague scribbled on a pad. She didn't recognise their insignia, a double helix – half silver, half red – with the earth in its centre.

Dan turned to her and said softly, "It's the GHO."

Rhyll nodded. "One of the good ones then?"

"Better equipped and more professional. We're lucky." He turned to the men. "Glad to see you—" Dan started.

"Sir, we have two here in the police lockup," one of them spoke into his headset. "A male and a female. They're alive ... Negative, the girl looks young and remarkably healthy. The other ... not so much sick but wounded." They loitered near the cells, observing the two prisoners and waving the instrument in their direction. He changed the setting a couple of times, and the other continued to write notes.

Rhyll stood up and pointed to Dan. "We need water, and my friend here needs a doctor. He's been shot and has a fev—"

"Good. You speak Anglo. Names, please. Who are you?" the one with the tablet asked.

"I'm Daniel Dobson."

"My friend needs a doctor," Rhyll insisted.

"All in good time, miss. Name?"

"Rhyllien Ellis."

"Spell it, please."

"E-l-l-i-s," Rhyll answered automatically.

"Your first name." He tapped his fingers in annoyance. He typed the letters as she spelt them. "Any middle name?"

"Aurora," Rhyll answered. "A-u-r—"

"How long have you been here?"

Rhyll answered first. "This is my third day."

"Same," Dan said.

"DOB?"

"19th August 2021," Dan replied.

"And you, miss?" he asked after a pause.

"1st April," she answered. She saw Dan give her a warning look, shaking his head. She shrugged with a grin. "2005."

"2005? There's always a wise-ass. So, miss, you're 53?" He typed on his tablet. Then returned his attention back to her. "Born on Luna, perhaps?"

"Luna? The moon? Can we do that now?" She looked to Dan, who shook his head, suppressing a laugh. "I was born on the Indian Ocean."

"The Indian Ocean? Fine. Have it your way. I can see why they locked you up."

"It's true," she protested. "On a yacht called the *Aurora*. It's where I got my middle name."

Two of the figures turned away and left. The armed one remained.

"Any chance of water and food? It's been two days now," Dan said.

At first, the soldier ignored them, not moving at all. Just watching them.

"Please?" Rhyll asked, putting on her best lost-girl look.

The soldier left for a few minutes. When he returned, he had two bottles of water and a couple of ration packs. Making sure he didn't physically contact them, or allow them to contact him, he got them to move back before passing the supplies through the bars.

"Thanks," they both said at the same time.

"Told you they'd look after us." Dan ripped open his pack.

She drank half her water before peeling her ration pack open, looking at the contents dubiously. "How processed is this?" She tentatively ate it. Full of flavour, but so little real nutritional value despite what was written on the label.

They'd barely finished eating when two more armed soldiers, all in EV suits and breathing gear, arrived with one of the original men.

"Okay," one soldier said. "We're going to move you to a safe place for examination. Behave and this will be painless." He directed the last words to Rhyll.

"Fine," she huffed.

He unlocked the cells, directing them to come forward. In silence, the soldiers escorted the pair out of the cells — one in front, two behind.

Rhyll wasn't surprised, but she was still sad to see the corpse of the police officer on the floor.

Outside, it was like a military camp. Four-wheel drive vehicles and armoured trucks were parked in formation, and everyone was in the same type of EV suits but in differing colours, probably denoting doctors, nurses, and those without a medical function. Some were in step, and she assumed they were a mix of military as well as civilian medical staff.

In pairs, people were conducting their own tests with various instruments on the air, water, and soil, while others were hunched over the bodies in the street. She'd seen the bodies at the mine, and it had been a shock. This was still a shock, but she was prepared for it, and therefore, she was slightly inured to what she saw. Like when she saw those in the mine office.

Dan almost tripped on the rough roadway as he stared at the gruesome sight. Again, it made her wonder why she was desensitised to it. *Am I that callous a girl?*

They continued following the armed escort down the road to a large, tented area. Everyone who saw them paused to look. Inside, the main tent was split into various sections, all walled off with large sheets of clear, double-layered plastic. Each unit had its own ventilation units.

They were separated and Dan entered one; Rhyll was ushered to the adjacent unit. There was an airlock to get into each unit; only one door could be opened at a time.

Two medical aides approached from another section, the male walking past her and going to Dan while a female aide came into her unit with a tablet.

"Any implants or enhancements?" the aide asked.

"Any what?"

"Implants or enhancements." She now spoke as if speaking to a child. "Are you all biological? No prosthetics?"

"I'm all biological." Rhyll looked confused. "Why wouldn't I be?"

"Raise your arms, please," the aide said as she put her tablet down. "I need to frisk you."

She saw Dan was struggling, going through the same procedure. "Are you blind? Can't you see the shoulder wound?" she called across to the other aide. "He needs a doctor."

"Miss"—the aide urged her to raise her arms—"it's procedural only. Nothing personal."

"Why is no one listening?" Feeling she had no choice, she raised her arms. The nurse was efficient, running her hands over the clothed area of Rhyll's body.

"What's this?" She felt something in her thigh pocket.

The armed escorts shifted their stance, becoming more alert.

"An old heirloom."

"Remove it, please."

"I'd rather not. It's very important to me."

"Rhyllien, is it? We'll put it in the safe after you're settled. You should realise, we don't have to ask."

Reluctantly, she reached into her pocket. The armed escorts were very alert now. *So tense. What's wrong with these people?*

Their eyes almost bulged when they saw the crystal.

"It's only glass, dummies." She giggled and rolled her eyes — as expected of a teenager.

Feigning indifference, they relaxed and resumed their previous postures.

"If you would enter here and change into these clothes?" Popping the crystal into her pocket, the nurse pointed to a set of lime green pyjamas on a table situated inside an opaque cubicle.

"I guess I have no choice?" she asked, rhetorically.

"Be quick. Come out when you're ready, but in four minutes, this door's opening. Put your old clothes in that yellow haz-bag." When Rhyll walked inside, the nurse closed the door behind her.

Taking the hint, Rhyll quickly removed all her clothes and slipped into the pyjama-like outfit. At least they were clean, which was a relief as her other clothes were getting crusty with mud and a bit on the nose. She was fixing her hair when the door opened.

"This way, miss," a guard said.

She was then returned to her cubicle next to Dan, who was wearing similar clothes.

"See, no harm done." Dan tried to smile reassuringly once she negotiated the entry.

"No harm done," she answered. "How are you?"

"I thought I'd seen some rough incidents around the globe but not so many corpses before … You seem to have coped well enough, though."

She shrugged it off. "So, what happens next?"

"Medical examination," a voice said. It was slightly muffled behind the double wall and through his EV suit. "We need to see why you two aren't affected by whatever it is going on here. I'm Dr Andrews. We'll cross-reference these details with anything on our database. Thank you," he said, accepting the tablet from the nurse.

Rhyll watched her leave, wanting to ask about her crystal and where it would be kept, but she also didn't want to seem overly concerned in case it brought undue attention to the "piece of glass".

"Can you see to my friend first?" she asked. "He was injured three days ago."

Andrews looked at the notes. "We can do that easily enough. I assume you've got insurance?"

"Through my work. What's going on here?" Dan asked as the doctor entered his unit. "Is there a plague or something?"

"Too early to be sure, except you're the only ones still breathing."

"And the animals?" Rhyll added. "We heard them yesterday." She determined this doctor wasn't military.

"Correct. Unbutton your shirt, please."

Dan did so, and the doctor helped peel the fabric over the shoulder, then the discoloured bandaging. "Looks infected."

"Facilities were limited." Dan winced at the probing. "And as you say, everyone seems to be dead, so they weren't much help."

"Still, you're in good hands now. Nurse, could you get hot water, swabs, and antiseptic?" he called to her, then focused on Dan. "The bullet grazed, but it will scar. How did it happen? Cleaning a firearm? Looting?"

"I'm an investigative journalist."

"That explains it. Everyone likes their secrets. Lucky you aren't an environmental journalist." He chuckled. "I understand they found you in the police lock-up?"

"Cops and I don't see eye to eye. I suspect something got lost in translation."

"Always does."

The nurse came back with a tray of equipment. Within ten minutes, the wound was cleaned and dressed. "I'll give you a shot of antibiotics, and we'll set you up on a course of medication. Right now, though, I'll examine you, then your friend."

"Sounds fair enough." Dan lay back. He gave Rhyll a wink.

"If you're going to poke and prod me, it might be best if I could use the bathroom first," Rhyll said.

"Fair enough." Dr Andrews pointed to the airlock. "Miss, if you would be so kind."

The nurse gave Rhyll a urine sample jar when she was let into the main area, then motioned for one of the guards. "Escort her to the quarantine latrines."

"Same for you." The doctor gave Dan a sample jar from the tray and directed an escort.

The examination procedure was fairly simple: checking the eyes, ears, temperature, blood pressure, heart monitoring, weight, taking several hair and blood samples, and asking a bunch of questions.

"How long have you been in Brazil?" Dr Andrews asked.

"On and off for several years." She briefly explained her parents' work.

"I must say, you look remarkable for a fifty-three-year-old."

She giggled. "Sorry about that. I was born in 2041, but it really was the first of April in the middle of the Indian Ocean."

"And the yacht?"

"The *Aurora*. Also true. My parents were anthropologists and archaeologists. We travelled a lot. We didn't stay long in any one area."

"Quite a life for a young girl," he said.

"Yes." Rhyll had to concentrate on something else before she started welling up.

"And where are they? Can we contact them?"

"They're ... deceased." As she said it, she realised the doctor would assume from this sickness going around.

"I'm sorry for your loss."

Dan returned shortly after, leaving his sample jar on the table by his airlock.

The soldier resumed his position by the main entrance.

Once the examination of Rhyll was complete, the doctor went to Dan.

"How widespread is this contagion?" Dan asked. "Is it localised to this area only, or are there incidents elsewhere?"

"An astute question. I'm sure someone with the appropriate clearance will come along later with an answer for you." When finished, he addressed them both before he left. "We'll arrange some food and water. In the meantime, get some rest."

When their lunch came, Dan moved his chair closer to the adjoining wall. Rhyll did the same so they could talk without shouting, eating with their trays on their laps.

After another hour, the armed escort was relieved. The replacements stood on each side of the door, quietly talking to each other, their voices muted through the helmets and by distance.

The escorts changed again two hours later. From the growing noise, there appeared to be some sort of ruckus outside; footsteps were moving fast here and there. Shouting was followed by the sound of rending metal.

"Sounds like a vehicle crash." Dan tried to see out the gap between the tent flaps. "Hey, man," Dan called out. "Know what's happening?"

They looked at Dan but ignored him. Then one of the escorts coughed.

"Same as before, unfortunately." Rhyll watched the soldiers with sad eyes.

"These people are totally covered with their EV suits. There's no way this sickness ... plague ... or whatever it is can get all of them at the same time."

"And yet, it's happening again."

As if to prove her point, the escort coughed once more, louder and harder. His companion turned to him, saying something.

More commotion outside could be heard — some of it clear and distinct, some more distant and muffled. They both jumped when there was rapid gunfire in the distance.

One of the soldiers left. They heard him yell, and the other one ducked through the flap. It was dim outside now, like dusk. They heard the soldiers running.

A couple of stray bullets penetrated the tented area. Nowhere near them, but unexpected all the same. As one, they ducked for cover; Dan a bit slower because of his shoulder.

"Might be wise to keep a low profile for a while." He climbed under his bunk bed.

Rhyll nodded her agreement and followed suit.

Outside was more running, yelling, coughing, and shooting.

They lay there and waited for what seemed an hour before the noise subsided. The gunfire stopped, then it was coughing, moaning, and cries for help, followed by silence.

After another ten minutes, Rhyll climbed up and made her way to the airlock exit. There was nothing to bar any escape, now that there was no armed guard. Dan joined her.

"Shoulder feeling better?" she asked. "You've got some colour now."

"It is, but I'll need more antibiotics." He headed to where the nurse had initially retrieved the tray of equipment. He rummaged through a medicine cabinet, and various containers of medicines, until he found what he recognised as antibiotics. He also grabbed a couple of packets of painkillers.

Rhyll waited by the entrance, noting the many sheets of printed paper pinned to the noticeboard beside the door. A quick read indicated they were the names and addresses of the town's inhabitants.

Dan came up behind her, stuffing the medication in his pockets. "There is a lot of them," he said quietly.

Rhyll nodded in silence and followed him to the main exit.

Outside was a tragedy, but it was one they were expecting, considering the noise and shooting.

Bodies lay in every direction. Quite a few of the body bags in this area had been arranged in an orderly fashion along the sides of the roads, but the GHO and military personnel were scattered. Some were lying behind vehicles as if sheltering from the bullets, and a couple lay sprawled in the streets with gunshot wounds.

Like at the mines, some were contorted as if in great pain. Others looked like they had sat down against the wall or a tree and simply passed away. Through the facemasks, many looked discoloured with one affliction or another, others with vomit or blood filling their helmets or leaking into their laps.

CHAPTER SEVEN

Rhyll and Dan remained silent, numbed by the death around them.

"Surely someone survived. We two cannot possibly be the only ones immune to whatever is occurring." Dan's voice caught in his throat. "Despite what the doc said."

Rhyll could think of nothing to say, though she had an inkling of why. It was all so overwhelming.

They walked on in sombre silence, intermittent lightning flashes brightening the sky. As they turned a corner, the area opened to a plaza with a large church at the eastern end. She remembered the way back to the police station. There was smoke above the buildings to the south, but not a raging inferno and nowhere near them.

"I saw our backpacks at the station when we left," she said to Dan before he asked. "Hopefully, they weren't moved. We'll never find them otherwise."

Approaching the police station, Dan slowed.

"What is it?" Rhyll asked, seeing him scrutinising several bodies.

"They aren't GHO uniforms," he declared, pointing.

At various locations down a side road, four men lay, all dead from gunshot wounds.

"I think this might have been what started the shooting." He started walking towards the closest body.

"What makes you think that?"

"The first gunshots we heard were from a distance — about this location, at a guess; corporations like GHO guard their turf well, hence the military presence."

The first male was wearing a dark-grey jumpsuit with armoured panels, and there was a small Velcro patch on the left upper arm. He pulled it off to show her. It was an image of an eye, with the world as the eyeball. "Firstly, these are mercenaries from a group called *ICON* ."

"ICON ?"

"Yes, a security firm based in Florida but with a worldwide reach. I'm curious what would bring them here; they wouldn't normally confront a large corporation like this."

"That looks like the same picture on the hoverpod at the mine."

"Maybe they are connected." He paused. "After the diamond, perhaps?" Dan started checking pockets.

"What are you doing?"

"I'm not stealing from the dead if that's what you're thinking. It's unlikely, but I was checking for ID." He pointed. "I've seen these in the field before. These are expensive weapons and top-of-the-line comms gear." Dan removed one of the headsets and listened. Only static could be heard. He dropped it. Moving on to the other bodies, they found all were dressed similarly and carrying the same weapons — a rifle, a pistol, and a knife. "Someone wanted something here badly. The cheaper companies have a militia, mercenaries for the highest bidder," Dan explained. "The large corporations have their own military."

"I'm beginning to hate 2056." She moved on.

"You're lucky you weren't around ten to twenty years ago. It was much worse."

I was. I was dead in a cave.

The police station looked the same as when they left it. Once the packs were collected and the contents checked, they went back outside. The body of the cop had been removed, but after their three-day incarceration, they'd had enough of the station. Rhyll donned her pack, and Dan hooked his over his good shoulder. With his camera in hand, he started taking pictures of the tragedy surrounding them.

"How do you think those guys got here?"

"Why don't we go look?" Dan headed back down the road towards the grey-clad military bodies. There was the noise of a slow vehicle, stopping and starting. They shared a look and went to investigate.

"Ah. A Reaping," Dan observed.

"What?" Rhyll asked as she looked on with equal horror and confusion. Body bags were spaced out along the side of the road. Man-like machines were collecting them and putting them into a large vehicle. "Are they ... robots?"

"Androids. But these are only basic models to do the menial tasks," Dan confirmed, taking photos.

"What are they doing?" She watched as the silver-and-red-painted androids collected another corpse. They moved like clockwork, each movement accompanied with the slight whirring noise of servos; each step a metallic clank. After an interval, the vehicle moved slowly, stopping every few metres where the androids would load up the next body. A funnel at the top blew a stream of grey smoke.

Dan moved around to take pictures. "First time I've seen them in action, considering I've not been in a plague-infected area before. To reduce contamination, the bodies are incinerated as quickly as possible. They're generally ID'd, but it isn't always the case. Especially in rural areas or third-world countries."

They moved on. At the end of the next block was a hoverpod, but larger than the one at the mine. It had an identical logo on the nose and sides of the fuselage, matching the ICON logo on the slain gunmen. As they approached, two laser cannons appeared.

Dan stopped, grabbing Rhyll's shoulder. "Back away slowly," he advised. "If we get closer without the proper ID, it'll open fire. I don't know about you, but I'd rather not try to dodge AI laser turrets."

The pair backed away and ducked behind the nearest building for cover.

"Now what?" Rhyll asked.

"We leave. There was no ID or remote on any of those guys."

"How would they get aboard?"

"A good question. Unlikely they'd lose it, so at a guess, there was someone else."

"But not in that group?"

"Correct." Dan popped his head around the corner to study the hoverpod. "I'm guessing it's a 6-8 seater; there could be four other men around here somewhere." He took a quick snapshot.

The streetlights, few and far between, came on automatically as the sun dipped below the horizon.

"That's funny," Dan observed. "All that lightning earlier, but there is not a cloud in the sky."

The pair wandered back to the centre of town where the bulk of the vehicles were near the plaza, each with the GHO company logo on the sides.

One vehicle, in particular, stood out: a prime mover with a large trailer. Several antennas and satellite dishes sprouted from its roof. There was a short ramp leading to a locked door at the rear. To the side was a card swipe console.

Dan strode over to the nearest GHO bodies wearing medical staff suits. A quick search found a lanyard with a security ID. He unclipped it, and one on the other body, and returned to the trailer.

"What are they?"

"You certainly have had a sheltered childhood. These security doors will only open to the correct swipe card or ID. We're lucky there's no AI laser security." He tried one card, then the other. Neither worked.

"What we need to do is find a higher-ranking officer." He turned back to the body-littered street.

"How can you tell the difference?"

"The more bling there is on their uniforms — shoulders or upper arms — the better chance they'll have the authorisation to get in. You go that way, and I'll go this way. Look for a lanyard around the neck or sometimes clipped to their belt." When she hesitated, he added, "It's either that or sleep outside. I've seen pictures; these command vehicles are generally well-equipped."

They went their separate ways, each returning with a handful of lanyards. Eventually, one of them worked. The unsuccessful ones were discarded.

"Ah. This is Dr Andrews' lanyard. I didn't really recognise him in the dark. Poor man. He seemed nice enough."

"We'll try more lanyards later. Better to have a spare or two," Dan advised. "I'm just glad we didn't need a retinal scan."

The doors unlocked with a click, and entering was through an airlock. There was a beeping sound, followed by a high-pressure blast of a neutral-smelling vapour shooting from the floor, ceiling, and side walls. When that finished, the vapour was sucked out in seconds, and they were bathed in intense blue light. There was another tone, and the inner glass door softly clicked open down the centre.

Inside there were three bodies: two seated and one on the narrow walkway between the bunks. Stepping over the latter, Dan did a quick walk down the length of the trailer's interior. It was designed as live-in quarters for four personnel, with an ensuite, fully functional kitchenette, a well-stocked pantry, and even a recreation lounge.

"I think we've found our accommodation for the night," Dan called back, leaving his backpack on the lounge.

"Yeah, true, but I'd prefer it if we removed *them* first." She pointed. "I have a great deal of respect for the deceased, but I draw the line at sharing sleeping quarters with them. You up for it?"

"I'll do what I can." Dan agreed, and together they dragged

the bodies one by one outside, going through the airlock procedure each time. It was a tight squeeze for three, and the proximity to a corpse was unpleasant.

"Mind if I grab the first shower?" Rhyll asked, grabbing her pack.

"Of course. Ladies first."

<hr>

Dan went to the nearest computer, putting the three ID cards taken from the bodies on the desk. Swiping one got the computer going.

With his journalist training, he managed to search the databases far more efficiently. He also turned on the monitor to get the news, swiping through the channels for an English-speaking one. The feed glitched frequently.

While the news was playing out, he started a search for *Rhyllien Ellis*. It took several minutes, but eventually, he followed a trail until he had a good understanding. He left each tab open so Rhyll could follow it later.

"GHO Manaus Command to mobile unit 45. Please respond." The radio was also garbled with lots of static. Taking Dan by surprise, the message repeated itself several times before he decided to reply.

Looking around the cabin first, he found paperwork referencing this GHO unit as Mobile Unit 45.

"Hello. This is Mobile Unit 45," he replied, cringing at the static.

"45? Who's speaking?"

Thinking quickly before he answered, Dan picked a random name and muffled his voice. "Umm ... this is Thomas Black."

"Thomas Black? What rank are you? Where are the designated personnel? Is Doctor Andrews there?" the voice over the radio asked.

"Everyone is dead."

"Repeat. The line is very bad. Did you say everyone is dead?"

"Yes. Everyone is dead. Roughly sixty-five GHO personnel and the whole town. No one is left alive."

"Mr. Black, why are you there?" The voice was barely understandable over the radio noise.

"Don't send anyone else. They'll all die the same way."

"What did they die from?"

"Some were shot, but most died of natural causes. Many vomited. I'm not a doctor."

"And there's no one to confirm this?"

"Only in a séance. Look, man, I'm a nobody talking to you on your radio inside your highly-secured command vehicle. You think I was invited? Something bad is happening. Nothing your people did made a difference. Everyone was still in their EV suits."

"Why are you still alive?"

"I have no idea—"

"You mentioned shooting? Who shot who?"

"There's a squad of dead mercenaries. They were wearing armoured combat suits with ICON patches. They're dead too. I repeat, do not send anyone." He shut off the radio, sighing with relief when the static stopped.

Rhyll came out of the shower in a clean set of clothes — the last from her backpack. "Maybe not as comfortable as pyjamas but far more practical—" She stopped when she saw his look. "What is it?"

"I was on the radio to the headquarters of these guys."

"Why?" she asked, sitting down.

"They called. If no one answered, they'd send someone. I had to let them know anyone they send would die. The line was bad though. No doubt this electrical storm is interfering with it."

He turned back to the screen, showing her the records he'd found. "I was looking you up. Have a read of this." Dan showed her how to navigate the tabs and left her to it. "I'll have a shower now. I hope you left me some hot water," he said as he closed the cubicle door.

Rhyll started reading. And crying.

According to the news bulletin dated August 2021, Professor Imogen Ellis organised a search when her husband, Professor Ken Ellis, failed to radio upon his arrival in Oriximiná. A search found the empty barge, and farther downstream, a capsized boat. No bodies were recovered, but by the amount of blood on the barge, it was deemed suspicious. Further searching of the area proved fruitless. The DNA was found to be that of Professor Ken Ellis and his daughter, Rhyllien Ellis. Other DNA found at the scene was inconclusive, but suggested there were three other individuals involved.

The article included a picture of Ken and Imogen Ellis and their daughter in Egypt in 2017 when she was fourteen years old. Her mass of red hair was prominent.

Following the trail using the surname "Ellis", Dan found more news, mostly regarding her parents and their academic achievements over the years. The yacht, *Aurora*, had been sold for US $2.5 million in 2022.

From that fateful day, her mother remained in Brazil, now known as the Brazilian Cooperative. After the bloody downfall of the corrupt regime in 2025, chaos reigned for over a decade and the many states separated or changed administration. Only in the last dozen years had the various regions patched up much of their grievances. In that time, the Brazilian Cooperative had swallowed up some of the smaller bordering countries including Paraguay, Bolivia to the southwest, and Peru to the west. In most cases, one corporation or another — whether from the medical or resources sector — bankrolled the takeover.

Corporations now owned countries.

Looking at the map, she saw the Argentinean Amalgamation included Chile and Uruguay. All the Central American countries had joined forces to incorporate Colombia, Venezuela, Suriname, and Guyana.

Scrolling on, she read the next article several times. In 2022, after selling the yacht, *Aurora*, Professor Imogen Ellis had secured a role at the São Paulo University as Curator of Antiquities and though now retired, she was still consulting with them on occasions.

Her mother was still alive!

"I need to find my mother and who murdered my father," she said as soon as Dan came out of the shower. "I thought, after all this time ..."

"We can do that." Dan tossed his clothes on a bunk and looked at the clock on the wall. "We'll have to wait until morning. Or ..." He went to the computer and searched for Professor Imogen Ellis and all variations of the name. "Looks like she's got a silent number. If I knew how to hack, I'd probably find it. We'll give the university a call first thing in the morning." He fought off a yawn. "For now, though, if you don't mind, I'm beat. And the shoulder's starting to ache again. Time for more painkillers."

He did look a bit paler and moved off, then turned back. "Are you okay?"

Rhyll nodded. "Tired. Surprised. Confused."

"I ..." He hesitated. "I was going to say I can imagine how you feel, but honestly, I can't. How can I?" Feeling awkward, he put a hand on her shoulder. "I'm sorry to have doubted you. Tomorrow, we'll start getting to the bottom of this and work out how to get you back to your mother. Just think on that and try to get some rest. Goodnight, Rhyll."

"Night." She reread the articles in case there was something she'd overlooked; then, out of habit, she reached into her pocket for the reassuring feel of the crystal, forgetting it had been taken. Deciding she needed fresh air, Rhyll searched for a torch. The moment she touched it, the light flared. She dropped it in surprise, and it went dark. She reached for it again, and the light came on. With a bit of experimenting, she worked out her *touch* was somehow activating it. "Or, it has a loose wire," she considered as she stepped outside.

With there being only one other person alive in the town, she felt no danger. Avoiding the worst of the bodies, Rhyll retraced her steps back to the quarantine section. In the distance, she could hear the stop-start of the Reaper patrol and shivered.

In one of the offices, she located the safe, then rummaged through the drawers for a key. Eventually, she found several on a keyring. She tried them until one opened the safe, but her crystal wasn't there. "Assuming the nurse had the opportunity to put it in?" Disheartened, she returned to the command vehicle and bed, deciding that finding the nurse's body in the dark was unlikely as well as distasteful.

Back in the vehicle, Rhyll had a quick wash and settled down in her sleeping area. Dan was snoring in the cubicle across the passage. Deciding to go through her pack and examine the other crystals, she laid them out on the pillow on her lap, all six of them. Other than different exquisite colouring, each one felt warm, gave a subtle vibration, and had a calming, even mesmerizing effect on her.

Stifling a yawn, she placed them under her pillow and went to sleep.

Dan woke and crept to the kitchenette, not wanting to wake Rhyll. He made himself a quick breakfast, taking a few slices of fruit loaf out of the freezer for toasting. He then put the coffee on while following the news headlines.

It had been four days since the mine incident, and only now were bulletins of a sickness being reported. Caroebe, São Lucas, Pitinga, Aracrua, Nova Sergina, and Laverto were all mentioned.

Dan had no idea about the other towns, but they were currently in São Lucas, and Caroebe was another thirty kilometres up the road to the west. He opened up a map and checked the other areas. One was directly east, and the others were towards the south. Whatever was going on was spreading over an ever-increasing area.

The even distribution was disturbing. Whatever was

happening, this new plague wasn't windborne, and the southern towns had no roads or obvious connections to the northern towns. The other weird anomaly being reported was how people weren't dying of any one thing in particular — some died of rampant cancer, others with severe cases of leukemia, chickenpox, measles, typhoid, and syphilis. Some of the diseases weren't lethal normally. It was like everyone's ability to fight the most rudimentary germs or infections was lost. It was as if their immune system just shut down.

Gleaning other news reports, this mysterious occurrence was happening in several other locations: north California, southern England, Egypt, western Brazil, and central Australia.

During his restless sleep, he heard the Reaper droids working through the night. With his coffee and last slice of toast in hand, he stepped outside for some fresh air and to have a look at the street. A lanyard secured around his neck, Dan opened the door and took a step.

He got no further.

It was an overcast morning. Standing all along the street were dozens of native women. Real native women in traditional garb, which meant very little other than short grass skirts. *Wai-wai!* He'd only ever seen the women in pictures, even when he was here ten years ago to cover the anniversary of the protest. And he'd only managed to interview one elderly male — a shaman.

They stood motionless, silent, watching him. Waiting.

"¡Buenos días!" Dan waved and smiled. "That's Spanish, you idiot," he muttered. He spun and re-entered the vehicle, wishing the airlock would hurry up. Try as he might, Dan couldn't work out how to deactivate it.

"Rhyll," he called once he was through. "Wake up."

"Hmm?" he heard her reply sleepily. "What is it?"

"Rhyll. Sorry, but you need to come and see this."

"What's wrong?" She climbed out of her bunk.

He turned away quickly, unused to seeing a teenage girl in only a T-shirt.

"Um. There's a lot of indigenous women outside." Dan

realised there was probably an outside camera for security purposes. Dumping his mug on the desk, he searched for a switch or button. "Here." He pointed as the screen came on. The vehicle had other views, and he switched them all on. The monitor broke into four images. Each showed the same thing from the different sides; the vehicle was surrounded.

While she looked at them in silence, he grabbed his camera, checking it had sufficient memory on the card since the reception was too poor to guarantee successful upload to his Cloud account.

When Rhyll stepped into view, they all bowed their heads, arms in front with palms up. They started chanting, *Collari. Collari.*

Rhyll leant against the doorframe in shock and confusion.

"What are they saying? What or who's Collari?" Dan asked, emerging behind her, camera at the ready.

"I think I am."

"You? Not Rhyll?"

"Not to them. I don't think it's a name, more of a thing ... an entity." She shrugged. "I've been hearing it in my dreams."

"I think they're waiting for something. They seem to respond to you. Say something."

"Me?"

"You speak Portuguese."

Without thinking, Rhyll spoke. "Bênçãos sobre você e seus antepassados. A mãe da terra ama todos vocês."

Immediately, the natives all raised their arms and shouted in their native tongue. As one, they turned silently and spread out through the town.

"Well, that worked, I think. What did you say?" He'd stepped down to the ground, taking photos of the event. None of the women had paid him any attention.

"Blessings upon you and your ancestors. The Earth Mother loves you all."

"And you just made that up?"

"It just came to me." Rhyll nodded. "It seemed appropriate.

The Wai-wai love nature and nurturing the land. They know they are stewards of the environment. Like all of us should be."

"Looks like it's working," Dan observed. "What did they say in reply?"

"'Blessed be Collari. We have long awaited your return.' I think it's Chawiyana. It's the Wai-wai language of the upper Nhamunda River."

"Right. But they just understood your Portuguese?"

"Again, I don't know. Maybe they got the *essence* of what I said. Maybe they *sensed* something ..."

It started sprinkling while Rhyll and Dan followed a couple of the women as they wandered through the town.

"It's like this," Rhyll continued, "they're all very connected to the land, as I am ... well, as I have always thought I was. All through my life, regardless of where I was, some old shaman or village elder would always comment either to me or my parents on how connected I was. And I have never been ill."

"But, pardon me for saying it, you're definitely not native. I mean green eyes, red hair — and a lot of it. Doesn't that mean there's Celtic blood in you?"

"Yes, Welsh, on my father's side."

"And your mother?"

"Australian, like you."

"How did you know? My office is in Melbourne."

"Your accent." She stepped down to follow.

"What accent?" Dan caught up.

The native women passed the dead villagers without a second look, making their way into some of the dilapidated buildings. When they emerged, they were holding children by the hands and carrying babies.

Dan and Rhyll looked at each other in disbelief.

"I never even considered there'd be children!" Rhyll looked shaken.

"But ... that's great they've survived. Why didn't they die ... and none of them cried or made a noise? What's with that?" He focused and shot more pictures.

Rhyll shrugged. "I haven't the answers for you, Dan."

They continued to follow the Wai-wai women, amazed the children were compliant and went happily with them. The children were aged from newborns to around twelve years of age. The women passed some children who had succumbed to the illness, barely giving them a look.

"I wonder why some are still alive and others not? What makes them different?"

Tears ran down Rhyll's face. "It's tragic, whatever the reason." She paused at an alley and looked down. She wiped her face.

"What is it, Rhyll?"

"I've found my crystal." She moved slowly but surely into the shaded laneway.

"Down here? Are you sure?" Dan followed. "I can't see the nurse, can you?"

She reached an intersection and turned. "I can now."

A few paces down another lane was a body with a familiar uniform and face down.

"How the hell did you know she was there?" Dan asked, incredulous.

"Not her ... I felt it. The crystal. Can't you feel its energy?" She reached into the nurse's pockets and withdrew it, holding it out to him.

Dan studied it before he took it. "Nothing more than before. It's warm and looks beautiful." He handed it back. "I might just have to do some research on it."

The native women had departed as mysteriously and silently as they arrived.

"I had no idea there were still so many of them," Rhyll said as they wandered back to the vehicle. "I got the impression they had mostly died out, and the remnants were moved elsewhere."

As they turned a corner, Dan stopped in his tracks, and Rhyll bumped into him.

She looked up. He was pale. "You okay? Is the fever back?" Then her eyes followed the direction he was staring.

"I wish it was fever. Looks like we have company." He started walking again.

They both approached the group standing on the road near the command vehicle. There were three men and two women. None were wearing EV suits.

Rhyll recognised a couple of them from the protestor camp. "Hello. I didn't recognise you without your placards."

One of the women separated from the group. She was slightly shorter than Rhyll, mid-thirties, with olive skin and long jet-black hair. She looked from Rhyll to Dan and back to Rhyll. "I'm Nala."

"I'm Rhyll, and this is—"

"Daniel Dobson," Nala finished.

Now it was Rhyll's turn to stare at both of them. "You know each other?"

"It's been over a decade, but we know — or knew — each other very well," Nala replied. "And you didn't call."

"Neither did you." Dan looked troubled. "I did miss you the other day when I dropped in."

"I was out in the field," Nala answered.

"Umm ... well. Maybe I should let you two catch up." Rhyll stepped away.

Nala turned from scrutinising Dan to Rhyll, looking her up and down and taking in the green eyes and mass of red hair. "Actually, it's you I came to see."

CHAPTER EIGHT

"ME? WHY ME?" RHYLL STARED IN SURPRISE. "WE'VE NEVER MET. I don't understand."

"Nevertheless, I'm here to finally meet *you*, Rhyllien Aurora Ellis, daughter of Ken and Imogen Ellis, missing these past thirty-five years. I admit I was sceptical when they said you would return. And then my group said a red-haired girl drove past the camp in Lewis' Merc ... and here you are, flesh and blood. Welcome back to the living and breathing."

"How? ..." Rhyll was shocked to the core. "How could you possibly know?" She turned to Dan. "Have you spoken to anyone else on the radio?"

"Not me," he replied.

"It's okay. Daniel hasn't said anything to me for years." Nala looked at the empty streets. "Our car broke down a few miles out. Anywhere with decent water around here?"

"Yes, sure!" Rhyll said, pointing to the command vehicle nearby. "It might be a squeeze, but we can get some for you and your friends. Isn't that right, Dan?"

"What? Oh, yeah. Sure thing. You lead and show them in."

"Come this way." Rhyll used the lanyard around her neck to swipe the door open.

Leaving Nala with Dan, the other woman and a male came through first. Cycling through the airlock was awkward with the three of them, and she became acutely aware neither had had a decent wash for some time. It didn't seem to bother them, though.

Rhyll showed them to the lunchroom area and poured glasses of cool, filtered water, then got a fresh pot of coffee brewing while the others cycled through. She raided the pantry for food, but it was mostly ration packs of some description.

By the time the others were seated, the coffee was ready, and there was a pile of food containers to choose from. Apart from small talk while eating and drinking, they listened to the news broadcasts with interest, especially regarding the snippets of information about the spreading sickness.

"We only get a few minutes now and then," a boy introduced as Bruno said. "Signal is quite bad at the favela."

After the food was eaten, Nala told her team to go and forage for whatever they could. "There should be a car to get going, grab extra fuel cells, and don't forget to ditch the transponders."

"Scavenging now?" Dan asked as he cycled the others out.

"Survival foraging. Times are tough." She turned her attention to Rhyll. "I'm Nala Xaschoal."

"That's a familiar name." Rhyll thought for a moment, thinking of the voices in her dreams. "That was the surname of a shaman in the tribe my parents were working with when …"

"It was. He was my grandfather."

"Whoa there," Dan said. "That's the guy I interviewed years ago!"

"It's the same man. He passed away two years after that."

"Oh … I'm sorry."

"Thank you, but nothing to be sorry about. He was a great man and did everything he had to do. His time had come, and he knew it." She turned back to Rhyll. "And you were introduced to me."

"I was? To you?"

"I had just been born. There was a ceremony during which

we both touched hands, like this." Nala put her hand out, palm forward, indicating Rhyll do the same.

The moment their palms touched, they felt a jolt and both staggered back. All the power shut down momentarily; the overhead lights blinked out, as did the monitors. Seconds later they flashed back on; the computer rebooted.

Wide-eyed, the two girls looked completely shocked.

"What just happened?" Rhyll asked in awe.

"Must be moisture in the fuse box." Dan got up to investigate. "I better check in case it happens again. I won't be long ... if I can find it."

"What just happened?" Rhyll repeated when they were alone. "I ... I've felt this once before but not as intense."

"Yes. When we first met." Nala was looking at the palm of her hand. After a few heartbeats, she held Rhyll's hand and turned it palm up. There was an identical pattern, illuminated but fading. She quickly got her phone out and snapped a picture before it disappeared completely.

Rhyll stared in wonder at it, then at Nala's. "What is it? What does it mean?"

"We are connected ... kindred spirits. Soul sisters, so to speak. My grandfather said it's been in our family for centuries, going from firstborn female to the next. My mother had it, now it has transferred to me."

"If it's transferred to you ..."

"My mother died during labour to twins. That ceremony you were at was not only celebrating our birth — twins are rare for us — but also paying homage to a departing soul."

"You've got a twin?"

"Identical, though ... we don't see each other. Our philosophical viewpoints are at odds."

"Oh. Sorry." Rhyll paused, rubbing her fingers over her palm while thinking of something to say without putting her foot in it. "What did you mean by soul sisters?"

Nala studied her. "You really don't know?"

"Know what?" Rhyll looked perplexed. "I mean ... sure,

something weird just happened, but lots of weird things have lately. Why am I still alive? Why am I here, now? Why is everyone dying? Why not me, Dan ... or even you and the protestors?"

"Actually, some have. The last one died yesterday," Nala said softly.

"Some?"

"Those that aren't true to their calling."

"Protesting is a calling?"

"No, the love and respect of the earth or nature. Protesting is just one physical manifestation of it. Like hugging somebody or smiling when you're happy."

"And Dan? I mean, I don't want him to die — I don't want anyone to die — but why isn't he dead or sick?"

"Because he loves nature too. What do you know about him?"

"Not much. He's an investigative journalist, he's Australian, and his dad hates him."

"He's more an environmental journalist, but they're despised these days, so he doesn't make it known if he can help it. He's here because he gets in the shit too much. He's working for Nexos magazine. His father sent him here as penance. Again."

"Penance? For what?"

"Dan has this knack of getting arrested. He goes to do an interview or to report on one thing or another, and the next thing, he's joining the protest."

Rhyll smiled at the thought of him in a protest rally. "But that doesn't tell me what just happened."

"I haven't had real coffee for ages. Make more of it and I'll tell you what I can."

"Before he comes back, how do you know Dan?" Rhyll and Nala sat opposite each other in the compact lounge area, a steaming pot of freshly brewed coffee between them.

Nala gave a warm, genuine laugh, looking into her coffee.

"There's nothing much. We were both young. He was surrounded by people he knew nothing about and could barely communicate with. We hit it off. He stayed a bit longer, but then he had to go back, and I had my people here—" She shrugged. "Thanks to your mother, I finished my degree and started as head of the protest camp. It had been going for a decade already.

"Dan was there to cover the story of our tenth anniversary and to dig into the atrocities of the indigenous people by the Erdany Mining Corporation. It was while he was doing this that he met my grandfather. He recorded a message from him, in fact, that might in itself explain your role."

"My role? What's this got to do with me?"

"You don't think you were in that cave for kicks? There is a plan, and you are part of it. Me too, now."

"Your grandfather had a plan?"

"This is much bigger than my grandfather, I can assure you. Throughout our history, every shaman had a role, but only when the time was right. He was the latest to warn everyone."

They turned as the airlock cycling started.

"Hey, ladies." Dan stepped out of the airlock and wiped his face. "Didn't appear to be anything wrong with the fuses." Dan trudged inside, dripping water on the floor. He nipped into the shower cubicle and grabbed a towel. "Weird. I thought these military-grade vehicles were built of tougher stuff." He looked at them, towel around his neck, stopping at their grins. "What did I miss?"

"Are you able to bring up that interview you did with Vitor Magalhães Xaschoal?"

"Umm ... sure." Dan was surprised by the question. "Why's that?" He leaned over and called up an old file from the cloud. He poured himself a coffee while it was loading.

As the old footage started, the two girls sat around the swivel table. Dan remained standing, leaning his back against the wall. He threw a couple of painkillers into his mouth and took a swig from his cup.

To Rhyll, the shaman looked older but recognisable, with his feathered headdress, woven reed necklace, and armbands. Seeing him now brought back many memories of the dig, her parents, and her once idyllic life. Another recollection came back to her, of the last conversation with her father, and she thought: *You know, for three goats I could have been your aunt.*

The vid started, and as the shaman spoke, she read the subtitles.

"I bring a message on behalf of Earth. You may call it Mother Nature, and you may call it Gaia — which is not entirely correct but will suffice for now due to your lack of comprehension of the natural forces which surround us all.

"The world has succumbed to a plague.
Mankind's ingenuity, believed to separate it from 'animals', enabled it to inhabit every niche of land, thereby spreading infection across the globe.

"Mankind has also developed a lust for wealth and power to the extent that the pollution and desecration are now global, threatening the very fabric of the world.
Just as a microbe cannot fathom the complex world in which it lives, Mankind is also incapable of fathoming the complexity of the world.
Every living thing on the earth has a role and is connected — or was.
Mankind alone has lost its connections, believing itself separate from everything else.

"A messenger will arrive — Mankind's one chance to survive.
Those who have lost their connection, who cannot bring themselves to

*attune, to live in harmony with the earth and the forces around them,
will perish.*

*"Resonating with all that is, she is Nature incarnate. It would be
foolish to thwart her, for Gaia's wrath is never subtle, always fatal.
Treat her well.
Mankind's continued existence relies on its ability to learn respect for
the world.
Adapt or die."*

Rhyll remained silent afterwards.

Nala had tears running down her cheeks.

Dan was sipping his tepid coffee. "Powerful stuff," he said. "I'm sorry to hear he passed away, Nala."

She nodded, wiping her face as she turned to Rhyll. "How are you feeling?"

"Me ..." She paused, breathing deeply. "My father was murdered. I'm feeling this could have been prevented."

"Prevented how? You were both victims of a robbery. People are responsible for that, not nature. Can't you see? It's you!"

"I can't be this messenger. I'm just a kid. How has this got anything to do with me?"

"You must be because of what happened to you, and because of what's happening now."

"What *is* happening now?"

"It has begun." Nala looked at her and at Dan. "Civilisation is dying out."

CHAPTER NINE

"You said my mother paid for your degree?" Rhyll asked Nala.

"Oh, she's done more than that. She's practically bankrolled the camp."

"Why?"

"Waiting for you. How about we call her?"

"We don't know her number," Dan said. "We searched, but it's unlisted. The university was our next option, but then you guys turned up."

"Lucky for you I have a direct line." Nala dug a sat-phone out of her satchel and thumbed through her list of contacts. It was small. She pushed a button and handed it to Rhyll. "Daniel, why don't you and I go for a walk?"

Outside, they followed the noises and eventually found Nala's colleagues. They'd purloined two all-terrain vehicles.

"You got rid of the transponders?" Nala asked.

"Sure, boss," Bruno answered. "We got two extra fuel cells, and we're just loading up all the goodies now. We scored a couple of tents, too."

"Good job. Look, once done, you guys head back. I'll join you soon enough. Then we can discuss what's going to happen from now on."

"What do you mean?" Bruno asked the question on the others' lips.

"Erdany is finished here. With this sickness, nothing will be the same. The tent city has done what it needs to do."

"You're sure?"

"Put it this way: my job's finished here. Everyone should consider what to do with their futures. My advice? Stay low for another couple of months. Things will have sorted themselves out by then — one way or another."

They were all looking worried and unsure.

"Look around you. You witnessed what happened back at camp. Trust your feelings, trust nature. Lose that trust, you lose everything."

Sullenly, deep in their thoughts, the group continued loading the cars.

"Come on, Daniel."

Surprised into action, Dan followed. "Anywhere in particular?"

"No. Just away. Give Rhyll some privacy."

"Good. I need to check on something. Rhyll and I were going to do it yesterday, but it got dark."

"And what would that be?"

He showed her the Velcro patch he'd taken from the mercenary's body. "We found this yesterday. I think there are more – maybe another four mercenaries."

"It can't be a coincidence. Mercenaries here, now, in this backwater town at the same time that this is happening? Did they know about Rhyll?"

As they walked around an area of the town not previously searched, Dan related the story of how they'd left the mine.

"So, this Grant fellow was under orders to kidnap Rhyll?" Nala asked.

"Someone seemed to be wanting both."

"What crystal?"

"I'm sure she'll show you when we return. You know a hoverpod followed us?" Dan continued at her nod. "It was automated, so someone was flying it remotely. I haven't found it yet, and I can't see why it would hang around for long. No doubt it returned when it saw us taken to the cop shop.

"When we were at the mine, the phone rang. The cop answered. From that moment, his attitude changed. I'm guessing these mercs are connected to that. I reckon they separated into groups to hit the cop shop from different directions. Maybe they weren't counting on the GHO being here. Anyway, something happened, and there was a shootout."

The pair arrived at the police station. "We've checked that way already; let's look over there." Dan strode along the street to the north, as Nala struggled to keep pace.

Half a block away, they came across three more grey-clad bodies, dressed like the others.

"Same weapons, same ICON patch." He started searching the bodies.

"We've moved down from environmental snooper to grave-robbing?"

"Looking for a remote. There's an armed hoverpod south of here. Rhyll and I nearly got toasted."

The third body had the remote.

"What do you intend to do with that? Can you fly a hoverpod?"

"No, but I'm thinking the thing will fly itself, once given the commands. At the least, this will get us onboard to deactivate the weapons. Maybe there'll be something to confirm what they were doing here or who they are."

They'd returned from their walk after returning to the hoverpod. The remote enabled them to access the pod's interior, but not to start it.

"I reckon it either has voice recognition software, maybe palm print, or even retinal scan. Looks like we're driving."

After cycling through the airlock, they sat in the lounge, catching up on the last ten years.

"How was your call to your mother?" Nala asked when Rhyll emerged from the shower.

"Wonderful. Scary. We both cried a lot. She's seventy-four now."

"What's happening next? You're going to see her, obviously," Dan said.

"She's in São Paulo and will meet me — us — at Manaus. She's saying there are flight restrictions into the area because of the sickness."

"We can get to Manaus; there are plenty of cars to choose from," Dan pointed out.

"Taking a GHO vehicle can either be a problem or a benefit," Nala advised. "No doubt with this going on, there'll be roadblocks and checkpoints. If by the GHO, they'll wonder about us using official vehicles; if by someone else, they'll probably shoot first, ask questions later."

"What about a local's car?"

"Good luck finding one that'll go the distance."

"I think I need to go back to the mine," Rhyll said nervously.

"The mine? Why?" Dan asked.

"Mum was asking about some disc. She said it went missing the same time I did. I did feel like something wasn't right. You all seem to think I know what I'm supposed to do. I don't. Maybe in my rush to get out of the cavern, I left something behind. I've had these recurring dreams, and there are a lot of unanswered questions. When they ... interred me, I don't think they envisaged the place would be falling down around my ears. I was confused, scared, and left in a hurry."

"Now we can take a GHO four-by-four. There's nothing between us and them, so no checkpoints."

"How about we head out in the morning?" Dan suggested. "The drive is a few hours, and it'll be dark soon after we arrive.

I'm not too keen on driving around an open-cut mine in the dark — lots of big drops. First thing in the morning will get us there before noon. Plenty of time then to explore this cave. You said it wasn't too far from the office?"

"Twenty minutes or so. And the place I was *sleeping* wasn't too far. It took longer for me to get out, but I was travelling slowly with only a dim light."

In a comfortable GHO ATV, the drive back to the Erdany mine didn't seem so long. They'd packed what they'd thought they'd need for an underground hike as well as food and water, but they could always grab something from the protest camp.

Nala examined the crystal, feeling the same vibrations and warmth as Rhyll. "And you've got six more of these?"

"Yes, but different colours, so I suspect they are different gems or crystals." She explained again how they were laid out on the crystal bed.

"I'm sure your mother will tell you more detail, but from what I know, after your disappearance — she never considered you dead, despite the evidence — she sold the yacht and got the job at the university in São Paulo. She vowed to remain in Brazil until your return."

"How did she know I would come back?" Rhyll asked quietly. "Why was she so confident I was alive? From what I've seen on the news, there was no distinction between either of our absences. Same with the robbers, for that matter."

"My grandfather never told me, but I think he knew much more than he let on. All I can say is your mother had absolute confidence you would return; she just didn't know when."

"How do we know anything different?" Dan asked. "If you're here, what're the chances the robbers have been hidden somewhere?"

"Because I killed them. Two of them, at least."

"You did?"

"Yes. I shot one and ..."

Dan waited. "... And what?"

"I called for the piranhas to finish the other one." It sounded ludicrous even as she said it, but she knew it to be true.

"Piranhas?"

"*Pygocentrus nattereri.* The red-bellied piranhas."

"Aren't man-eating piranhas a myth?"

"Normally, but there was a lot of blood ... and I summoned them. I know it sounds crazy."

"Just a bit."

"As does being interred for thirty-five years and coming out no older than when I went in; or thousands of people dying from every and any known disease under the sun."

"True enough."

They continued in silence, and Rhyll watched the passing forest.

"So, my mother started the protest camp at the same time Erdany came on the scene?" she spoke up later.

"Soon after, yes. Erdany were ruthless then — moreso than now. After bribing the local officials and a couple of environment ministers, they started bulldozing the forests and driving the people out."

"What were they looking for?"

"Tin, mainly, but it wasn't the most profitable mine. The job of the protest camp was to highlight the continued forest destruction and decimation of the first nation peoples. It seemed the main reason they were here was to destroy as much as they could."

"I'm glad they didn't, but why didn't they force you guys out?" Dan slowed for a tight bend as they were getting into some hilly terrain.

"The university owns the land we're on, for research purposes. The dean at the time had influence in high places; he is the brother of the current president.

"Over the years, Erdany simply ignored our presence." Nala looked out the window. "We'll be at the camp soon."

• • •

The tent city came into view a few minutes later. One of the GHO vehicles her group had taken was parked to the side, all the provisions removed.

"Is it normally this quiet?" Rhyllien asked, stepping down from the vehicle.

"No, but we did lose a few to this sickness." Nala reached over and hit the horn. After a few minutes' waiting, there was still no response.

"I thought they'd be suspicious of another GHO car, but this isn't right." Nala climbed out of the cab, joining Rhyll.

"You wait here," Dan offered. "I'll go and—"

"These are my people. I'll go."

"Do you feel it, Nala?"

"Feel what?" Dan asked, looking at them.

"Death."

Nala spun, calling out names. There were no replies.

"Would they have left?" Dan asked.

"Not without taking a perfectly serviceable—" Nala stopped at the entrance to a large tent. A swarm of flies erupted with her shadow in the doorway. "Ah ... *shit no!*" Inside were three fellow protestors. Tied up and bloody.

"Who would do this? Why?" Nala turned to Dan, weeping on his shoulder as he held her.

"Take Nala back to the car. I'll check elsewhere." Rhyll walked away. She moved through the camp, finding two more bodies before returning to the car. Like the first three, each victim was the same: broken fingers — evidence of torture — and their throats were cut.

Silently, Nala passed her a water flask when she returned, slumping on the seat in the doorway of the car.

"Thanks." Rhyll sipped, then reached out and held Nala's hands. "Where's Dan?"

"Being a journalist. Horrible as it is, this needs to be documented. It's never been this bad."

Rhyll nodded, taking another drink. "I found two more. How many were there?"

"After the sickness, there were nine others left."

"So, we have four unaccounted for. Those you were with yesterday?"

"Bruno, Sanchez, Ngaio, and Yvette," Nala told her, regaining some of her composure.

"As Dan asked, do you think they left? Or do you think they went to the mine?" she asked Nala.

"We didn't pass any other car, only our old one that broke down earlier. The only other road out of here is a goat track heading south to Pitinga."

Dan returned, putting his camera away. "Is there a shovel?"

Nala nodded. "I've got to help."

Together the three of them dug graves and buried the bodies.

"Did you know them well?" he asked.

"As much as you could really know anyone here. Many of them preferred to keep the past to themselves. I do have a list of their details. Their next of kin need to be informed when we get to Manaus," Nala said as they washed their hands and arms in the nearby stream.

"Shall we go to the cavern?" Rhyll asked as they made their way back to the camp. She untied her hair, which had become a hindrance when digging the graves.

"It's what we're here for," Dan replied. "Though we might run into whoever did this."

Tyrone contemplated the latest updates as he went over the file on his desk — copies of everything he had from his father's work, including the list of artefacts the Ellis family were believed to be digging up. The originals were dog-eared and stained, but there was no way he was going to digitise it; nothing digitised was safe.

These notes were all he had left to remember his father. The file stayed in his safe, in his office, for his eyes only.

Ellis' last dig in the rainforests of the Trombetas-Mapuera

region was purported to be an ancient ruin pre-dating the Incans by thousands of years. When he died and nothing was found to prove their case, it was believed Ken was desperately grasping at the limelight of his dwindling career, since he had been less successful in his later years.

No bodies were ever recovered, but the circumstances were deemed suspicious. His death and that of his daughter were a tragedy put down to foul play and a botched robbery.

That was the official story; his father knew otherwise. Ken Ellis wasn't unsuccessful. It was the other way around — he was keeping very tight-lipped on his recent success for fear of jeopardising the indigenous natives' health and lifestyle. Any artefacts found were quietly being donated to the more local universities and museums. If he'd made it public knowledge, there'd be far more interest in his digs and less chance for the likes of his dad to grab it.

"*Carpe diem*," his grandfather drummed into him as far back as he could remember.

Tyrone believed in that motto. It made his grandfather so successful, and he was building on that success. Many wannabes fell by the wayside dithering and worrying, letting opportunities slip by. This was an opportunity not to be missed!

His father had questioned some locals working on the Ellis dig. If the translations were accurate, they overheard Ellis had uncovered what he referred to as the sun-disc. There was nothing official about this discovery.

According to supposition and guesswork on pseudoscience websites, the sun-disc was reputed to be part of the myth where an Incan priest, Amaru Muru, used a golden disc to open a doorway carved into a rock. The myth also said it was a gateway to the gods.

"Preposterous," Tyrone scoffed, reading the entry again. No matter how many times he read it, he couldn't bring himself to believe the nonsense. What he did believe was the ability of Ellis; and that if he was on the trail for a relic, then he'd find it.

Any artefact pre-dating the Incans would be worth millions. Especially one made of gold.

"Father died for this. I'll get it for him."

As impossible as it was to believe, facial recognition finally came up with an eighty-five per cent probability this girl was the missing Ellis daughter, Rhyllien.

"But how can she be? This girl's a teenager, not a 53-year-old woman."

Tyrone had them run it half a dozen times using images from different angles and got the same results. Eventually, he put a call through to his grandfather.

"Opa? Are you sitting down? I've found the girl who killed Dad."

CHAPTER TEN

IT WAS AN UNEVENTFUL DRIVE BACK TO THE MINE COMPOUND. THEY stopped near the busted boom gate, and Nala looked over the site with a pair of binoculars she'd found in the glove box.

"There's the burnt-out excavator. I can't see any movement. Doesn't look much different from the last time I was here."

"No hoverpod? No GHO car? No sign of your friends?" Dan asked, accepting the binoculars. He scanned the local area, then looked farther afield. "There is something over there." He pointed to the northeast.

"Might be good to have a map of the mine," Rhyll suggested. "I know there was one in Lewis' office."

They entered the compound, stopping near the ruined building.

After burying the bodies earlier, Rhyll's gloomy mood didn't improve when the dead earth permeated her every nerve. She climbed out of the car and stopped, breathing slowly while she clenched the crystal.

"You okay, Rhyll?" Dan asked from the open door of the ATV.

Rhyll nodded and moved on. It took several minutes climbing over the fallen timbers, cladding and insulation to avoid the worst of the bodies. Only portions of the structure showed any signs of fire damage. She recognised Lewis' carpet, then his upturned desk. She saw one of Lewis' red sneakers underneath it. From her recollection of the office layout, she located the area where she'd seen the map.

Sifting through roof insulation and rolling a filing cabinet, she soon found it, slightly torn and discoloured with water damage. She unpinned it from the corkboard and headed back to the car. "Got it."

The trio left the compound and followed the path into the mine area, stopping on a rise overlooking the devasted landscape.

"Whereabouts is this cavern?" Dan asked, looking over the back seat to the others as they perused the map.

"Can I borrow the binos?" Rhyll scanned the horizon, looking for telltale landmarks. "It's supposed to be in Sector 32, which is more or less north of here. I was in a excavator for about quarter of an hour, but it was very slow, and then I was in a jeep for about twenty minutes."

Dan started driving again. "Does it show a path to whatever it was we saw earlier? It's big enough to be a hoverpod."

Nala, in the back seat with Rhyll, gauged where they were in comparison to where the object was. "The road looks like it goes close."

Following the road, they found the hoverpod, the wreckage blocking the way.

"Ah, that's fan-bloody-tastic!" Dan slowed to a halt.

They got out to investigate. There was minimal fire damage, but the cause of the crash was easy enough to determine by the state of the bodies within. Noting the ICON logo on the side, he took a couple of photos.

"Even in their EV suits, they got the sickness," Nala observed.

"Like all those GHO people back in town," Rhyll agreed.

"I hope they suffered for what they did."

"How much farther to the cave?" Dan asked, coming back to the vehicle.

Rhyll pulled the map off the seat. "About another ten kilometres."

"I don't feel like hiking." He returned to the wreckage and checked the road shoulder conditions. The path was on a ridge between two deep pits. There were signs warning of weak edges and dangerous drops. "Maybe we can push the hoverpod a bit, just enough to get through. These things are supposed to be lightweight." He pushed against the tail, and it rocked marginally. "If you ladies wouldn't mind waiting back there"—he pointed several metres behind them—"I'll see what I can do."

As they stepped away, he climbed back into the ATV.

"I'd engage low-range four-wheel-drive," Nala called through the window.

"Well, of course I'm going to engage low-range." Dan waved her away with a smile. When she turned, he looked for the low-range four-wheel-drive option.

Nala joined Rhyll, laughing.

It took a few minutes, but the car edged forward until the bull bar touched the side nearest the tail section. Dan gradually increased power. As gravel started to spray from the wheels, the hoverpod shifted slightly. With a bit more encouragement, the tail suddenly spun around as the car pushed through.

The hoverpod slowed its spin, the tail section now hanging over the rim of the cliff-face.

"There. Easy!" Dan called back from the side of the ATV.

Now closer to the other edge of the road, the extra weight of the hoverpod was enough to weaken the shoulder. There was the peculiar rending noise of rock breaking and cracking, reminding Rhyll of the columns in the cavern falling.

"Get back," she warned, "it's going over!"

The pod fell away with the shoulder, and it tumbled and rolled down the steep slope to the bottom of the pit, thirty metres below, partially buried by the falling rock debris.

Wary of more of the shoulder dropping unexpectedly, they stepped away from the edge and quickly strode to the ATV.

"That's that, then." Dan was happy with his success. "Let's go," he said when the girls slid back inside. The gears started grinding as he drove off.

"You can disengage low-range now," Nala chuckled.

"Hey. I'm a journalist." Dan deselected the option and continued in silence.

In the pits they passed, the mining equipment remained motionless. Two trucks were on their sides, having driven off the narrow roads spiralling out of the pits.

"That looks familiar," Rhyll said ten minutes later, quickly referencing the map and their surroundings. She climbed out when the car stopped, and looked down into the deep cutting. "That's where I got into the excavator, which means the cavern is over there." She turned. With her binoculars, she examined the cliff face where the rock had split open. "There it is." She passed the binoculars to Nala. "Dan, look for a track leading down there."

Dan followed the spiralling road, seeing where it merged with the rim, and drove there as quickly as safety allowed, then began the descent. The roads had been built wide enough for the biggest of trucks; it made the drive relatively easy. At the bottom, he drove to where Rhyll had pointed. Before long he saw the rift she was talking about and parked a few metres away from it.

They climbed out and looked at the area.

Rhyll was both excited and nervous about going back inside.

Nala put her hand on her shoulder. "You're not alone in this now."

"You can feel it?"

"I can sense your feelings, not the source."

Dan dragged out the backpacks, putting one over his good shoulder.

"Rhyll's leading the way." Nala took the pack off him. "I don't know if you're trying to be an idiot or a gentleman."

"He doesn't have to try too hard," Rhyll joked as she grabbed her pack and strode to the entrance.

"But for which one?" Dan asked. He took a quick photo of the entrance before catching up.

Rhyll entered, Nala following a couple of paces behind. Dan turned his torch on almost immediately.

"The path is narrow and angles down. It's damp, so watch your step," Rhyll warned.

"And no heroics here," Nala added. "If it's too slippery, get on your ass and shuffle along. No one's going to laugh."

"Why do I get the impression you two ladies are talking to me?"

"Because you're only a journalist," Nala retorted, but he couldn't see her smiling.

For Rhyll, retracing her steps was easier than expected, though Dan found some of it arduous until the path widened and levelled out.

Their voices echoed as they entered a larger space. Sweeping the high-powered torch revealed large crystal columns. On occasion, the ground on one side or another of the path dropped to a depth even the torch failed to illuminate.

"And you did this in the dark?" he asked.

"Not entirely. I'll show you. Turn off your torches and don't move."

"Umm, OK." Dan hesitated. He stepped back from a crevice and leant against a solid column for security before dousing the light.

"Now wait for your eyes to adjust." Rhyll's voice seemed softer in the darkness.

"Wow!" Nala exclaimed after a few minutes.

"That's amazing. The columns are glowing." Dan joined Nala's amazement. "But only near you?"

"So it seems. And then there's this."

In the eerie gloom, they saw Rhyll's dim silhouette dig into her pocket. A green glow eerily lit up several metres around her.

"So, as long as I moved slowly, I wasn't completely in the dark."

Her image dimmed when she replaced the glowing crystal. They saw her turn and walk away. As she did so, the columns in front began to glow as the columns behind gradually faded.

Nala and Dan had no effect.

"There is something definitely happening with you," Dan stated. He turned his torch back on, ensuring he covered it with his hand first so it wasn't too intense.

He rejoined Nala, and they both continued.

Finally, they arrived in the chamber where Rhyll had initially awoken. They saw it from a distance, the ambient violet glow emanating from the large, flat column in the centre.

"Here's my bed for the last thirty-five years."

The trio stood around the large crystal platform, and Rhyll pointed out the depressions on the surface. There was a large, body-shaped recess with several smaller niches down the centre.

"And that was comfortable?" Nala asked.

"I was unconscious, but there was no discomfort after."

"Definitely a good advert for a firm bed." Dan ran his fingers over the surface. "Any idea how you got to this cave?"

"None. My last memory before this was dying with my father in my lap on a broken-down barge on the Rio Mapuera. I do remember vague dreams of a native ceremony, but that could have been one of the dozens I've experienced over the years … except I recognised the shaman from where we were doing the last dig."

"My grandfather," Nala prompted, continuing after Rhyll's nod. "Can you show us where the crystals were placed?" Nala asked.

"Sure." Rhyll removed her pack and brought out the other crystals, now wrapped individually in socks found in the drawers of the command vehicle. She pulled out her notebook to check. Starting at the lowest one, she placed them in order: red, orange, yellow, green, blue, indigo, and violet. They all glowed.

"And you slept on those? Maybe I could get a photo or two of you lying there?"

"Sure, but I was naked."

"Ah, maybe we could just recreate the position clothed?"

"Where's your professionalism?" she laughed.

"Considering your age, I'd rather not have photos of you naked in compromising positions."

"Prude."

"Prudent is the word you're after," he answered.

"Chronologically speaking, she's 53. Older than me." Nala laughed, then turned to Rhyll. "Have you heard of chakras? Used in meditation, yoga? For health and wellbeing?"

"I have many times. In fact—"

Nala was looking at the crystal bed. "Because this is very much like how the chakras of the body are situated, according to various images I've seen."

"Meaning what?" Dan asked as Rhyll climbed onto the crystal bed.

"I've no idea, but considering what we've seen, it's very important: the vibrations, the warmth and feeling of wellbeing, and all these crystal columns glowing. It must be all connected somehow. There is truth to what they say about crystals and the healing energy they can provide."

Dan moved around, taking photos from different angles, then climbed onto the bed to take overhead shots. "You can climb off now, unless you feel like another nap." He stepped to one side as she slid off, then took a few shots of the crystals in situ.

"In my dreams, a voice — it sounded like your grandfather's — mentioned geo-stones." Rhyll read from her notebook. "I wrote it down here." She started reciting, "*'Earth Mother is within you. You are in complete harmony with all that is natural. By re-energising the world chakras with these geo-stones, those also in a resonating harmony will survive.'* In my dream, the dots separated from the planet and grew bigger; they resembled different coloured, eight-sided crystals."

"World chakras?" Dan repeated. "The world has chakras?"

"There are many that believe in them," Nala informed him. "Some say seven, and some say twelve."

"And you?"

"I believe there's something. There are many things science can't explain—"

"Doesn't mean mumbo-jumbo is true," he argued.

"No, but science is limited to the questions the scientists ask. Once the right question is asked, then they can follow the next path."

"Science, like everything else today, is only about money."

"You're a cynic."

"I'm a realist—"

"Explain *her*," Nala said, pointing to Rhyll. "Explain all this."

"I'm not a scientist."

"Exactly. But get a scientist to explain it — one that wants answers and isn't guided by greed — and you'll start getting answers. We not only have to ask the right questions but the right minds."

"We came here to search the cave, not argue," Rhyll intervened gently. "There are people dying out there. There must be a way to save them."

Dan took a deep breath. "You're right. I'm sorry." He moved to the far side of the cave and shone his torch through all the crevices, high and low.

The others did the same, moving to different areas to begin their search.

"I've found something," Nala called out after crawling around for ten minutes. She had searched toward the "head" of the crystal bed. She was down on her stomach, reaching in up to her shoulder. Some of the columns here had cracked and shifted. "I can't reach it, though. Daniel has the longer arms."

"Sure thing." With assistance, he got down onto his stomach and reached in with his good arm while Nala shone the torch inside the crevice. Dan stretched as far as he could, putting his face into the dust. His fingers closed around a leather strap, and he dragged it out scraping through the grit.

Dan pushed himself away from the niche and got to his knees before a coughing fit took hold.

"That's my father's!" Rhyll swapped it with a water bottle. "You okay?"

He nodded, wiping his face and mouth. "Relax. It's just the dust."

"Not dying on us, then?" Nala helped him to his feet.

"Thanks." He took another quick swig, gargled it, and swilled it around his mouth before stepping to the side to spit it out. Then he drank more before joining Rhyll and Nala by the bed, their torches illuminating the area.

Aware of the cracked leather, Rhyll carefully opened the flap and removed the contents gently. "Looks like time and the air in here dried it out."

Inside the satchel, she found his old compass, his notebooks, and a silk bag tied at the top. The notebook had maps, notes on each with arrows, and many sketches of the items he'd found or those he was looking for. As she flicked through, a couple of family photos fell out.

There were copies of images pasted or folded within, depicting similar objects to what he was seeking at the time. Not all his digs proved successful, but several times he'd revisited a site whenever he came across new clues.

"May I?" Nala picked up the silk bag. "It's quite heavy. Whatever's inside is solid."

"Be my guest." Rhyll was slowly flicking through his notes, tears welling in her eyes at the memories. She sniffed, wiping at them with the back of her hand.

Nala untied the pull-strings. Once loose, she carefully emptied the bag into her other hand. A palm-sized disc slipped out.

"Is that an Incan artefact?" Dan whispered.

Rhyll looked over. "Looks like it, though my father found many that predated the Incans who simply adopted the glyphs and ideograms, like many cultures in history have done. It's tarnished, so it's not gold."

"It isn't?" Dan asked, disappointed.

"Pure gold, twenty-four carats, doesn't oxidize or tarnish. If it does, it isn't pure gold, but you'd have to get to a very low percentage of gold to get that much tarnishing." She reached for it as Nala passed it over.

At her touch, it vibrated and flared brightly. When their eyes readjusted, the tarnish was gone; the disc's surface was now bright and clean. Rhyll swapped hands and examined her palm. The image she'd seen when meeting Nala was fading.

Nala dug out her phone and scrolled through to her photos. "The image on the disc is the same." She showed the picture taken when she and Rhyll first touched. "It must be something important to all of this; some connection."

"It might still be gold if that wasn't tarnish," Dan suggested. "Is that what we came here for?"

Rhyll sat back for a moment and waited silently, eyes closed. "I think so. That feeling of something out of sync has gone. Maybe it was the disc or Father's notes. Keen to go, are you?"

"On the practical side, we took longer to get here than anticipated. I'd rather not have to drive out of that pit in the dark if I can help it. Yeah, I'm happy to leave whenever you ladies are ready."

"Sounds fair to me." Rhyll put the disc back into the silk pouch, which joined her father's notes and compass in her backpack. His leather satchel was cracked and falling apart so, reluctantly, she left it. After checking they had everything, the others followed, torches sending beams down the path.

Dan turned, taking a couple of departing pictures.

The return trip seemed quicker, but as they neared the exit, a new sound reached their ears.

"Sounds like a lot of water," Rhyll called back. They were now approaching the narrower section. A torrent of runoff flowed, emptying into one of the many deep crevices on either side of the path. It was a wet and slippery climb, but eventually, they emerged to the teeming rain, sodden, scratched, and tired.

Stomping through the mud and rain, they climbed into

the ATV.

"This is going to be fun," Dan said sarcastically as he started the car. He turned the fan high to get the warm airflow to dry them, then carefully followed the spiralling path up and out of the pit.

Nala reached back and found a couple of towels in the gear they'd stowed. "Here you go." She tossed one in Dan's lap. "Don't crash." She used hers to wipe herself down, then passed it to Rhyll.

As they made the arduous trip back to the main road, Rhyll spoke more about the disc.

"We know it isn't pure gold, which is quite soft and therefore not a good metal to make jewellery out of anyway." She tapped the edge of the disc against the doorframe, then ran her fingers along it. "No change; I still say it's bronze. Not so valuable in metal, but very much so as an ancient artefact."

"You getting this info from your dad's notes?" Dan called back.

"Of course." Rhyll laughed. "You think I know that much about ancient artefacts and metallurgy? Most of it's in here, but I do know some of it." She turned to Nala and showed her an entry. "Do these look like the lines you mentioned earlier?"

Nala looked at the sketches. It was the earth, with myriad lines covering it. There were numbered asterisks next to several places where these lines intersected.

"Yes. Or at least, they look similar to what I've seen."

"I saw something similar in my dreams; they were called spirit lines."

"Some ancient cultures called them that," Nala agreed. "The aborigines in Australia call them song lines. We can confirm it once we get a reliable signal."

During the drive, they flicked back and forth through the book, comparing references and sketches to other entries.

Eventually, the main road where it met Nala's camp appeared.

"You mentioned a road going south to Pitinga and then on to

Manaus," Dan said. "Want to go that way? Going back to São Lucas will take us over a hundred kilometres in another direction."

"It's a goat track at the best of times. With this downpour, it's guaranteed to be flooded again."

"Fair enough. I didn't feel like sitting in these soggy clothes for ages." He turned north to São Lucas, leaving the mine and the tent city behind.

Rhyll looked out the window, seeing discarded placards in the mud. "Why the torture?" she wondered aloud. "What did these bastards think your people knew?" She realised they never did catch up with Bruno and his colleagues.

Nala wept, and Rhyll reached out to hold her hand. "Sorry. I should have kept quiet," she said softly.

It was a quiet trip back. She dozed lightly, disturbed by vague dreams interspersed with glimpses of the passing, dark forest. The car came to a halt, and she woke up fully. Nala stretched beside her, having slumped against her shoulder.

"I'll unpack the car," Dan offered.

"Was he such a gentleman when you knew him before?" Rhyll asked Nala as they slipped out the back door.

"There's a slight improvement, but he's no smarter." She smiled to soften her joke. "Dan, you've got an injured shoulder and drove all night while we've been sleeping. How about you go in first? Rhyll and I'll deal with the packs."

Dan fished out the ID to swipe the door. "I bow to your wisdom and accept."

"Maybe he is getting smarter," Nala whispered to Rhyll.

"I heard that." Dan cycled through the door and disappeared inside.

Nala and Rhyll moved to the back of the ATV.

"Can you sense that?" Rhyll whispered.

"No. What is it?

"Wait ..."

As they paused, a jaguar moved silently around a corner of an alley onto the street.

"My goddess!" Nala started.

"Keep still. She's only curious."

The jaguar sniffed the air, letting out a low rumble. It wandered closer to the two women, its long tail slowly swishing back and forth.

Rhyll took a step forward.

"Rhyll ..."

"It's OK," Rhyll assured. "Watch."

The large, spotted cat sniffed her palm, then incredibly, it pushed its head against it. Rhyll obliged by scratching behind the ears. She then ran both hands over it, scratching the neck and down its back.

"If you step forward slowly," Rhyll said in a soothing voice, "you can scratch it too."

"I've always wanted to ..." Nala said hesitantly, slowly moving forward. "But I preferred keeping my limbs."

The jaguar ignored her, revelling in its bliss. Soon, both were rubbing it down.

"This is wonderful!" Nala whispered.

"Look over there." Rhyll indicated with her head as two cubs bounced around the corner. After a few playful tumbles, the cubs were entwining around their legs as well as their mother's.

A few minutes later, mum continued its wandering through the town, her cubs rolling and scurrying after her.

"How did that just happen?" Nala asked, wistfully.

"I'm not sure. I've always been able to get close to animals; they never give me the impression of fear or anger, but I've not done that before. I've never even been bitten by a spider, ant, or mosquito."

As they chatted, they both heard other noises as more animals ventured from the forest into the now-deserted town.

"It didn't take long for nature to make a comeback." Nala smiled.

"Given a chance, it rarely does."

CHAPTER ELEVEN

Rhyll was the first one to wake the next morning. She had a quick wash, set the coffee to brew, and turned the news broadcasts on softly to see what had changed since yesterday.

According to the GHO, access to Caroebe was now cut off due to the continuing spread of the mysterious plague — "death-wave" was what some stations were calling it. No one, as yet, had confirmed what the actual virus was, though rumours of it being a newer strain of Ebola conflicted with previous reports of people dying from many other diseases.

There was no mention of any children surviving. Rhyll hoped the local indigenous cared for them as they did in São Lucas.

Other reports of similarity were the electrical storms preceding the event which interfered with radio transmissions, making it difficult for up-to-date reporting.

Having finished her breakfast, Rhyll began looking up crystals to learn what was so special about them; she wondered why Lewis and Grant — or his boss — were so interested.

• • •

"Morning. What are you up to?" Dan asked as he poured himself a coffee and made toast. "I wish they had some Vegemite here." He searched the cupboards in vain.

"Good morning. I've been checking up on crystals and gemstones."

"Did you find anything?" Dan picked the diamond up again to scrutinise it.

"I think you better sit down," she advised, before reading off a webpage. "Green diamonds are rare; a deep green diamond of one carat and of good colour and clarity can go for as much as one million dollars."

Dan sat down. "That's ... unbelievable! What's a carat, exactly?"

"So glad you asked." She read off the screen. "In general mass terms, a carat is 200mg, so one gram is five carats."

"This weighs much more than five grams."

"Surely, it must have more significance than mere dollars."

"Credits of that amount will always count to someone." He handed it back. "Of course. I think Lewis must have been either joking or wrong."

"More than likely, but with all the interest, I somehow doubt it was a joke." Rhyll laid out the other crystals. "We have six others: red, orange, yellow, blue, brown and violet."

"Without a professional assay, these others could be mere crystal, not diamonds. Probably only glass," Dan continued, giving them a casual glance.

"I know, but how do you explain the glowing? They *feel* more than glass, considering where they came from — a crystal cave that kept me alive for thirty-five years. My mother did a bit of gemmology in her day. It was always exciting on a new dig when they uncovered some new relics. Ancient civilizations didn't use mere glass to adorn their kings. I can't wait to see her again; she'll have a better idea."

Dan examined the others in the light. "They do look very nice. Better not lose them then, just in case."

Nala stepped into the lounge area, hair dripping as she finished drying.

"Morning, you two. Who's next?"

"You go have a shower," Dan offered Rhyll. "I'll finish my coffee and listen to the news for a bit."

As Rhyll left, Nala poured herself a coffee.

"I've been thinking about our trip to Manaus. Depending on where the checkpoints are, it should be a fairly straightforward drive."

Dan brought up a map on-screen, and Nala leaned forward to peruse it. "We can cut across from São João da Baliza and go to Nova Carolina, making it a nine-hour drive over 550 kilometres."

"There are reports Caroebe is now affected and cut off."

"If it's like here, there won't be anyone around to stop us. I think the next roadblock will be São João. That'll cut off anyone from the north or the south. It's all jungle, otherwise."

"And they won't be expecting anyone coming from Caroebe."

"If we do take the ATV, we can be almost through before they realise we aren't GHO personnel."

"Won't they shoot?"

"Possibly." Nala picked up one of the crystals on the table. "What's happening with these?"

"Rhyll was checking their value. We've decided Lewis must be wrong."

"Why?"

"He reckons this is a diamond." Dan started sliding the crystals into a small bag.

Nala stood and went to the window, sliding the gem across its surface. "Maybe he's right." She pointed to the long scratch.

"How accurate is that test, though? Doesn't quartz scratch glass?"

"Doesn't look like quartz." Nala tossed it to him to put away. "Whatever they are, they are important."

"That's what Rhyll says."

"You should listen to us girls then — especially if we say the same thing."

"He should." Rhyll entered, towelling her hair.

"That was quick." Dan stood up for his shower.

"Probably because we ran out of water. Sorry."

An hour later, they arrived in Caroebe. It was a larger town, but otherwise much the same as São Lucas. No one looked to have died from gunshot wounds, indicating ICON must have been after something in particular only in São Lucas or the mine. Villagers and GHO personnel lay everywhere.

Other than grabbing a couple of spare fuel cells, they continued through the depressing sight, hardly saying a word. The road continued, mostly sealed, but there were stretches washed out by heavy rains and yet to be resealed. Several times they passed bodies on the roadside, either fallen from a bike or motorcycle, and cars at odd angles against an embankment or in a ditch. Dan was in the back. When he wasn't taking photos, he was writing on his tablet.

In the silence, Rhyll brought her tablet out of her pack. She was thinking about the torch the other night. When Dan used it, it worked like normal. With the tablet in her hands, she waited to see what it would do.

"You know your way around here well enough," Rhyll said to Nala, breaking the depressed mood.

"Don't let these clothes and way of life fool you. I'm indigenous. I've been on and around these roads all my life, which is why I insisted on driving. Like I know we'll turn left when we pass this sporting field coming up."

They were on the outskirts of the town. There was no sign of life or traffic ahead. Nala slowed down as she approached the turn.

"Oh look. You've found a muddy goat track," Dan complained from the back as he was tossed around on the bumpy road.

"Maybe so, but it's just a precaution. It will get us around the town and onto Route 460. Then we'll only be 80 kilometers from Nova Carolina."

Rhyll's tablet lit up in her hands. "Hey, somehow I charged it!" She showed Nala and Dan.

"That's ... weird!" Dan examined it. "How?"

She explained about the torch incident. "When I realised the torch wasn't faulty, I thought I'd experiment."

"There is something about you, no doubt," Dan said.

Route 460 was a better maintained arterial road, and like earlier, the drive was uneventful, with farmhouses and fields interspersed with rainforest. With no traffic — and little concern for a speeding ticket — Nala took forty-five minutes. She slowed as they approached the outskirts.

"There are farmers in the field!" Dan pointed. The click of the camera could be heard.

"And there are people on the road ahead." Rhyll handed Nala the binoculars when she pulled over.

Nala studied the town. "At least no one's paying attention to us."

"Probably not expecting anyone from this direction. Know another shortcut?" Dan asked her.

"The best I can do is take a few side roads." Nala handed the binoculars back to Rhyll and slowly moved off, keeping the revs down until a side street presented itself. She turned and meandered through the south end of the town, slowly wending her way west towards the main road. As they passed the houses, curtains moved, and faces peered through the windows.

They were roughly a hundred metres from the main road access when several people in EV suits came out of a building. One of them began speaking into a radio.

"They look like GHO uniforms," Dan noticed.

"Maybe we'll be lucky," Rhyll suggested hopefully.

Nala drove on like they were supposed to be there. At the intersection, they turned left and headed south. A few kilometres farther along a couple of trucks were positioned at the far end of the bridge, blocking any further travel. Several armed men were lined up on the sides of the bridge.

"Unfortunately, the Rio Jauaperi blocks our southern exit, and there's no way through those trucks." Nala slowed.

Dan looked over his shoulder. "And there's now an ATV behind us."

Nala continued at a steady pace, stopping when one of the soldiers put his hand up.

He motioned them out of the car. At all times, several weapons were trained on them as they climbed out of their ATV.

"Where are you from?" a soldier called out.

"São Lucas," Nala replied.

"That's impossible. Everyone east of BR-174 is dead."

"And yet, here we are." Dan shrugged.

Ignoring him, the soldier indicated with his weapon they were to walk forwards. Other soldiers frisked them efficiently before they were ordered to move.

"Where are you taking us?" Rhyll stepped off first following the leader seeing a couple of soldiers grab their gear.

"I reckon the commander would be interested in having a word," he called over his shoulder.

Nala and Dan followed, a few paces separating them. Beyond the trucks, many tents were lined up on a flattened field. The trio was herded into a tent similar to the one in São Lucas. They then followed the same procedure — stripping, washing, and being isolated in separate cubicles. Medical staff came in and took blood samples and the other tests, like before, without saying a word. Their packs were placed in bio-hazard bags along with their clothing.

"How long have you all been here?" Rhyll asked.

"The CO will talk to you when she's ready," the same soldier replied.

Several hours later, Rhyll was escorted from her cubical.

"Name, rank and serial number only," Dan called out to her.

She was taken to another, larger tent across a muddy path by two armed soldiers, where she was seated in a plastic booth in the centre of the tent. A trestle table was erected, and a dark woman in an EV suit sat opposite with an open folder. She was shuffling through sheets of paper.

"I can assume from your description you must be Rhyllien Ellis?"

Startled, Rhyll only nodded.

"It's okay. You're not in trouble," she said in a kind voice. "But you must understand you three are intriguing, to say the least."

"How did you know my name?"

"We know much more than that. Your mother is Professor Imogen Ellis, and your father was Professor Ken Ellis. He died in 2021."

"Murdered, you mean."

"True. My apologies. What we don't yet know is how you came to be here."

"In São Lucas?"

"In 2056."

Rhyll slumped. "I can't explain it. How do you know who I am?" she asked again.

"Maybe I have a crystal ball." She smiled. "Unfortunately, it's all very mundane. Everything you or Daniel sent through the computer went through our server. We followed your progress here via satellite."

"You knew we were coming?"

"And where you are going; who you are going to meet."

"We didn't do that over the computer," Rhyll pointed out.

"This transcript of your phone call is fascinating reading." The CO pointed to her notes.

"Then you'd know I have no idea of how or why I'm here. I just want to see my mother again."

"It sounds like your mother was somehow expecting your return. How is that possible after all these years?"

So much for name, rank and serial number; it seemed pointless holding anything back. Rhyll told her everything she knew, from the moment the robbers shot her father to waking up in the cave at the mine.

"There may be a chance the anomalies surrounding you can explain your immunity to whatever is happening, but it doesn't explain your friends. Daniel and Nala are ordinary — no different than myself — yet they too seem to be immune."

"What do I call you?" Rhyll asked.

"We don't need military rank here. I'm Ayar."

"Ayar, how connected are you with nature?"

"Nature? Like do I go for walks, get my toes in the grass?"

"I guess without trying to sound crazy, it's more spiritual. How do you relate to your surroundings?"

Ayar paused.

"Put it this way," Rhyll tried to explain, "Daniel and Nala are both environmentalists in their way. They feel nature around them. They may not say it — Dan certainly won't — but they're attuned to the earth, in harmony. I've always been told I'm 'one with nature'." She shrugged. "I think — I believe — what's keeping me, the others, the indigenous and children alive is that we still feel our connection — our roots — with the earth, to the land and everything in it."

"So, you're saying this immunity is like a religion? A belief system?"

"No. It's not a system, nor do I think it a religion. There is no praying, devotion, or homage to a god or goddess, but more a simple recognition that we — you and I — are a small part of something much, much bigger."

One of the soldiers sniggered behind her.

Ayar scowled at him, but before she could say anything, Rhyll continued, "How long have you been here in Nova Carolina?"

"We got here yesterday. Reports stopped coming in from Rorainópolis, so we set up our post at a safe distance. Why?"

"Before the sickness arrives, there'll be an increase in lightning, probably preceded by static over the radios. Within an hour after that, everyone not attuned to the environment will begin coughing or feeling unwell in some way. Those already ill will succumb first. Some will take longer, but everyone not in tune with nature will follow. EV-suits are no protection. Everyone here other than myself, Nala and Dan will be dead."

"How does it get in? How is it we are affected ... if what you say is true?"

"I don't know, but I saw it happen in São Lucas. It isn't airborne; there was no breach in quarantine. People died completely enclosed in their EV suits, even personnel within the command vehicle. The only survivors were the local indigenous, young children, and the wildlife."

"Wildlife?"

"No animals are affected by this. This is nature making a comeback against the one thing that is destroying it."

Ayar made notes.

Rhyll continued, "If I were you, I'd pack up and leave before it's too late. Not that there's anywhere to hide. It will just delay the inevitable."

"How much time have we got?"

As if on cue, a soldier's radio hissed.

"I'm guessing about an hour," Rhyll said.

CHAPTER TWELVE

It took forty minutes to clear the camp. Leaving the tents behind, the medical equipment was a priority, then all personnel boarded the trucks and they moved south.

"What about the villagers?" Rhyll asked. The three of them were sitting in the rear of the command vehicle with Ayar, her lieutenant manning the radio and computer.

"We've got an AI-drone overhead. If what you say is true, we'll know about it soon enough."

"You aren't going to help them?"

"With what? If our medicines or EV suits don't stop this, we can do nothing for them. And, before you ask, we haven't the transport to shift three thousand villagers. The same thing is happening in a few other places around the world. What we discover might save millions."

Tears welled, but Rhyll realised how pointless it was, feeling in her bones anyone not connected to the land would perish. Running would only delay the inevitable.

"Maybe get your satellite to watch natives within the affected areas," Nala suggested. "You'll see the indigenous are immune."

Ayar made more notes. "I'll get onto that after we see what happens."

A vid was playing on the monitor. They could see the village of Nova Carolina, recognising the road they used from São João da Baliza.

"How high is the drone flying?" Dan asked.

"Three thousand metres," the lieutenant answered. "We can zoom in well enough to read the paper if needed. This is a remote-controlled drone."

Already, they were witnessing the effects. People were staggering in the streets, and a car veered off the road, but any young children outside appeared unaffected.

"Lieutenant, put a call through to HQ. Tell them to pull everyone back and use AI drones to keep us updated, then arrange for one of our hoverpods to meet us at Jundia to fly to Manaus." Ayar then went to the internal comm to the driver. "Pull over at Jundia."

"You're going to Manaus?"

"No, you are. My job is to help here. I couldn't do much in the timeframe with the information we gathered, but with this footage, I've got enough to order evacuations now."

"If this continues to spread, you realise nowhere will be safe?" Rhyll asked.

"Then we better learn how to beat this."

The convoy arrived in Jundia a short time later. When they left the vehicle, there was a hoverpod coming in to land in an adjacent field.

"This will take you to Manaus Airport. I have a brother in the city. I'll arrange for a car to meet you and take you wherever you need."

"I can't thank you enough ... but why are you doing this?"

Ayar raised her voice as the pod landed. "Call me crazy, or maybe I'm superstitious, but there's something happening here we have little control over. We have your file, and you have piqued our interest, Rhyllien Ellis.

"We've analysed your bloods, and while rare, there is nothing in it to use against whatever's attacking us. How you're here still as a teenager after going missing decades ago is impossible; how you're surviving when everyone else is dying is unexplainable, so I won't waste my time trying. There's obviously something about you ... Others may not agree, but here and now, this is my call."

Soldiers came over with their backpacks, stowing them inside the pod.

The trio thanked Ayar and boarded the hoverpod. The doors closed, and they were airborne in moments, gaining altitude with ear-popping speed and turning south. Looking down, she glimpsed Ayar returning to the command vehicle.

"What the hell's going on?" Dan asked. "Are we prisoners or what?"

"Nothing like that." Rhyll laughed. "We're going to see my mum."

The craft they were on was a larger version than the one at the mine. This pod was much more spacious, with eight seats. There was a steady vibration, and the background noise was softer than expected.

She was thinking about Manaus when she felt a nudge.

"—better check for your crystals," Dan was saying to her. "No telling who's been rummaging through them."

"They're there. I can sense them."

"All of them?"

Rhyll nodded. "They all feel slightly different."

"Where are we meeting Imogen?" Nala asked.

"Mum said she was staying at the Novotel, but she'll now meet us at the airport. Ayar let me make a call."

A GHO officer wandered back from the cockpit. "I'm the co-pilot. There's a fridge with drinks and snacks if you want them. Weather is good, so we should be in Manaus in forty minutes. You can change back into your clothes in there." He pointed to a cubicle. "If you need anything, press the green button in the armrests." He waved and returned to the cockpit.

"Is it always this humid?" Dan asked within five minutes of the hoverpod landing at Manaus International. He wiped his brow, and his shirt clung to him, making him pull at it constantly.

"This *is* the Amazon," Nala reminded him.

He looked at Rhyll, seemingly unfazed, and swore under his breath. She poked her tongue out.

Following the co-pilot, they walked the short distance along the tarmac and entered the building through automatic sliding doors. Immediately, the positive airflow washed over them with its cooling relief.

Dan sighed loudly, lifting his arms up to get the cool air into his armpits.

They were allowed through without their bags being checked once the co-pilot showed his GHO credentials to the security officer before he went off to find the GHO driver.

"Can you imagine the shitstorm if Security found those gems or the sun-disc?" Dan whispered.

"There she is." Nala shook Rhyll's arm, pointing.

Rhyll looked in the indicated direction. The terminal was busy, and if not for Nala pointing her out, she might not have recognised her in the crowd. Tears came unbidden to her as they moved closer.

It was crazy, but she felt nervous. *This is my mother!* Even though the reality of the missing years had finally sunk in, she still yearned to see her mother like the last time she saw her — a fit and tanned thirty-nine-year-old woman dressed in khaki with a streak of mud on her face when she wiped the sweat away.

Her trepidation melted away the moment their eyes met. Her mother's smile of delight and love banished any nervousness or hesitation. Before she realised it, Rhyll had run to her and wrapped her in her arms, weeping into her shoulder.

They stood there for a long time, tears streaming from both. Like the waters of the Amazon, people flowed around them, focusing on their own concerns, not knowing a reunion of almost four decades was taking place.

Nala and Dan stood nearby; she had a huge smile on her face, and he had to wipe his eyes.

"Damn dust," he said. When he pulled out his camera, he felt a hand on his arm.

"Let them have this for themselves."

True to her word, Ayar managed to organise a GHO driver. The co-pilot found the trio with Imogen, and they were efficiently chauffeured to the Novotel. Dan folded his lanky frame into the front passenger seat while Rhyll and Nala sat in the back with Imogen, catching up on all that had happened.

On the night of Ken Ellis' murder, she had been woken in the camp by Nala's grandfather — the shaman — and was told the story.

'The time is upon us. Collari is now sleeping in the embrace of Earth Mother, in preparation for her reprisal,' he had said.

Imogen told of how she raged at them for taking her daughter away, but they persevered against her wrath. If not for Earth Mother's intervention, Rhyll would have perished alongside Ken. It would have been a straight-out double murder and robbery. The killers would have survived, perhaps even coming to the village, killing her, and taking the remaining relics.

With a couple of canoes, the Wai-wai natives took Imogen to the barge. "You were nowhere to be seen. All we found was your father and the remains of his murderers; one was on a speed boat, the others were mostly skeletons picked clean."

Rhyll added her bit of detail. "I thought I dreamt it, but I called piranhas to finish them off."

"How did you do that?"

"I sensed they were near. I was furious and distraught about what they did. I was dying — or thought I was — and the one responsible was standing there in the water, waiting for me to take my last gasp. I think he was dying too, but I called them forth to take him," she finished.

Imogen held her hand. "The Wai-wai tipped the last man into the water. We wrapped your father's body and took him back with us, burying him at the village with all the honours befitting a chief." She wiped away tears. "The shaman did not know where you were taken. There are yet other natives who have never seen a white man; it was they, the ones who have never deviated from the Earth Mother, who took you.

"I packed up everything in the camp and left for Oriximiná. I've not been back since. When I arrived in the city, I tried to organise a police search, but only influence from the university got the ball rolling."

"But if you buried Father ..."

"An investigation had to be done to legitimise his death, otherwise he'd just be missing, presumed dead. I wanted the record clear that he died at the hands of robbers. I then donated all our relics to the university, but the one item I most wanted wasn't found: the one you and your father were taking for authentication."

"You mean this?" Rhyll dug into her backpack and showed her the sun-disc. With all her handling over the last days, no more zapping sensations were felt since the initial shock.

"You found it!" Imogen held it longingly.

"Father's belongings were in the crystal cave as you hoped. And I was on this massive crystal bed. Daniel has pictures of it all. I can't wait to show you."

"Gee. I'm feeling so good at this moment to be a prude," Dan muttered.

Nala burst out laughing, kneeing the back of his chair. "You idiot."

"How long will we be here?" Rhyll asked. She was looking out the window that faced to the south; her view held a leafy, affluent suburb with the Rio Negro in the distance.

"When I got your call, I arranged to visit the Federal

University tomorrow morning. I hadn't planned the GHO getting you all down here so soon. After that, it depends on what we find."

Rhyll nodded. "It just feels ... wrong."

"You never did like cities."

"There's absolutely nothing natural about them, as if they were purposefully designed to separate people from the natural environment. These 'green zones' might look pretty, but they are fake and pointless."

"They are all that, but don't let it spoil this time. We have so much to catch up on." Imogen joined her by the window. "I promise, once this is sorted, we'll go camping. I've only been working at the university to keep tabs on discoveries and anything related to our previous work. Now you're back, I don't care. I'll leave and we'll go bush again; anywhere you want."

"You only had to hear about my week; I've got decades to hear about, and I'm looking forward to every minute of it. The selling of the *Aurora*, your posting at the university ... and did you find out anything about the robbers?"

They moved away from the window and settled on the lounge, next to one another.

"The selling of the yacht was a regrettable necessity. We had been travelling the world for so long, and we had no permanent address — except your father's family residence back in Wales. I couldn't handle the yacht without you or your father, and the drive to search for unknown cultures left me. I started working at the SPU as Curator of Antiquities more to keep a tab on new discoveries."

"And Father's murderers? The robbers?"

"It took a lot of bribe money, but I did eventually find some information. Two of the killers were low-key thieves with a list of crimes and misdemeanours going back to their youth; the one you shot and somehow sicced the piranhas onto was John Stradjek. He wasn't much of a criminal mastermind, but his father, Viktor Stradjek, is the founder of the Volaris organisation. They're involved in many philanthropic activities, but it's believed to be a front for organised crime, especially in the arts and antiquities trade. If there is a relic wanted, they have the knack of providing it, even if it wasn't on the market."

"So why are they still operating if it's known that they're organised crime?"

"Knowing it and proving it are two different things. No one has given evidence — or more precisely, anyone who was going to give evidence has changed their minds, disappeared, or had an unfortunate but very fatal accident. They also have influence and friends in high places."

"And they were after the sun-disc? How would they have known about it?"

"Maybe they were, or maybe they just knew your father was onto something big."

"So, if these three killers weren't the brains, who was? Were they working for this Viktor?"

"I can only assume so. John wasn't freelancing; it's very unlikely he'd go against his father." Imogen stopped to answer the phone by the bed. It was a quick call, and then she hung up. "Dan and Nala were just checking if we were going to have dinner. Shall we join them?"

"Great. Where are they? Dan can show you the photos of the cave I was in, and the crystals."

"They both had to get rooms on different floors. It being the weekend, I was lucky to get these adjoining rooms as it was."

"So, the university is open on the weekend? I thought a museum would be better."

"Museums are wonderful for storing and displaying cultural artefacts, but we need to analyse, study and tabulate each item first — make sure they are what they are. Having said that, we work hand in hand with each other. With their affiliation with the SPU, I've arranged access to their new Archaeology and Ethnology Department."

CHAPTER THIRTEEN

After breakfast, the Saturday morning traffic was light, making it a quick cab ride to the university, passing the security checkpoint with minimal questions once Imogen showed her ID and authorisation from the institution's dean.

A pre-arranged contact, Antonio, met them at the entrance to escort them to wherever they needed to go. He was a tall, dark-haired man, with Hispanic origins and a dazzling smile. His casual attire, this being a weekend, was loose-fitting, lightweight trousers and a polo shirt.

"You look familiar," Imogen remarked. "Have you ever been to SPU?"

"Me, only once, many years ago. I have younger brother in São Paulo doing Humanities. Maybe you are mistaking me and him?" Antonio flashed his smile and moved off. "Please to forgive. My English not so good."

Rhyll had to suppress her smile at Nala, who was admiring his robust physique as they walked behind.

"You are doing fine, Antonio," Imogen complimented.

"What's up first?" Rhyll asked her mother as they were shown into the building.

"We need to check the authenticity on the sun-disc, and once that's done and we're awaiting the outcome of the tests, I'll use their facilities to check these unusual crystals."

"You've come to right place. We have one of latest Multi-Sensor Spectroscopes in Brazil — and indeed all South America. Only Smithsonian has better device. Please, this way."

They followed Antonio down the long corridor, the floors and walls gleaming with fresh paint and newness. There were large, wood-panelled doors to the left and right, each with a small square window to see inside the room.

"The cafeteria is closed, but there is kitchenette down to the far right, just after washrooms and exit to car park." He stopped. "Before we go any farther, I point out the emergency exits, for safety.

"As mentioned, there is exit to car park; at the north end of corridor is green space which will lead to an emergency evacuation area. To our south, past the cafeteria and where we just entered, are stairs to either basement or upper floors and hover-pad on the roof, which also is designated emergency evacuation area."

"Thank you, Antonio," Imogen said. "Your English is very good."

Antonio smiled at the compliment. "Now, to lab for your first analysis." He moved off.

"Aha." Dan looked relieved. "There's the loo ... I'll catch up with you in a moment."

Antonio's ID unlocked the door to the lab. Inside, the far wall was a bank of windows from the top of the long bench to the ceiling; island workstations ran down the centre, and there were cubicles at each end.

"The MSS is enclosed in the cubicles. I trust you familiar with device?"

"I am. We have one at SPU, though that one is a couple of years older. I'm sure we can take it from here now. Thank you."

"A pleasure. This sun-disc sounds intriguing. Incan origin?" Antonio didn't notice the hint.

"That's what we're here to determine. Thanks for your time,

especially at short notice on a weekend." Imogen nodded and strode towards the cubicle, leaving him by the entrance.

Rhyll saw his smile drop when Mum walked away without offering to show the relic to him. It was brief. The smile reappeared instantly, and he turned to the corridor and left, much to Nala's disappointment.

"Why don't you go after him? Maybe ask if he's married?" She nudged Nala.

"What?"

"You may as well. It looked like you'd have his babies at the drop of a hat."

"I would not!" Nala thumped her in the arm. "That is ... so untrue. He's simply a good-looking male specimen; part of my degree was physiology, remember?"

"Right ..." Rhyll chuckled as they followed her mum.

A window to the cubicle allowed those outside the opportunity to view the procedure.

Imogen entered the cubicle and turned the MSS on, and a display lit up in moments. She made some entries via a keypad and simply placed the disc on a tray that slid out automatically. It then retracted, and she stepped out.

"It will undergo a full spectrum analysis. The results will come through in about thirty minutes. One great thing about these devices is that they can also do crystals. I'll use the other one, which will do them all at the same time. I didn't want to say anything in front of Antonio. I thought the sun-disc a sufficient reason."

Rhyll gave her mum the bag of crystals as they walked to the other cubicle. Imogen entered and repeated the process.

"We have time for a coffee," she said when exiting.

"What if they are real diamonds?" Nala asked.

"Then I'll be drinking something a lot stronger."

Ensuring the door remained wedged open, the trio made its way across the hall to the kitchenette.

"Damn ... only instant." Imogen searched the other cupboards.

"I might stretch my legs. There could be another kitchenette elsewhere," Nala offered.

"Why don't you join her, Rhyll?"

"Oh, I don't think Nala needs my help ... not for what she's looking for, but I might look at this green space Antonio mentioned."

"Good idea." Imogen poured two glasses of filtered water and followed.

The green space was a garden oasis. A large pond with water features meandered through a densely foliaged garden. Already vines entwined the tall pylons, which held a mesh canopy, filtering much of the harsh sunlight. The result created a cool, shady microclimate.

They found a bench to sit on next to the pond. Their quiet small talk stopped when Dan wandered out.

"There you are." Dan looked around. "And Nala?"

"Off to find some real coffee," Imogen answered. "There's only instant, otherwise."

"I'd rather have water. I won't be a minute." Dan went back inside.

Antonio swiped into the office on the first floor, putting in a wave to Volaris Corp. "Mr Stradjek, they here. What your orders?"

"Did you find out what they're working on? Do they have the diamond?"

"She claims to have sun-disc—"

"Did you see it?"

"I did not, but—"

"If it looks like this, I want it." Tyrone Stradjek showed him an image. "I'll double the payment if you get both the disc and diamond and kill them both. That will be the last piece of business with us."

"Very good, Mr Stradjek." Antonio finished the call, wiped down the desk and keyboard, then opened the drawer and proceeded to check his weapons.

He stopped when he thought he heard a noise outside. As quick and as stealthy as a cat, he strode to the door and whipped it open. The corridor was empty in both directions. Antonio relaxed, putting the pistol in his ankle holster, then he checked the dagger in the other sheath and finally the taser in his pocket. He was keen to get the job done, but he also wanted to confirm the authenticity of this sun-disc. Knowing Professor Ellis was the expert in the field, if she authenticated it, the extra time would be well worth it.

Antonio returned to the desk and grabbed a palm-sized monitor, slipping it into his other pocket. His reflection in the mirror showed no sign of his weapons and nothing out of the ordinary. Satisfied, he left the office and headed for the stairs.

***

Nala heard the door to the stairs open and close — she recognised the squeak of the new hinges. She counted ten seconds of silence before quietly looking out from the toilet.

The corridor was empty as she crept along to the door where she had glimpsed Antonio at his desk. She felt stupid now, thinking to blunder in by mistake with her search for another kitchenette. The conversations she had thought up to explain her appearance now seemed silly and pointless. Nala chuckled in embarrassment at her sudden nervous dash away when she bumped the door.

Why did he have a pistol? Was he part of the weekend security? He was certainly built like it. Passing his office door, the idea of a quick look to see if he did in fact have a picture of a wife or girlfriend crossed her mind.

She stepped in to walk to the desk. Something out of the

corner of her eye made her glance to her right. There was a body lying in the corner, the front of his shirt matted with dry blood from his cut throat!

Screaming wasn't in her. She paused, taking a deep, measured breath, then turned to warn the others.

Antonio was in the doorway. His taser made her body spasm before dropping to the floor, and he kept it going until she lost consciousness.

Antonio regretted having to do that; it was not a good trait in his line of work. Innocent bystanders were one thing, but unexpected witnesses had to be dealt with, especially those that would recognise him.

He dragged her to the wall behind the door and lay her next to the real security man. He was swapping his taser for his dagger when he heard the stairwell door squeak.

"Nala?" He heard the other male call out as his silhouette passed the small window in the door.

Antonio opened the door softly and tasered Dan into unconsciousness before dragging him into the office and laying him beside Nala.

He swore at the sound of a car pulling up, then voices outside in the car park made him pause. He left the office thinking to return later. He had his main job to do, and the sun-disc would be authenticated very shortly.

Nala came to, groggy and aching. She tried to lick her dry lips, but her tongue felt swollen and numb. Her head flopped to the side. *Why is Dan here?* She flopped her head the other way. "Yep, dead guy. I'm not dreaming."

Willing herself into motion, she awkwardly rolled over almost on top of Dan.

"Dan! Wake up!" Movement slowly came back to her extremities, and she managed to push herself onto her hands and knees. She crawled to the desk to lean on. Spying the bar fridge farther along, it was easier to crawl.

Inside she found bottled water; her eyes focused on a tin of coffee beans on the shelf. She worked the lid off a bottle and drank half of it. The cool of the fridge revived her somewhat, enough to stand, though unsteadily. Every muscle ached. Her legs felt like they belonged to someone else. Someone drunk.

Nala grabbed another bottle and staggered over to Dan, pouring the contents on his head. "Dan! Wake up!" she cried.

Like her, when Dan recovered, he was unsteady and groggy.

She slapped his face a few times.

"I'm awake! What was that for?" He stumbled to his feet.

"Ten years, and you didn't call once!"

Dan turned, partly falling, partly hugging her for balance. "I'm sorry."

They stood there, briefly lost in the moment.

"Rhyll! Let go, idiot," she said, but not unkindly. "She's in trouble."

There was a refreshing, subtle breeze making the foliage rustle; dry leaves on the path spun briefly in an eddy before dashing up against the garden's rock formations.

"Nala seems to be taking her time." Rhyll smiled at the possibilities.

"Speaking of time, I believe the analysis should be ready."

As they both turned, they saw Antonio strolling towards them, an enigmatic smile on his face. He held a printout in his hand.

"My apologies. I came looking for you in lab. I saw this and thought to bring to you."

"Thanks, we were about to check ourselves." Imogen didn't sound overly impressed.

"Is it as you expected?"

"You seem curious." She read over the print, her face splitting into a grin.

"Only that it would be so good for Manaus University's reputation to have played some small part in a significant discovery of our ancient history."

"From your smile, I gather it good news?" Antonio prompted.

Imogen turned to Rhyll. "Your father was right! It's everything he hoped for. All those years of searching. If only he was here today to see it."

"You mean ... that sun-disc is from Amaru Muru?" Rhyll asked, gobsmacked.

"The one who used the Gate of the Gods — yes!"

Antonio shared in their joy. "That is great news to hear." He then pulled out the taser, stunning them both.

When Rhyll recovered, she found herself on the bench with her arms tied behind her. Her mother was tied to one of the pylons, head down, still unconscious.

"Mother?"

"She older; recovery slower." Antonio returned from the building, holding the disc in his hand. "This fascinating."

"Is that it? You're just a thief? You'll never get away with it. We have documentation going back to the original find. It will clearly show my father as the true discoverer."

"My dear, is not for me. I have no use for such thing."

"Then why are you still here? Does your feeble ego need to gloat?"

"I have a message from employer." Antonio put the sun-disc into one pocket and pulled out a small tablet. He activated it and placed it in Rhyll's lap.

It was dim footage — like it was night. They were approaching a familiar barge with a lean-to. She saw a man. Her father? "Is that ..."

"Professor Ken Ellis? Before death. Yes. I believe you were in reeds."

"How did you get this?"

"The man on boat had this quirk of *vlogging* everything. A stupid thing in his work but it help now. Once we had this, began watching your mother's movements."

She heard the gunshot and saw her father's head knocked back as he crumpled.

"No!" she cried in anguish, thirty-five years after the event.

The boat cruised closer. Two men jumped across as the sound of the engine died.

She heard a gruff male voice. "Wasn't there another with him?"

The tall reeds swayed as the boat's wake swelled through them.

"The daughter. Maybe she's hiding in the shelter," a second, rougher voice said.

Her nightmare replayed itself. She saw how she was hauled out of the water by her hair, reliving the pain even now.

"Look what we have here," John was saying.

"Good," his partner had replied. "We got what we came for." He held up the box containing the relics that had been hidden under the blanket in the shelter. "Let's go, John. Remember, no loose ends."

"I can only guess this sun-disc was inside box?" Antonio asked. "That's what they after?"

Rhyll heard him, but she was too engrossed in the vid. Her worst nightmare. Again, she couldn't drag her eyes away. Tears flowed down her cheeks as she watched herself raising her father's pistol and shooting John in the chest.

Her body fell to the deck as John collapsed on top of her. The vid blurred and jolted as the engine suddenly came to life, and the boat spun around, Harry just in view hanging onto the sides as more shots — her return fire — were heard over the revving of the motor.

The vid played on. The boat turned, and the rifle came into

view. She fell sideways. Her body shuddered at the memory of the impact.

Rhyll's vision became hazy; she closed her eyes in an effort to forget.

John was in the water, talking to her when she refocused on the monitor. Suddenly, the water boiled around him. He writhed and screamed, disappearing under the surface.

"See that?" Antonio rewound the vid a few seconds and turned the volume to max. "This is interesting part. We even enhance audio. Listen." There was hissing background noise. John and her previous self were talking, and she could hear it faintly over the distance.

"Watch out for the piranhas."

"Oh, I'm not worried about fish."

"Not worried about piranhas? You should be. They haven't feasted for a long time."

"How could you possibly know?" Antonio was asking.

She heard her voice, indistinct ... *"Piranhas, piranhas."* She heard thunder rumbling.

"Rhyllien?"

"Mum!" Rhyll's head snapped up, vid forgotten. Her mother was looking at them, dazed and confused.

"What's going on?" Imogen struggled against her bonds.

"Ah, Professor Ellis. It a shame you woke." Antonio unsheathed his knife.

"Rhyllien?" Imogen repeated. "What's going on?"

"This low-life is a thief after the disc."

"Oh no, dear girl. I much more than thief. Today, he say I am to be 'harbinger of retribution'. My employer has given me grave task."

"Stealing my father's life work is pathetic, but not what I'd call a grave task."

"Stealing life, though, is."

Rhyll's face paled.

"Ah. Penny is dropping. You see, John — in video — was my employer's father. He was child the last time he saw. Can you imagine distress his young mind went through, watching his father die such horrible death?"

"Actually, more than you realise."

Antonio moved closer to Imogen, not listening to her. "You won't have to imagine, you can experience yourself." His hand lashed out, cutting Imogen's throat.

"NO!" Rhyll's scream burst from her lungs full of shock, outrage, and anger. Her mother gasped, her blouse becoming red.

Rhyll struggled against her bindings, her wrists becoming raw and bloody in the attempt. The monitor slipped from her lap to the paving. The screen cracked, but the vid played on ... *'Piranhas, piranhas ...'*

Antonio examined his work. "Not deep as planned. It will take longer." He moved back to Rhyll, standing over her. "I greatly respect your mother's work. Your father's too. You understand, this nothing personal."

Rhyll ignored him, her attention solely on her gasping mother, her head lolled forward, knees bent as she sagged. Only the bonds kept her upright.

Why, why, why? "Wait until I get my hands on you, you bastard! I'll make it very personal." She was shouting over the rising win and thunder.

"The diamond. Where?"

She shook her head to remove her tears. "You'll get nothing from me."

"Your friends still alive. That can change."

"We've all seen your face. None of us will be walking away from this."

The vid replayed on a loop, her voice faintly heard. *"Not worried about piranhas? You should be. They haven't feasted for a long time."*

... One with nature ...

"You know, Antonio ... Is it really Antonio?"

"Bahlam," he responded.

"I thought I was crazy thinking I could call for piranhas. Do you think I can do that?"

"You are mystery. I fortunate to not be waist-deep in river."

Rhyll remained silent, concentrating.

"Now, back to diamond ..." Bahlam continued, moving behind her.

If I can really do this, do it now! she wished feverishly.

... You are Collari ...

Prove it! she challenged the voice in her head.

"Where is diamond?" Bahlam had his hand entangled in hair, pulling her head back.

An inexplicable calm took hold. She felt no pain or discomfort. If she hadn't opened her eyes, she'd be unaware of his presence. Staring up at him, noting now how one of his eyes looked a different colour. She felt a strength within herself.

"I am Collari. I AM one with nature."

Bahlam shook her head violently. "You not making any sense—"

"You'll never get it from me," she mumbled repeatedly, "I am Collari. I am one with nature."

"Fine. I get information from friends. Die, *vadia loucah!* Join your mother." He moved his arm to slash her throat. Or, at least, he tried.

A shot rang out, and the knife's edge grazed her forehead as Bahlam fell back.

Rhyll heard footsteps.

"Miss Ellis, are you alright?" The stranger moved behind her. She heard him shuffling in the undergrowth. Then her bonds were loose.

"What? ... Mother!" Rhyll lurched forward to her mother across the path. The man joined her. He cut Imogen's bindings as Rhyll took the weight, lowering her to the ground.

"Lay her flat," he instructed. He immediately pulled off his shirt and applied pressure to the wound. "She's weak but alive. You have to get out of here!"

"Are you crazy? I'm not leaving her!"

"Your friends have been taken in a van. Kidnapped."

"What are you talking about?"

"Nala and Daniel. Two men — I believe they are freelancers — dragged them into van."

"Why didn't you stop them?" Rhyll wiped the trickle of blood from her forehead with the back of her hand.

"Because you are my assignment, not them. I couldn't do both in time."

"Assignment?"

"I am GHO — or a branch of it. There's no time to explain. Your mother is alive. I can make sure she is cared for, but if the authorities find you, they will have many questions and much paperwork. Considering your history, you do not want to be asked any questions. You will probably not see your friends alive again unless you go now. Follow them." He fished out a small remote. "An AI hoverpod is on the roof. It can be voice-activated. If you are quick enough, you will see them leaving the campus grounds."

Rhyll looked at her mother, caught between two decisions.

"My sister said you had a role to play. Go play."

"Your sister?"

"Ayar. Now move," he said, his voice full of authority.

In the distance, sirens could be heard approaching.

"How will I find you?"

"You will not. I'll find *you*." He nodded his head. "Go after friends."

Climbing to her feet, she clutched the remote. After two paces, she turned to where Bahlam was lying. With a quick search of his pockets, Rhyll had the sun-disc and the report in her hands. After the briefest hesitation, she also grabbed the gun strapped to his ankle. She had to untangle it from the vines ... *wrapped tightly around his arms and legs* ... Rhyll shook the thought from her head and moved.

"Thank you," she called out over her shoulder as she dashed toward the door.

Inside, she raced to the lab with the cubicle and the crystals. There was a report sitting in a tray. Rhyll snatched it and shoved it in her pocket with the other printout. The crystals slid off the tray into a small bag, and then she was moving again, running along the corridor to the far stairs.

Panting, she finally reached the top. The dark blue pod gleamed in the sunlight. Fishing the remote from her pocket, she pressed a button.

The pod's side door lifted and opened. Much like the one at the mine, this was a compact two-seater.

"Rise," she commanded.

Nothing happened.

"Take off. Rise. Lift-off!"

"Ignition sequence commencing." There was a slight rumble as the drive started, and the doors closed as the craft lifted off the roof. The campus grounds became visible. The Antiquities Department was in the centre of the university grounds.

Avenue Octavia Hamilton snaked north and south. She spied a black van driving fast to the south. It was the only vehicle heading out. There were three vehicles with flashing lights parked next to the building she'd just left, and two at the security entrance. The van swerved around the police vehicles; one remained, and the other gave chase.

"Fly southwest."

"Designate altitude," the AI voice said.

"Umm ..." She studied the display, looking at the options. Currently, they were at two hundred metres. "Five hundred metres."

"Altitude designation too low over urban areas unless in landing configuration. Revert to landing configuration?"

"No! Fly minimal allowable height, you stupid machine."

"Ascending to fifteen hundred metres."

Below, the van turned left onto an arterial road. It zigzagged south before driving steadily along Avenue Biriti. By the time the pod reached cruising altitude, the van was very difficult to define amid the other traffic.

"Has this thing got a camera?" She was thinking about the ICON pod at the mine that followed them with its camera.

"Visual device activated." A previously dark display lit up. The image was slightly jittery. She could see directly in front but not the van or the road below.

Thinking there had to be a method to direct the camera, she discovered the joystick in the right armrest. Hoping it didn't change their flight path, she tapped it slightly and the camera moved. Rhyll spent a few minutes adjusting the focus and direction before she had the van in view, helped by the flashing lights of the pursuing police.

"Are you able to follow that vehicle?"

"Designate subject vehicle."

"What the ..." Rhyll stared at the screen. There was a cursor. "How the hell do I adjust that?" she muttered.

There was no response.

"How do I designate subject vehicle?"

"Activate thumbwheel, left armrest."

There was a ball inset in the left armrest. The cursor moved incrementally as she toyed with it. Eventually, the cursor was above the van. She depressed the wheel, the van became outlined.

"Subject vehicle assigned." Without needing her input, the camera adjusted to follow the black van, now a pulsating amber dot.

Out the window, other flashing lights could now be seen. Several police cars appeared to be zeroing in on the van.

"Where the hell are you going?" she wondered out loud.

"Displaying possible destinations based on current data." Roads on the display appeared highlighted.

"Wow," Rhyll chuckled in awe.

The trailing police vehicle was closing in. Suddenly, it veered off the road and crashed into a store. A fire started. The van raced through a roundabout, causing other cars to veer and collide, and then it proceeded along Avenue dos Oitis. It had now been heading northeast for a few minutes without deviation.

On-screen, different roads highlighted possible routes while others faded. As the van sped farther away from the built-up areas, fewer roads became available.

"Can you work out where it's going?"

"*Probable destination ... calculating.*" An array of highlighted roads flashed on and off as the AI crunched numbers. Eventually, one route was brighter. "*Probability of destination is 77.4%, based on current data.*"

Experimenting with the thumbwheel, she moved the cursor over the nearest cop car and clicked the button; the cop car became outlined like the van. It was now a red dot.

"*Secondary vehicle assigned.*"

"Are you able to work out if and when they'll catch up?"

"*Probable intercept primary and secondary vehicles ... calculating.*" Now the roads between the two highlighted vehicles flashed. "*89.2% probability of intercept based on current parameters.*"

Rhyll studied the map. "Can you work out when and where it is best for us to intercept the van?"

"*Define 'best'. Fastest, safest, or most fuel-efficient?*"

Rhyll considered briefly. "Safest."

"*Probable safest intercept for GHO pod ... calculating.*" Instantly, a section of road lit up in a different colour. It was a section curving around a hill. There was a green zone before entering an industrial estate.

She looked out the window. "Do it now."

"*Optimising rapid landing configuration.*"

The harness snapped around her, pulling her tightly to the chair. With her stomach in her throat, the pod dropped out of the sky. At the last minute, it slowed and spun, dropping the pod onto the road just around a bend and over the crest. Towards the industrial area, a bus began the climb up the windy road.

"How long?"

"*Primary subject vehicle ETA 43 seconds; secondary subject vehicle ETA 138 seconds.*"

The harness clicked open, and Rhyll pulled herself to her feet and wobbled outside. She waited in the bright sunlight at the side of the road inside the curve of the quiet, remote area. The sound of the van accelerating up the far side of the hill soon reached her ears.

Holding the gun in a relaxed manner as her father always instructed, she waited.

The van appeared around the bend, slamming on its brakes and veering to the side to avoid the pod, hitting the curb with its front right-hand wheel. If not for the rising embankment, it would have rolled. Instead, it ploughed into the dirt and foliage, grinding to a halt at an angle, then slowly toppled back onto all four wheels.

Rhyll raced to the back doors, pulling them open.

Nala and Dan were bunched up against the back of the seats. They were moving and bleeding from scratches. They were alive. The driver was motionless, and his passenger was groaning. Sirens could now be heard in the distance.

"Hey, you two. No time to dilly-dally."

"Wha— How?" Dan mumbled, echoing Nala's confusion.

Rhyll made the weapon safe and shoved it in a pocket, then she reached in to help Dan to his feet. He sat on the tailgate instead, woozy.

She did the same with Nala. Both had their hands tied in front.

"I'll explain later. Can you move, or do I have to carry you?"

"Can ..." Dan leant forward to get the momentum to stand. "Where?"

Rhyll led them both by the arms, aware of their light-headedness, mindful of the approaching sirens and the bus chugging up the hill.

"Watch your step." They climbed single file into the pod. "Grab a seat, both of you," she instructed firmly.

"Maximum lift-off," she commanded as she stepped inside; her two passengers barely had time to slump into the chairs.

"*Unable to comply. Safety protocol breach.*"

"What safety protocol breach?"

"*Safe passenger limitation surpassed. Recommend passenger disembarkation to rectify.*"

"I'll give *you* rectify," she muttered. The sirens were almost upon them. "Do whatever you need to do to get us in the air. Now!"

"Emergency safety protocol override engaged."

The pod doors slammed shut as she became one with the deck. The craft screamed into the air, making her ears pop, the cabin pressurisation slightly lagging with their rapid ascent. Nala and Dan groaned in the front, holding their heads.

They soared to fifteen hundred metres and slowed. *"Previous cruising altitude attained."*

"Are you guys okay?" Rhyll sat up. She felt her face, sure the pattern of the textured deck was permanently embedded in her cheek.

"Define okay," Dan mumbled, trying to look over his shoulder.

"Don't you start. I've had enough of that from the pod's AI."

"Where are we?" Nala rolled her shoulders with difficulty and looked out the windows. "How the blazes did we get here?"

"I ... I'll explain later. I'm just glad you guys are safe. Pod, can you take us to the Novotel Manaus?" She worked at their bonds.

"Novotel Manaus ... destination confirmed; ETA 5 minutes." The pod sedately turned and accelerated back to the southeast and the city. On the display, a dotted line represented their flight path.

CHAPTER FOURTEEN

THE POD LANDED BETWEEN THE IBIS AND THE NOVOTEL IN A discreet corner away from the main entrance, crowds, and prying eyes.

Common sense told them it was too dangerous to stay here, but they needed to get their gear from their rooms. As they entered the lobby, the concierge got their attention.

He turned to Rhyll. "Pardon, miss. I have a message for you." He brought out an envelope with her room number on it. No name.

From the look on his face, their bloody and dishevelled appearance had him curious.

Nala allayed his curiosity. "Our taxi was involved in a car accident. Just a few scrapes."

Rhyll had a quick look at the message. "And we'll be finalising the bill."

"Oh. Checking out early? I hope nothing is wrong with the rooms."

"No, the rooms are great, as were the meals. Just news here to change plans." She indicated the note. "Sorry for any hassle."

"None at all. I will organise the account now."

"Oh. How did you know the message was for me?"

"Miss, I take pride in my work and to know all our customers. And your startling red hair certainly makes you prominent."

Rhyll nodded, leading the others toward the elevators.

"What's in the note? There's still so much you need to explain," Nala asked.

As they awaited the elevator, she let them read the note.

"You've got friends in high places, it seems." Dan read it over Nala's shoulder.

"Beats me. Ayar's brother, I think." Rhyll shrugged. "I'm glad Mum's not as bad as it looked, but I'm not sure I like the sounds of 'military barracks'."

"The Jungle Warfare Instruction Centre isn't just army barracks," Nala said. "They're one of the elite units of the Brazilian armed forces — and the best in all of South America when it comes to jungle warfare and general sneaky shit. If it's safety you want, you couldn't ask for more."

The elevator arrived.

"Let's stick together," Dan suggested. "No splitting up. We go to Rhyll's room first, then yours."

"What about you?" Nala asked Dan.

Dan patted his pack. "All my important gear's in here. I need nothing else."

The lift took them to the eighth floor, and the suite she'd shared with her mother was near the end of the corridor. The key card didn't work, no matter how many times she tried it. One of the cleaning staff working in another room came to their aid, swiping them in.

They stepped inside in shock. Imogen's room was a mess, the place ransacked.

Nala spied sudden movement. She pushed Rhyll with a yell of warning as a gun went off, and the cleaner screamed, clutching her arm.

Rolling to the floor, Rhyll saw a woman in dark, loose-fitting clothes slip into the bedroom. "Get outside, everyone."

Dan and Nala helped the crying woman into the corridor, using the cleaner's radio to call security.

Since they shared adjoining rooms, Rhyll raced to her own suite. It hadn't been touched yet, so she assumed they'd only just arrived and not had time to do both. Her backpack was still there under the table by her chair, a cold half cup of coffee on the table.

Rhyll pulled the gun from her pocket. ICON had been armed, Grant had been armed, Bahlam had been armed, and now this woman. It seemed only fair she was too. Worst case scenario, it was better to shoot than be shot; she clicked off the safety and got down low.

She noticed the outline of the assailant's shoes under the connecting door. They were clear and distinct, indicating proximity. The door handle turned.

"Stop or I'll shoot," Rhyll warned.

The assailant fired through the door several times. If Rhyll had been standing, she'd be dead. Again.

It was bastards like this who had murdered her father and tried to kill her and her mother. Remembering her father's training, she aimed and gently squeezed the trigger. The bang was very loud within the enclosed space.

She heard the body on the other side of the door crumple to the floor. Rhyll got up and pulled the door open to check. The woman was gasping, holding her stomach, another pistol by her side. She was trying to reach for it.

Rhyll kicked it away. "Who are you? Are you working for ICON?"

The woman remained silent, other than her short and fast breathing.

"I will stop you all, you know."

That made the woman laugh. "We are far bigger than you can imagine."

As big as the world? Hearing loud voices in the corridor, Rhyll left the woman, closed her door, and locked it. She grabbed her pack and exited her room while hotel security entered her mother's suite.

Dan and Nala were still by the cleaner, looking frantic. Other staff had come to help.

"Let's go," Rhyll whispered, waving to them as she scurried past, heading to the elevators.

Without a backwards glance, they followed. Nala had the foresight to grab a towel off the room-service cart to wipe the blood from her hands before passing it to Dan to do the same.

As luck would have it, the lift was still on their floor, and it opened almost immediately.

"What happened? We heard more gunshots." Dan asked as they bundled into the lift before anyone could see them.

"She shot at me, and I shot back."

"You did? How?"

It was probably an inappropriate time to laugh, but the question sounded so ludicrous. "With this." She pulled out the gun, explaining briefly how and why she had it.

When the elevator arrived on the ground floor, she quickly pocketed the gun, and they casually made their way to the concierge.

"You have the account ready?" she asked.

"Miss Ellis, of course, but I heard there was a commotion in your suite."

"Was there? Ours is fine. It must be the one next to us. We've just come from there. Is that the account?" Rhyll signed for it, forging her mother's signature.

They were outside and halfway across the car park before the alarm was raised. Security came out and started chasing them.

"Why did we park so far away?" Dan complained.

"Is your leg bothering you?" Rhyll asked, concerned.

"I'll make it."

The trio reached the pod and climbed inside, panting and sweating.

"Sit quickly. You've got five seconds. Pod, maximum lift. Engage emergency safety protocol override."

Once again, they were pushed into the seat as the pod surged into the air.

"Plot a course for ..." She dragged out the message. "Avenue São Jorge, São Jorge, Manaus. AM, 69030 460, Brazil."

"Course plotted. Destination, Home. ETA 4 minutes."

Four minutes, thirty seconds later they stepped out of the pod onto a large, flat grassy area. Three soldiers separated from a group of armed troops and joined someone dressed in blood-stained civvies — the mysterious GHO officer from the university.

"I'm Pachacutec Bocaiúva. Pacha though is good. You all made it, I'm glad."

"Where's my mother?"

"She's in surgery and won't be available for several hours. How about we get you all tended? Cuts and scrapes, I see."

They all climbed into a military ATV — not totally dissimilar to those of the GHO — and sat in silence until it stopped outside a long, low white building.

"Is a military hospital. Your mother getting the best medical attention outside Rio."

Following him inside, they entered the admissions centre. Each had a cubicle separated by curtains. Male and female medical staff were in attendance ready to deal with them. A quarter of an hour later, bandaged and treated, they sat in a waiting area where snacks were available from the kitchen.

"I think it's time we got some answers," Rhyll said politely when Pacha joined them. "Don't get me wrong, I'm very grateful for all you've done, but why? Why all this and not a public hospital? You referred to me as 'your assignment'; what's that about?"

"Here you are. Anywhere else not be safe." Pacha placed a large folder on the low table between them and took a deep breath, looking at them all. "You all meet my sister, Ayar, who furnished my CO with everything of you." He studied Rhyll. "You are not what you seem is my understanding."

"Are we referring to my ... age?"

"Si."

"Then you'd know I can't explain—"

"Understand. With the blood samples, we checked the database. Considering your parents, it was not difficult. Your hair sample is 100% match to where your father was murdered. You are who you say, little doubt."

Rhyll sighed with relief. "I knew I wasn't crazy, but—"

"This is why you are my assignment," Pacha confirmed. "There something happening we cannot explain, and then you appear."

"I didn't cause it!"

"Not what we implying. You are not in danger from us. None of you. Our concern is with the others who are after you. What were your reasons for visiting the university?"

"We have an artefact that needed to be authenticated."

"With this death-wave happening, you needed to check on a relic?"

"I ... I feel it's vitally important, and so does my mother." From the little Rhyll knew of this man, he was no doubt formidable and professional in what he did. She trusted him, sensing the sincerity.

Rhyll told him about her father's digs and ongoing search at the Incan site for relics, especially those mentioned in myth. "He felt in his bones there was always a bit of truth in myths." She pulled out the artefact. "This is the sun-disc of Amaru Muru."

Pacha's eyes widened at the sight of the gleaming disc. "I have not seen so much gold."

"You still haven't. The sun-disc looks like gold but is predominantly orichalcum, an ancient mix of copper and bronze, but the report from the Multi-Sensor Spectroscope shows 5% of an unknown element." She handed it to him. As it left her hands, it dimmed noticeably.

"Still heavy for its size. This 'unknown' element?"

Rhyll shrugged. "There's no record of it, but that's what makes my mother believe its authenticity — the fact it contains an element that science hasn't found yet."

Pacha marvelled at it. The image on the disc was not particularly exotic or unknown. Many Incan relics had similar depictions of a face. This one included seven arrows — denoting rays of the sun — glyphs, ideograms, and stars.

"Did you know or check on the man that attacked us? Bahlam, I think he said." Rhyll held the bag open, and Pacha slipped the disc inside.

"Bahlam Tupinambás. Low-key assassin from Rio. The last information had was a sighting in São Paulo four years ago. He disappeared after. We also found a hand-held screen where you were tied." Pacha brought it out of his pocket.

"Did you watch it?"

Pacha nodded.

"That man in the water — 'John', his son—"

"Tyrone Stradjek. I know of him, and Viktor, his grandfather. They both run Volaris."

"Volaris? The philanthropic organisation?" Dan looked surprised.

Pacha nodded. "Suspected involved with organised crime. Never proven. They have powerful friends."

"And you know all this in Brazil? Are you Interpol?"

Pacha turned to Dan. "As journalist should know information across the globe is instant."

"I ... sorry." Dan blushed. "What's on the vid?" He changed the subject.

"Maybe Nala and Dan should see it?"

"It quite disturbing," he cautioned.

Rhyll turned to her friends. "I know you both trust me — and it's only been a week — but I want you to see everything I've been telling you is true—"

"There's no need, really." Nala reached for her hand. "The connection we have is beyond mere trust."

"Oh, yes, of course. We don't need to see it." Dan sounded disappointed.

Rhyll smiled in thanks, then continued. "This disc is what they were after thirty-five years ago. Knowing my father's reputation, anything he felt the urge to take to the museum immediately was worth stealing."

Pacha nodded at the obvious connection. "Volaris deal in many antiquities."

"And they sent Bahlam for revenge—"

A buzz in Pacha's other pocket stopped her.

Pacha looked at the message. "Your mother awake. Shall we?"

Leaving Nala and Dan in the waiting area, he led Rhyll down a long, tiled floor. The doors on either side had mostly blank labels on the doors. They went into one, still unlabelled.

"Dr Alvarez, this daughter, Rhyllien."

The doctor, dressed in standard white scrubs, shook her hand. His hand was soft, like his voice.

"Your mother was very lucky; firstly, the cut wasn't so deep, and as she was upright, her drooping head prevented much blood loss, and, of course, Major Bocaiúva's first-aid. If the larynx or windpipe is penetrated, then the struggle to breathe is the main issue, depending on if there was much blood being aspirated—"

"Obrigado, Dr Alvarez. Perhaps Rhyllien could have a private word?" He made it sound like a question, though from the doctor's response, it wasn't.

"Of course." He nodded to both and left.

"I'll be with your friends. Take your time."

Rhyll moved to the side of the bed and reached for her mother's hand, relieved to feel its warmth.

Imogen's eyes flickered open. "There she is." She smiled. Her voice was hoarse and scratchy.

"Are you okay?" Rhyll asked, concerned.

Her mother nodded briefly. "They did great. Have you got the disc?"

"Here." She patted her pocket.

"You need to take it to the Hayu Marca. The final proof of it being the authentic Amaru Muru disc."

"Volaris is behind all this because of the robbery and death—"

"I suspected as such." Imogen coughed.

Rhyll passed her a glass of water. "The man who did this, Bahlam, is dead."

"I thought I recognised him from SPU," Imogen said after sipping from a straw.

"Probably following you to get the disc."

"Or you. They knew your body was never recovered and may have suspected you were in hiding and that I knew of it."

"Is that why you set up the protest camp?"

Imogen nodded. "Vitor Xaschoal convinced me you would return in that area, just not when. No one was expecting the mine to open."

Rhyll told her what happened after the incident. "Things are getting out of hand. The GHO ... the Brazilian Army interest, and no doubt the police are investigating."

"This is why you've got to go to Hayu Marca. To test the disc once and for all."

"It's in Peru. It's thousands of kilometres away ... and I haven't a passport—"

"It's all Brazil now. Are my old clothes here?"

Rhyll looked around, finding them in the cupboard, washed and fresh.

"I hope the key is still there."

"No key here." Rhyll checked several times, patting down the pants. On a whim, she looked in the drawer by the bed. "This?" She found a key, but there was no indication of locality, just a number.

Her mother nodded. "Keep it with you. I've learnt not to carry everything with me. At the airport ... a small locker." Her eyes drooped.

"I should let you rest. Love you, Mum."

Imogen opened her eyes momentarily and smiled. "You too."

Rhyll made her way back to the waiting area where Nala and Dan were talking to Pacha.

"How is she?" Nala asked.

"She's doing fine."

"Pacha was saying we can stay here until we decide what we want to do." Dan got up and poured a fresh coffee for her.

"It's in everyone's interest, considering the threat against you," Pacha said.

"Do we know who the kidnappers in the van were? And how that happened hasn't been explained to me. Nala, you went looking for ... coffee ..."

"Oh yes, coffee." Nala turned to Dan. "They only had instant in the kitchenette, so I went to look for more upstairs."

"And I went looking for you and got zapped," Dan added.

"And when we revived, we started to head back, then these clowns jumped us—"

"Tasered again!"

Pacha nodded. "And that's where I come. Was looking for you, heard your scream, and as I ran, saw the kidnappers bundle these two in the van. I believe would come after you and mother, except heard the sirens."

"How did you know where to find us?" Rhyll asked him.

"Simple. We knew you were planning to meet your mother in Manaus. When Ayar got you on the pod, arranged to drive you to the motel. Our driver placed bug on you, and we followed. The rest you know."

"What are we going to do now?" Dan asked.

"I'm not in a rush to leave; I've not seen Mum for over three decades, and I think we all need a couple of days to recover. Your shoulder, all the bumps and scrapes from the van ride, and my wrists. And we need to go over Dad's notes; compare what he wrote against what we know now to determine 'what's next'."

"Maybe make a list of things?" Dan suggested.

"What about you, Nala? You've not said much."

"I'm with you, regardless. I'm now unemployed."

"What makes you say that?"

"My job was at the camp; that's finished."

Rhyll laughed. "You can be my chaperone since I'm still only a child. I'm sure we can negotiate fair rates."

They all chuckled with her.

"It'd better include danger money — I've been tasered twice and kidnapped. And that's week one."

Pacha cleared his throat. "Suggest you take conversation to your rooms, I have some duties to attend. If you'll follow me, is only a short walk to accommodation area."

"Do you know what happened to the woman I shot?" Rhyll asked.

"Or the kidnappers?" Dan added.

"The woman is umm ... surviving. One kidnapper died, and the other is serious but stable. Your assassin is at morgue. It is unusual — vines covered him."

"That does sound weird." Rhyll nodded.

CHAPTER FIFTEEN

Following a winding path through a section of natural rainforest, they came to an area with several buildings. Other personnel were seen, either on balconies or walking the path. When they passed the group, they paid their respects to Pacha.

Their adjoining ground-floor rooms were simple, yet clean and comfortable: king-single beds with ensuite, a small kitchen, and a TV monitor and computer.

When Pacha left, the trio sat around the table in one of the units and started a list of all the things they knew. Dan had a pack of peanuts in his pocket from the snack bar, and he tipped them into a bowl.

Rhyll began writing. "So far: there's a spreading wave of death starting at the mine—"

"At the same time as you appeared," Dan added. He got up to turn the TV on to see the latest news, failing to see Rhyll's scowl.

"All those unaffected seem to have a connection with the natural world in some positive way." She continued, "There are seven vibrating diamonds, which apparently correspond to the seven chakras, there are my father's notes, my dreams make reference to grid lines and earth chakras, and then we have the sun-disc of Amaru Muru."

"And not forgetting Volaris is after you, the sun-disc, and the diamonds. Mercenaries are out for us too," Nala added.

"And those ICON mercs in São Lucas came after us at the cop shop," Dan reminded them. "Assuming they were the 'gringos with muchos denhiro' the cop was talking about."

"You mean muito dinheiro." Rhyll laughed with Nala.

Dan flicked his peanuts at them both. "Hey, listen." He pointed to the TV, bumping up the volume.

"Earlier today in Manaus, a van was pursued by several police vehicles after leaving the scene of a crime at the Federal University of Amazonas. The pursuit, going through Japiim and Amando Mendes districts, came to an abrupt halt when the van lost control, veering into an embankment on Avenue Cosme Ferreira. The driver was pronounced dead at the scene, and the passenger is in a serious but stable condition."

On-screen, they saw the entrance to the university where several police vehicles were parked, as well as an ambulance. As they watched, another ambulance from inside the campus grounds raced out, sirens blaring.

"A spokesperson stated a blue hoverpod was seen leaving the area moments before the police arrived. The back doors of the van were open, indicating at least one passenger fled the scene. Witnesses in the vicinity claimed two people from the back of the van joined the pilot of the hoverpod."

On the monitor, there was an aerial view of the police chase before the first police car crashed. The skycam followed the van to where it ran off the road on a bend in between an urban area and an industrial estate. The footage clearly showed a blue hoverpod and three people entering the pod before it surged into the sky, almost colliding with the drone.

"The crime scene at the university included the shooting of one Bahlam Tupinambás, the death of two security guards and a university lecturer, Dr Antonio Brandeas, who was believed to be meeting with a Professor Ellis from São Paulo University. Security video shows Mr

Tupinambás meeting Professor Ellis with three other people at the Antiquities Department. It is believed Mr Tupinambás murdered and impersonated Dr Brandeas to kill Professor Ellis.

"*Police are investigating the identity of three other visitors, who have a similar appearance to those leaving the van crash site. Manaus Police request they come forward to assist in their ongoing enquiries. Professor Ellis was severely injured and taken away to an undisclosed location.*"

"Well, that's just shit. Now everyone knows about it." Dan muted the TV.

"All they know is Mum's name, the assassin, and the dead lecturer."

"Wait, there's more," Nala noted.

"*In other news regarding Professor Ellis, there was a shooting at the Novotel Manaus today. An unnamed woman believed to be a thief was shot in the abdomen. Witnesses say three people seen running across the car park resemble the three figures from the university. Hotel records report they are Daniel Dobson, Nala Xaschoal, and Rhyllien Ellis. Police are on the lookout for these individuals with a warning they could be armed and dangerous.*"

"I'm dead! My dad, or someone from the Nexos office, will be scanning world news. They'll either hear my name or see the drone footage, I have no doubt."

"They'll be concerned, right?"

"The exact opposite. Knowing my history, they'll see the worst side and assume I'm up to my neck in this."

"You are." Nala nudged him.

"Yes, but this isn't my fault!" Dan argued.

"So let them know. Talk to them."

"I'll have to do something." He sighed. "I might head off and compose my story. I'll see you ladies later."

"We'll call you for dinner," Nala offered.

Dan nodded his thanks and left.

"Where does that leave us?" Rhyll asked.

Nala looked around. The TV was now showing the weather

forecast for the week. She considered Rhyll's question as the map was overlayed with isobars and temperatures.

"Ley lines and earth chakras." She got up and turned on the computer. It took a few minutes before she had a web browser open displaying various hits on ley lines.

"See how when you do a search for ley lines, energy lines and spirit lines also appear? Here's a site I remember from my uni days when I did a semester on biogeology." She clicked the link, and a new window opened. "It goes on in detail about what they're supposed to be."

"I see a subtitle calling it all pseudoscience."

"True. Because they can't prove their existence scientifically, it's all conjecture. Myth."

"Like how they couldn't scientifically prove how a teenager could sleep for three decades without aging."

"Exactly. So to buggery, I say, to pseudoscience; there has to be something, even if we don't know how to measure or quantify it — you're proof."

"And this death-wave too, I guess. Not even the top epidemic organisations know what's happening."

"Back to the ley lines." She read off the screen. " ... A series of metaphysical connections linking a number of sacred sites around the world. Essentially, these lines form a grid or matrix and are composed of the earth's natural energies."

"It says here ley lines were first theorised in 1921," Rhyll pointed out.

"So they say, but there are cultures going back thousands of years with something similar in their mythos; the aborigines in Australia are one of the oldest known cultures going back over sixty thousand years, and they called them *song lines*. South American shamans call them spirit lines, druids in Europe called them mystical lines, and Asian cultures call them dragon lines. There are as many names for them as there are cultures."

Rhyll looked at the list. "Okay then, what about earth chakras?"

"You know in yoga they say the human body has chakras?

Well, it's the same with the earth. If you consider the earth to be a living entity—"

"Which we do. Hence my presence, apparently."

"Exactly ... See here?" Nala pointed and read. "We're connected to Mother Earth through the subtle electrical current that runs around the planet. In many places where these ley lines intersect, the energy is increased, and you'll find many of our greatest sacred temples and monuments: the great pyramids, Machu Picchu, Stonehenge ..."

Rhyll read on, "It says 'ley lines can take information or energy around the world from these nodes'. Do you think it's somehow carrying this death-wave?"

"It's too early to tell, but we know at the moment it's spreading more or less evenly in all directions; it's not airborne, and penetrates the very things designed to keep it out." Nala shrugged.

"What's that picture?" Rhyll pointed as Nala scrolled down. "Earth chakras. Physical locations super-charged with energy to help keep the planet and all life on it balanced. The map shows seven."

"They're coloured the same as the crystals," Nala said. "The chakras have the same reference as the body: root, sacral, solar plexus, heart, throat, third eye, and crown. As you can see here, there are several sites all with the same colouring."

"And it correlates with what's in my father's notes. There has to be a connection somehow."

"There's one more unexplained anomaly. These reports of sickness in other areas all correspond to earth chakra locations: Mount Shasta, Glastonbury, Giza, Lake Titicaca, and Uluru."

"But why is this death-wave here?" Rhyll wondered. "According to that info, there's no earth chakra near here."

"I don't know. There has to be some connection ..."

While Nala performed further searches, Rhyll was feeling peckish and checked the fridge and pantry, noting a selection of packet and canned foods. "Hey, real coffee!"

"I'll have one," Nala responded, eyes glued to the screen as her fingers tapped away at the keyboard.

Several minutes later, Rhyll returned with steaming mugs. "What more have you found?"

"This and that. I saw some intriguing images and followed the breadcrumbs." The one now displayed was dozens of lines criss-crossing the globe. There were many places where they intersected — some more than others.

"And that is ... what?" Rhyll couldn't make out what she was looking at.

"Another version of the energy line grid. Take a look at this." Nala moved the image until it was over Brazil and zoomed in. "See here where all these lines intersect?"

Rhyll nodded, sipping her coffee.

Nala opened a hybrid world map, naming locations. She zoomed in to mirror the image on the other map. "There's São Lucas ... and there's the mine."

"So, you said where these lines intersect there's more earth energy?"

"And a place where the earth energy can be accessed efficiently — if you know where to look and how to do it."

"I don't—"

"But the ancients did — as do the shamans today."

"Your grandfather put me in that cave?"

"Not him, but there are other Wai-wai tribes. They all communicate with each other. He would have known about it."

"And he told my mother?"

"And knowing you weren't dead, she employed someone to stay in the area to keep an eye out for your return. The protest camp, while doing good work and bringing attention to the plight of the indigenous, was a front." Nala started drinking her coffee.

Rhyll looked at the screen, waving her hand to slide the image across.

"My mum wants me to go to Hayu Marca—"

"At Lake Titicaca? Obviously, because you have the sun-disc?

Which, coincidentally, is where one of the chakras is supposed to be."

Rhyll nodded. "But these lines don't go anywhere near it."

"There are myriad ways Earth energy moves. Take a look at these dragon lines." Nala enlarged a previous window. "As you can see here, there are the Rainbow Serpent and the Plumed Serpent lines."

"Only two of them?"

"But they do cover earth chakras, except the fifth one." Nala shrugged. "I don't know how or why, but it's a start. There has to be something to all this."

Rhyll considered the options. "Seems like Lake Titicaca is the next step. There were other items from the dig in the box we had on the barge, but they haven't turned up. Only the sun-disc. If it was buried with me, there must be a purpose for it."

———

Rhyllien was sitting on a log, enjoying the morning sun in the garden. It was humid, and the insects were buzzing, but none bothered her. She sensed the three commandos hidden in the foliage, and thought it amazing how they managed to move without the slightest hint of sound. No threat was intended, as they were not after her but testing each other's skills.

It made her think of what happened at the university. *When Bahlam was shot, was it an accident he managed to entwine himself ... maybe in his death-throes?*

On a mischievous whim, she closed her eyes and tried to concentrate on the closest soldier, to see if it was really her doing or coincidence.

Not knowing exactly what or how to do it, she focused on the area where one of the soldiers was hiding and *encouraged* the vines and undergrowth to wrap around a leg. Everything around her seemed to grow dim, like when a cloud blocked the sun. A moment of weariness overcame her, and she felt herself about to doze off.

At that same moment, she heard footsteps approaching. Eyes still closed, her senses registered a familiar form. Pacha.

"Good morning, Pacha," she said without opening her eyes.

There was a pause before he replied. "And to you." He was standing in front of her now. "How did you know?"

She opened her eyes, smiling. "Lucky guess. Would you like me to tell you some other guesses?"

"Sure."

"There are two males and a female hidden within ten paces of us, trying out their skills."

"Are there? And why you say that?"

"I can sense them, like I did you." Discreetly, she pointed as she spoke. "The female is over there, hidden underneath the *otacanthus caeruleus*, and the two gentlemen are over there amongst the *cubitanthus alatus*. I think it was a dare to see who she would date."

"*Impressionante*. Assuming you guess correctly."

"And I believe one of the males is entangled in vines."

Pacha studied the areas for a moment. "Benigno, Felipe, Cataleya. *Desapontado*, when teenage civilian know you there." He winked at Rhyll.

Two of the named individuals silently rose out of the foliage. Their camouflage was so good that even standing there your eyes could easily slide past them. Felipe had difficulty rising. When he did, it was like he was wrestling with the vines.

Pacha kept his face straight, but Rhyll could see he was controlling his mirth.

"Cataleya ... not that what you do in your own time is my business, but surely you can do better than either of these two?"

"Sir, I'd rather take the girl for drinks and find out how she knew before I share my time with these *putos*." She winked at them.

"Better make it a coffee. I'm not allowed alcohol for a couple of years." Rhyll chuckled as the soldiers made their way into the open.

The two males were roughly the same height as Rhyllien,

lean but well muscled; Cataleya could be the poster girl for female warriors, and she was a hand taller than Rhyll.

"Miss Ellis, I have some news you should know."

"Sure." Rhyll waved to the soldiers and joined Pacha in walking back to the units.

The three soldiers met, watching the departure of their commander and the red-haired girl.

As Pacha escorted Rhyll back to the living quarters, he spoke quietly to her. "Results of the autopsy regarding Bahlam came in late last night. He was how you say ... *conectado* ... wet-wired ... with bio-lens."

"What do you mean?"

"He had vid-cam for one eye. A fairly common prosthetic, but this was top of line. Too expensive for him. Someone is footing the bill."

"I thought I saw something weird. Does that mean someone saw what he saw? One of the Stradjek's, perhaps?"

Pacha nodded. "Assuming he was transmitting. If so, they may believe your mother is killed but realise assassin was captured or killed. They will want confirm of your death."

"And they'll also want the disc."

They arrived at her unit, and Nala was on the balcony stretching. "Morning."

"Miss Xaschoal," Pacha greeted her.

"Hey, you." Rhyll waved, then turned back to the commander. "Will it be okay to visit my mother again?"

"I'll leave word with the nurses to expect you."

"Thanks for all your help. Especially yesterday."

"Ayar would hound me for anything less." Pacha nodded a farewell to both.

"Coffee?" Rhyll offered.

"Need you ask?"

Dan joined them on the balcony a few minutes later with a mug in his hand. "Hi, ladies."

"All good with your dad now?" Nala asked him.

"Seems so. He wasn't at first, but once he saw my report—"

"You didn't mention us or—"

"I'm really not as stupid as I look," Dan responded. "All I showed him were some shots of the natives and the victims in São Lucas."

"Did he ask how you were alive?"

"He didn't, and I didn't offer." Dan drained his mug, seeing three soldiers strolling along the path and Rhyll giving them a quick wave.

"Who are they?"

"Benigno, Felipe, and Cataleya."

"How do you know them?"

Rhyll rolled her eyes. "One should know her bodyguards."

Leaving them to wonder how she found bodyguards, she went to visit her mother. Imogen was in good spirits and on the mend. It was a pleasant surprise that they were able to go for a walk around the grounds.

"Have you decided on your next plans?" Imogen asked. "Not forgetting to get to the airport and that locker."

"I'll see Pacha about the airport today. Otherwise, we've been researching as much as we can regarding other things mentioned in Dad's notes: ley lines and spirit lines. But, as you suggested, Lake Titicaca is the most obvious choice. It's the one thing we have a solid lead on. That and the diamonds, which have something to do with the earth chakras."

"Those crystals are really diamonds? They did look spectacular."

Rhyll unfolded the report from her pocket. Her mum went through it.

"If you were after money, these would be worth a fortune!" she said in surprise.

"We priced them, but thought you'd have better luck."

"I doubt it, not being active in gem appraisal for years."

"One billion, three hundred and fifty thousand dollars."

"We use geecees now. Global credits. And yes, it's a ridiculously huge amount. If Volaris — or anyone — knows of it … nothing will stop them from coming after you."

For the first time in her life, Rhyll saw her mother worried.

Rhyll tried to soothe her concerns. "We've got the best commando unit in Brazil looking after us, and you're forgetting the message from Nala's grandfather: I'm 'Nature incarnate' and 'Gaia's wrath'. No one dare." She knew it was stretching the truth to say the commandos were looking after her, but she convinced herself it was worth it to stop her mother from fretting.

"Darling"—Imogen turned and took her hands—"they don't understand or believe in Gaia, and will no doubt pay little credence to any message from an aging shaman of the first nation's people." She hugged her tight. "Mark my words, if they've been following me for thirty-five years, they will definitely dare."

CHAPTER SIXTEEN

Several hours before dawn, Rhyll, Nala, and Dan dozed fitfully in a GHO hoverpod.

The previous day had progressed well — food, company, and another medical check-up of their injuries. With the current news and police alerts, it was deemed too risky for any of them to be seen in public, so Pacha grabbed the locker key and made a quick trip to the airport to collect Imogen's items.

Then late-night breaking news came in. The sickness had hit the Manaus area near the south-eastern sector. It was a shock to everyone because the initial death-wave was still several hundred kilometres to the north. No one knew how it had jumped the distance.

The trio had been woken up by Pacha and told to pack up all their gear. As they did so, Dan turned on the monitor. Not only was the sickness here, but it had also caused panic among the Manaus population — at least, those that were awake at the time. Those that could either arrange a flight, drive their car, or catch a boat anywhere did so.

A Brazilian Army ATV took them to the airfield, where a large hoverpod was waiting. To their surprise, Rhyll came face to face with the three soldiers she'd seen the day before, along with another female soldier. Introductions were made, including Ileana, the fourth soldier.

"I thought you were joking when you said they were your bodyguards." Dan laughed.

"You should trust me more, Daniel," Rhyll said, suppressing her own surprise.

After the initial excitement, their disrupted sleep, along with the long, tedious flight, had them dozing within the hour.

"Everybody wake up! Todos acordem!"

Rhyll opened her eyes, instantly awake, as was Nala beside her. Dan was wiping his eyes, still drowsy.

"O que está acontecendo?" Rhyll called out, concerned why the soldiers were alert and tense.

"We have bad weather. Turbulence," Cataleya answered. "The pod has engine trouble and is going down."

"Where are we?"

"Almost over the Andes," José, the pilot, called back.

Outside, barely discernible through the heavy cloud cover, rugged mountain peaks came into view. The hoverpod was buffeted by crosswinds as it navigated through the deep valley. From the gloom and infrequent rose tint on the clouds to the west, it was dawn.

"Look on the bright side,"—Dan was fully awake now—"at least we aren't crashing in the dark."

Nala reached out silently to hold his hand.

Rhyll looked out the window beside her. The rough terrain was still a few thousand metres below, but the normally soft buzz of the pod drive now had a high pitch to it, rising and falling in volume. They were still travelling quite quickly, but descending rapidly as well.

"José will get us through the worst of this," Cataleya was saying confidently.

Rhyll sensed she believed it. She also sensed how the other

soldiers were feeling — maybe not as confident as Cataleya but not panicked. She heard the pilot say something in his headset.

Cataleya nodded, then repeated it to her. "There is a town ahead. He thinks it best to put us down there and not risk flying farther."

Rhyll nodded, then looked down to see if she could see it too. It was still dim within the valley in the shadow of the mountains. She could, however, make out distant streetlights.

The pitch of the drive increased, as did their rate of descent. It looked too fast for a safe landing, but she had to trust the professionalism of these army elites.

All too soon the ground became clearer and nearer.

José called out over the headset, but she heard him anyway. "Prepare-se para a colisão!"

"Brace for impact," she told Dan.

The view outside was now cliff and rocks, and treetops flashed by. The pod's angle of descent matched that of a hill. Terraced fields and then farmhouses came into view.

Rhyll remembered as a younger girl, the moment just before a jet landed on the tarmac, there was a brief moment of calm before the jolting of the wheels on the ground. That didn't happen this time.

Screeching metal assaulted her ears as the pod slid over rocks and gravel, softening momentarily when they crossed ploughed ground, then a series of bangs and drops jarred her. The pod finally came to a stop with a massive jolt that took the wind out of her, snapping her head down. She bit her tongue and immediately tasted blood.

Rhyll could smell an electrical burning odour, and a small amount of smoke issued from a back panel. The pod was at an angle, and the soldiers on the high side were held in by their straps.

"Everyone okay?" Cataleya called out, snapping her restraints open and moving as fluidly as a cat, despite the tilted floor.

Rhyll looked to Nala and Dan. They were both shaken but gave the thumbs-up.

"Your mouth's bleeding," Nala said.

"Bih mah toh," Rhyll answered, trying not to dribble, with her mouth full of saliva and blood. She unbuckled her belt and reached for a paper cup, spitting into it. "I bih my tongue," she repeated unnecessarily, touching it with her fingers.

The other soldiers looked okay, but when Felipe moved, he groaned. "Minhas costas doem."

"Felipe hath damaged hith back," Rhyll translated.

José was slumped in his seat, head to the side. Cataleya stepped quickly to him.

Marco, the co-pilot, reached across to check his pulse. "He's alive. Unconscious."

Ileana grabbed a fire extinguisher and checked the smoking panel while Benigno helped Felipe to his feet. Once upright, he could move, albeit slowly. Benigno guided him to the door across the skewed deck.

Finished with the panel, Ileana tossed the extinguisher and opened the door, but it only opened halfway, hard up against a hedge.

Dan climbed out of his seat and slipped past the others to help Ileana force the door open farther, but it was wedged firm. "There's no way out," he called back. "Door's jammed against some scrub."

Deciding what to do, they turned at a loud banging; Marco was kicking out the front window.

It was awkward getting José out in the confined space. Benigno and Dan climbed out first, then together, Marco and Cataleya managed to pick the pilot up and pass him through. Felipe grimaced when it was his turn, but he remained stoic throughout the ordeal.

Once the others climbed out, Ileana passed the weapons and bags to them all.

Still spitting blood, Rhyll gazed with interest at their new location. The terrain was hilly and rugged — understandable for the foothills of the Andes. She had seen many methods of farming in her travels, but this terracing amazed her. Other than vertical cliffs, the vast majority of the accessible slopes around them had been utilised for cropping.

Dan and Nala joined her.

"Well. That was interesting." He already had his camera out.

"There's a town down there." Nala pointed.

As they watched, locals emerged from their homes to investigate the noise.

Rhyll's tongue finally stopped bleeding enough that she could speak more or less properly. "I heard Marco say we are in Amarete. We're still east of the lake by about 60 kilometres." She took a sip from the water bottle to rinse her mouth.

"Maybe we can get a vehicle from these guys?" Dan suggested. "Or we could wait for another pod to get us from La Paz."

"Will that happen?" Nala asked.

"As far as everyone is concerned, we're not here," Rhyll said.

"What do you mean?" Dan turned to her.

"It's what they do. These guys aren't your regular troops. The only people who know we're here are the few back in Manaus — and we don't know what's happening there, either."

The three watched as the soldiers went about their business. Once José was settled comfortably, they did a thorough check of the pod for anything left behind, then regrouped.

"Hey, Nala," Dan piped up. "Where's your sat-phone?"

"We left it in my room at the Novotel. I didn't think I needed it, and under the circumstances, I thought it to be too much trouble to get it back from police forensics."

Cataleya spoke quietly to her people, and they nodded in response. Felipe kept lookout while Ileana and Benigno walked down the path to greet the villagers.

"We'll stay here until help arrives." Cataleya walked over to join Rhyll and the others.

"Help from Manaus?" Nala asked.

"Assuming the message got through. The storm fried some of the electrics, so we aren't sure."

"This keeps getting better." Dan vented his frustration by swishing the branch he was using to keep the buzzing insects away.

Nala dodged Dan's fly-swatting. "When will we know?"

Cataleya watched the villagers stomping up the slope towards them; kids, as well as a few of the village dogs, were dodging between them all. "Benigno and Ileana will make a call from the village and see about a place to stay. We'll get a doctor to check on José as well."

"How is he?" Rhyll asked.

"Concussed, but nothing too serious from what we can tell. The pod is a goner, though."

The villagers were very helpful when they arrived, assisting in carrying the pilot down on a stretcher. Felipe was able to walk, as long as he stayed on the even surface of the track that zigzagged down the hill. The children swamped him, with several holding each hand.

Looking back at the crash site, they were very lucky. The pod had slid downhill, ploughing through the fields and taking out terraced walls, which accounted for the bangs and sudden drops. They were fortunate the hedge prevented their plummet down a much steeper embankment.

"Those three seem to be paying attention to us," Dan observed.

Rhyll and Nala looked. They saw two women and an aged man in traditional clothing, hats adorned with beads and feathers, large colourful coats and leather sandals.

"Looks like they're paying more notice to Rhyll," Nala suggested.

"Probably just the hair." Rhyll laughed.

In the town, the group had to split up to fit with the available accommodation. The mayor, Eduardo Ramos, graciously offered his house for the injured and arranged for a doctor to visit; all they had currently was a retired nurse and a midwife.

"Felipe and José will stay here. A doctor visits every week but isn't due for two days," Cataleya translated for them all. "His cousin has a boarding house farther up the road which he says has vacancies. He also hopes we like cats."

Leaving Felipe and José behind, Rhyll, Nala and Dan wandered into the village with the soldiers and Marco. Many people were out and about setting up their roadside market stalls or opening shops to sell their produce — fruits, soybeans, corn, rice, potatoes as well as many other vegetables. It wasn't long before fires were going and food was being fried, boiled, or grilled.

The market was bustling, and many children were running about and playing games, just like kids in a market or public space anywhere in the world. When they saw the new arrivals, the children swarmed around them, giggling and pointing, but all were in awe of Rhyll's long red locks.

As Rhyll was enjoying her mote pelado, she was amused by the antics of Nala and Dan. Not game enough to try unusual foods, he was making a real mess of his tortilla, trying to emulate Nala's casual style and ending up wearing most of it, which put the kids in hysterics.

"You're wasting good food, Daniel." She wiped her own mouth before the juices dripped on her shirt too, glad she'd let it cool so her cut tongue didn't cause too much pain.

"Those dudes are watching you again." He indicated with his head.

Without being obvious, Rhyll looked in their direction. They all looked as old as Nala's grandfather in his message. On a whim, she decided to go speak with them.

"I won't be a minute." She licked her fingers, then wiped them on her pants as she wandered over. Most of the kids followed but curiously, when she neared the three elders, they left her and played games elsewhere.

"Hola. Buenos días."

The elders bobbed their heads to her, gently reaching out to touch her. She remembered when, back in the jungles, the elderly did that to her, touching her hair or resting hands on her shoulders and arms briefly.

"Collari," they murmured.

She nodded with a smile. *There's that name again. I should remember it.*

"Qué significa eso?" She decided to ask them what it really meant.

"Reina inca. Guardián de la vida y la muerte," they answered.

"Incan queen? Keeper of life and death?" Rhyll translated dubiously.

They then spoke to her softly and earnestly for several minutes before a final bow. Surprised at what they'd said, she turned back to Nala and Dan. The whole market had stopped to watch, and now they all bowed to her too.

Rhyll was too stunned to say anything, feeling her face warm with the blush, her heart racing. Before she knew it, Nala was by her side, Dan too after he took photos.

"What's going on?" he whispered. "Did someone drop some coins?"

Nala punched him. She didn't say it, but he knew what she was thinking. *Idiot.*

Rhyll ignored him, nodding to everyone and putting her hands out, palm towards them. "Bendiciones para ti y tus antepasados. La madre de la tierra los ama a todos."

"Is that the same as what you said in São Lucas?" Dan asked.

"The Spanish version. My Quechua isn't great."

"It sounded very nice," Nala complimented, watching the crowd as they slowly stood and continued their daily routines, all smiles.

"These are villagers though, not like those natives." Dan put his lens cap back on his camera.

"True, but like you and me, they have still a great affinity with their land and nature." Rhyll motioned with her head, and they wandered back to the boarding house, which had as many cats as rooms. She saw the soldiers relaxed but watching from the balcony.

"What did those old guys say?" Dan asked, opening the door for her and Nala. Two of the house cats darted out between their legs.

"They reminded me who I am, or who *they* think I am."

"And that is ...?" he prompted as he followed them inside.

"Collari. Their Incan Queen." She turned as Dan tripped on the doorstep.

CHAPTER SEVENTEEN

Tyrone paced back and forth in his apartment overlooking Key Biscayne Beach. The failure to kill the girl and her mother in Manaus, compounded by the failure to collect the diamond or disc, made his blood boil at the ineptitude. Williams suggested he go home, and he'd let him know of any further updates.

"How could this one girl be such a nuisance?" he raged to himself. "At least that Bahlam fool had the decency to die, saving me the hassle."

When the comm chimed, he exhaled. "This better be good. On-screen."

Williams' face appeared. "Sir, there's been some positive developments—"

"The girl's dead?"

"Not quite, but we know where she is — or, at least, where she's headed."

"Where and how?"

"We know one of her companions, Daniel Dobson, is a journalist. He's got a bit of a tendency to get arrested, so it was easy enough to track him down. We contacted his agency in Melbourne, Australia, and made them an irresistible offer. Nexos is a leftie-environmental magazine. Using the cover of representing the San Francisco Daily, we offered inducements on his stories, especially regarding his current assignment."

"And?"

"They're heading for Lake Titicaca."

"What the fuck are they doing there?"

"Sir, ludicrous as it sounds, I believe the girl might be trying to use the disc at some Incan mythological 'star-gate'. It's in her father's notes."

"Have we anyone there?"

"We have a team en route, and they should be on-site in a few hours," Williams said.

"I saw the news of some kidnapping attempt in Manaus. What was that about?"

"I'm looking into it. We know two of them were ICON mercs, freelancing."

"ICON? How the hell did they find out?"

"They have global resources — as we do — but I will be keeping tabs on their feed, just in case."

"Excellent. Keep me appraised of anything further ASAP."

"Will do, sir." Williams ended the comm.

Other than Ileana, whose turn it was to be the lookout, everyone was in the upstairs guest lounge; four cats moved from lap to lap.

"This is why the major wants us to look after you," Cataleya explained after Rhyll repeated to them all what was said at the market. "Not that we've done great so far."

"But I'm no Incan queen!" Rhyll protested.

"Maybe not physically but spiritually," Nala considered. "If you take into account everything that's happened to you and everything my grandfather said, what they say — or believe — has to have some truth."

"You have to face it," Dan added, "like it or not, extraordinary things have occurred."

"Plus, you are now in possession of the sun-disc of Amaru Muru and those geo-stones," Nala added.

"We don't know if it's the real sun-disc—"

"I'm sure your mother would disagree, and from what I hear based on your father's reputation ..."

"Can't I just be a kid?" Rhyll grumbled.

"Why are you being like this now?" Dan asked. "Ever since we met, you've been able to do or say things you yourself didn't know you could do. When you told me you were born in 2005, I wanted to laugh; yet you seem to know things you shouldn't—"

"And that wild jaguar came over to us in São Lucas." Nala shook her head. "I nearly peed my pants, but you calmly reached out and pet it."

"She did?" Dan looked at them. "No one told me."

Nala continued, "You said yourself, we'll know one way or another once you've tried the disc. See what happens after that."

"What am I supposed to do with it?"

Dan opened his tablet, glad they had some service out here. "According to this website, Amaru Muru was evading the Spanish, who were after anything and everything made of gold. He fled to Hayu Marca — the Gate of the Gods — where we were heading before we crashed. They say he put the disc in a depression in the wall, there was a bright light, and then he vanished." He scrolled through other websites. "They all more or less say the same thing; I can find no record of where he went, nor any other sighting recorded afterwards."

"All I hear about is the Incans. This ... power, this spirit of Mother Nature, is vastly older," Rhyll argued. "My father, in his work, found so many similarities with many cultures and their religions. The next culture simply took over the previous one's beliefs, modifying it as they went to suit their interests. This is still happening today."

Dan passed his tablet to the soldiers to read over. "Perhaps this artefact is the only one we know about; records of others may have been lost and now become nothing more than myth.

There might be many things to use, but the sun-disc is what we have now."

"If it works, what am I supposed to do then?" Rhyll repeated. "Does it say that anywhere?"

Nala shrugged, as did Dan, though she did reach out to hold her hand. "If the disc works, maybe something will happen and reveal the next step," she suggested. "But what we know from our previous discussions is the Lake Titicaca area is where one of the chakras is situated. Maybe these two things are connected."

They discussed it in depth while Benigno poured them all Api Blanco, a local beverage. It tasted surprisingly creamy. He and his colleagues then spent some time studying maps of the area on the tablet.

Afterwards, Cataleya left with Marcos to check on the condition of Felipe and José while Benigno went to relieve Ileana's watch.

Frustrated, Rhyll needed to get outside. The trio went for a walk around the town, and Dan took the opportunity to take more photos.

———

Rhyll woke up from an unusual dream. She was running through the darkness, and there were several armed people chasing her. The weird thing was that it looked very much like the village outside, and dawn was approaching. She got up to get a glass of water and drank it on the balcony.

She'd had those vivid, running dreams before, where she was being pursued through dark alleys and tunnels by someone or some*thing*—dreams so weird a psychiatrist would probably love to explore them—but this one made her tense and wary.

A shadow on the balcony made her jump before she remembered the soldiers were keeping watch. She did spill her water, though, and was glad the darkness hid her embarrassment. Rhyll had grown used to being able to sense the four soldiers, and realised how disturbed she must be to have missed this one.

"Hola," he whispered, and moved silently over.

"Hola." Rhyll looked over the plaza, feeling the warm breeze and admiring the horizon with the dawn. *Dawn?* The feeling of impending doom remained. She hesitated before saying anything, but her father always said she should trust her instincts. "Ben, this will sound crazy, but I have a bad feeling something is about to happen."

Without another word, he stepped inside to wake the others. He was back in moments, activating the ninox goggles. He saw her look.

"With what's going on, better to be safe than sorry." Benigno used the night-vision goggles to sweep the area. "Get friends up. Now!" he warned.

Her heart skipped a beat as she turned and swiftly went to Nala's and then Dan's room, waking them. "Get dressed and grab your gear!"

"Again? What's going on?" Dan grumbled, throwing the covers back.

"We have company." She raced to get dressed and grab her stuff.

By the time the others were ready, Cataleya was downstairs at the front window, scanning the street with her ninox and whispering in her link, "What are they doing?" She turned and waved her hand for Rhyll and her friends to stay low and quiet. She nodded at something she heard, then spoke to them. "We have four, maybe more, figures sweeping through the village."

"Not farmers, I gather." Dan adjusted his backpack nervously.

"Not by their movements—" She stopped to listen to another report.

"Ileana has found an old truck in a lane out the back." Cataleya turned to the co-pilot, standing behind the trio. "Can you clutch-start a truck?"

His head silhouette moved with a nod.

"Good. We're leaving. The road out of town is mostly downhill. We'll roll as much as we can, then clutch it, and you can drive like you're flying the pod."

"Yeah, without crashing this time," Dan muttered.

"What about José and Felipe?" Rhyll turned with the others and made their way to the back.

"Ileana and Benigno are going to them now. They'll meet us on the road."

A loud hiss and mewling made Nala and Rhyll jump; Dan had stepped on a cat's tail.

Cataleya shook her head in annoyance, taking point as they quickly exited the boarding house.

They crept along the back lane. After a short distance, a truck loomed in the shadow of a small warehouse. Marco climbed in behind the wheel while the others clambered onto the back, unhitching their packs and stowing them against the back of the cabin. They sat to the side as Cataleya braced herself and kept vigil behind. There was the framework for a tarpaulin arching over the back tray, but from the corrosion on the metal and the weathering of the boards, it obviously hadn't been covered in years.

As the truck was already on a slope. Marco put the truck into neutral and eased off the handbrake, but nothing happened.

Hearing his cursing, Cataleya got Nala and Dan to hop off and check. They found a rock, but the weight of the truck was now hard up against it, making it impossible to budge. Dan put his shoulder to the grill and tried to push the truck back while Nala got down to pry it loose.

"Hopeless," she whispered. She scurried along the edge of the building, coming back with a rusty metal rod. She slipped it between the tyre and rock while Dan strained to push the truck, trying to keep quiet, but in the peaceful darkness before dawn, his grunts of exertion sounded loud enough to wake the town.

With a lot of intense wriggling from Nala's metal rod, the rock finally tumbled free. When they both climbed back into the truck, Marco released the brakes again, and they slowly rolled.

"That's probably the hardest I've seen you work. Ever," Nala congratulated him.

"I could say the same for you."

"Quiet, you two." Cataleya kept her vigil.

Using the buildings and fences as cover, Marco did wonders in steering the truck around the narrow lanes toward the mayor's residence a hundred metres away. They now had to go onto the main street, as the lane finished.

"Marco, no headlights," Cataleya ordered.

The others were waiting by the fence. José was conscious but unsteady, and he and Felipe sat inside the cabin while Ileana and Benigno climbed on the back. Now three rifles were aimed at the dark village.

The terrain meant the village of Amarete was built in two sections, with the larger portion on a ridge. The truck slowly gained speed as it began its descent to the lower part of the village. Halfway down, Marco clutch-started the truck.

The engine burst to life with a backfire, but they were moving faster.

"That's fucked us," Cataleya muttered.

It would be naïve to think that noise in the dead silence of the morning in a mountain valley hadn't alerted anyone.

Rhyll sensed the soldiers were more on edge, though on the outside they remained calm, alert, and professional.

Sure enough, within a couple of minutes, they saw headlights from the upper part of town come over the ridge and down the hill at speed.

"We've got company," Cataleya warned everyone.

"Mierda!" The other soldiers added their curses to the mix.

Everyone hung on as Marco navigated a sharp bend, braking hard, then gunning the engine to get their speed back up. The road wasn't paved in any way, and as the speed increased, so did the discomfort, especially for those sitting on the boards in the back.

Rhyll turned her head to look through the small, dirty window at the road ahead. The road levelled a bit as they entered the built-up area. A couple of stray dogs yelped and bolted as the truck raced past. In just a few heartbeats, the buildings and houses began to dwindle.

They were now heading roughly westward; the land sloped up to their right and down on the left with barely any vegetation, just more dirt and rocks.

"Pegue a estrada para a direita!" Benigno banged the top of the cabin and yelled down to Marco, waving to take the track to the right.

Ahead, the road forked, and a trail barely discernible and only marginally better than a goat track appeared.

"Are you sure, Ben?" Cataleya asked.

There was a lot of Portuguese going back and forth.

"Rhyll, what are they saying?" Dan asked.

"They'll expect us to stay on this road. It's better but longer. If we go right, it's shorter but bumpier ... By the time they realise, it will be too late. And he's counting on them not having studied a map like he has," she translated.

"Do it!" Cataleya confirmed loudly to Marco.

The pursuing car was hidden momentarily behind the village buildings, and that meant that the pursuers couldn't see then, either. The truck lurched to the right faster than advisable, but applying the brakes would activate the rear brake lights and possibly give their position away. Marco ground through the gears, preventing a stall as they chugged uphill.

In a few more seconds, they'd be over the hump and out of sight. He took it slowly once he was over the rise; the road was narrower, bumpier, and it was still dim. With judicial use of the gears and handbrake, he negotiated the sharp bends without incident.

Their goat track took them gradually up the barren slope.

"There they are," Cataleya pointed.

Below, they could see the taillights of the car moving farther away along the main road to the south.

"Boa ideia, Ben. Nice driving, Marco." Cataleya looked inside to check on Felipe and José. They appeared well enough.

Rhyll decided her rump wasn't going to take much more of the jolting, so she stood up, hanging onto the railing. The truck was rumbling along, but the speed felt too fast for the conditions.

Try as Marco might, the handbrake was no longer as effective. He was forced to stand on the brakes, so they didn't go off the road; there was a steep slope inches away, and it was a struggle to keep the speed down.

"That is no good!" Ileana pointed to the distant car. The brake lights of the other car were on; it was slowing. As Ben described, the other road was relatively straight.

"They probably realised that they should be seeing us by now," Rhyll deduced.

There was a pause for a few heartbeats before they saw it turn around, awkward with the road conditions but eventually successful. Now the headlights were facing their direction.

Cataleya called to Marcus, "Looks like they're onto us. May as well do what you can now."

The speed increased marginally and remained that way for several minutes until, finally, the sun rose above the mountain peaks. Now Marco could see much more of the road, enough to give him the confidence to drive faster.

Their trail levelled out, following the contour of the slope. A few tight bends appeared where centuries of erosion had created gullies. Hard braking and wrenching on the steering wheel kept them moving, but they were close enough to the edge for gravel and rocks to tumble down the slope.

The next bend in the opposite direction had them grabbing hold of whatever they could find. They could see the lights of the pursuit car, now on their trail.

"We have about 2 kilometres before we reach *Ruta Nacional* 16. Looks like we might make it," Cataleya judged.

As if on cue, the front wheel hit a deep rut, and the left tyre blew. The truck lurched towards the steep slope. Marco wrenched the steering wheel frantically to avoid the drop. He was successful, but ploughed the right hand side into the rising embankment.

The truck ground to a sudden and dusty halt. Dan and Nala, still sitting, and those in the back near the cabin, were thrown. Ileana, farther towards the rear, tumbled, falling heavily onto the boards.

She screamed in pain. Strangely, so did Rhyll, who was still standing and unscathed.

Concerned for both Ileana and Rhyll, Cataleya knelt beside her colleague while calling out for a report on everyone's condition.

Nala, Dan, and Benigno were slightly bruised, Felipe had struck his head but was okay. There was no change to Marco or José.

Dan and Nala stood to see what happened to Rhyll, but nothing was visible.

"What's wrong?" Nala asked.

Rhyll felt it all. When the pod crashed, she'd felt pain too, but she thought it was her injuries, only to realise later she had none; she was picking up the pain of others. She now recalled feeling it with her mother, but she'd put it down to the shock of seeing her throat sliced open.

"It's not me," she answered. The pain she felt now was in her left elbow. Reflexively, she moved her arm. *Nothing wrong.* She shuffled over to Ileana, helping Cataleya sit her up.

"I can deal with this." She surprised herself by saying it. "You've got soldiering to do."

Cataleya looked at her. "Are you sure?"

Rhyll nodded, then focused on Ileana. "I'm going to roll up your sleeve to look."

Ileana bobbed her head, gritting her teeth as her discoloured arm was revealed. "Cat, you need to go and stop them," she said.

After a pause, Cataleya called out, "Benigno, with me!" She grabbed her weapon and leapt off the truck, Benigno a second behind. They ran to the nearest rise.

Rhyll could sense Ileana's injury as well as her pain. More instinctively than anything else, she lay her palm over the swollen area and closed her eyes. In her mind, it was as if she could physically *see* the problem.

"It's not a break; more of a hairline fracture," she said. "But painful, nonetheless," she said in empathy.

Dan and Nala watched, astounded.

"How can she know that?" Dan muttered.

Nala nudged him to shut up.

Again, in her mind, she felt something ... Rhyll concentrated, inhaling and exhaling slowly and deeply. "Ileana, relax and match my breathing. Feel the rhythm."

It took several minutes for the soldier to match, having to override her pain as well.

With nothing else to do, Dan dropped off the back and ran around to assist Marco as he climbed out of the cabin, then they both helped José and, finally, Felipe.

"What is doing?" Felipe asked as they looked over the side into the back of the truck. Very little appeared to be happening; Rhyll was holding Ileana's arm.

Oblivious to her surroundings, Rhyll sensed Ileana's heart rate slow, beating in rhythm with hers; her breathing matched. In her mind, they were joined, subtly different from when she and Nala met the first time. The moment this equilibrium was reached, energy flowed.

Ileana gasped, not in pain but in surprised relief.

Cataleya dropped to the dirt just short of the crest and crawled the remaining couple of metres, with Benigno doing the same. They weren't staring into the sun, but the glare still posed a problem.

She checked her weapon as Benigno brought out his binoculars and sighted the dust trail. The car was a 2039 classic, and it would be a shame to damage it.

"They're still eight hundred and thirty-eight metres and closing. See that shoulder?"

"With the right-hand bend?"

"Si," he said, reverting to Portuguese. "That's three hundred and twenty-eight metres. They'll be there in about twenty seconds. Hit them there. If we're lucky, they'll go over."

"This isn't a sniper rifle."

"But you are our best shooter."

Cataleya aimed at a rock formation this side of the shoulder and fired one round. There was little wind to worry about. She zeroed her sight, set the rifle on auto and waited for the car as Benigno counted down.

"Eight seconds ... five, four, three, two ..."

The car came into view. She fired a burst. The spray took out the windshield, and the car veered and skewed across the gravel. A wheel must have struck an outcrop of rock or a deep pothole. It lurched onto its side and slid to a halt, smoke streaming from the engine.

She put a couple of bursts through the roof, then waited and watched.

Benigno aimed and put a burst through the bonnet. "Just in case."

"Cat, you ... you need to come and see this." They recognised Felipe's voice over the comm.

Benigno kept his eyes on the upturned car. "You go back and check; I'll wait to see if anyone still wants to play."

CHAPTER EIGHTEEN

Rhyll was sitting inside the truck, resting, a bottle of water in her hand.

When Cataleya returned, she saw them milling around the driver's door. Ileana was there, looking healthy. In fact, they all looked in good condition. Even José looked better.

"What's going on? Ileana, I thought you were injured."

"I was ... She fixed me."

"Fixed you? What did she fix? Splinters?"

"No. It was a fracture. It's still tender, but ..." Ileana moved her arm easily.

Cataleya turned to José. "You too?"

"I'm feeling better than before our flight."

"Rhyllien? You did this?" Cataleya studied Rhyll closely.

Rhyll didn't answer immediately, as if still coming to terms with what she had achieved. "Let's say I took part in it. There was ... something else. It was like I was a conduit ... something channelled through me." She struggled to find the right words. "Like this water bottle. It only provides the water because water was put in it. It didn't make the water."

As Cataleya was trying to work out what she'd said, they all heard weapon fire from Benigno. "What's happening, Ben?" Cataleya commed him.

"Still some movement. I think one or two got out before the car rolled, and they are using it as cover."

"Can you guys hear that?" Felipe grabbed his binoculars and climbed onto the back, then onto the roof. After sweeping the west he said, "I thought I heard a vehicle. There's the main road, Route 16. You can barely see it beyond that ridge."

"Are we all good to move then?" Cataleya looked around at everyone, who shrugged or nodded. "Grab your gear." She then spoke to Benigno. "We're close to the road and heading out."

"Coming." There was another burst of gunfire.

By the time he jogged back, they were ready to go. "We should be okay now."

"Famous last words." Dan trudged on, camera in his hands.

The trail sloped gradually down. There was a tight bend followed by a sharper descent, and the strip of black bitumen became visible.

"I keep look here. No one sneaks," Benigno offered at the crest of the steep descent. "No telling how long a vehicle comes."

He got comfortable and waited in a cleft of rocks as the remainder carefully negotiated the rough trail. It was less than forty metres, but no one wanted a snapped ankle.

They waited on the side of the road with little cover from the rising sun. Like most of the area, there was hardly any vegetation larger than weeds. The section of road they were on was a hairpin bend, so there was no issue of trying to flag down a speeding car.

"Reckon we'll be needing another truck or a bus," Cataleya said. "Nine of us is too much for a car."

"Several cars in a convoy?" Dan suggested.

"I don't like it, so only if desperate."

Several vehicles passed, but they were few and far between. All were old cars with several occupants. After about thirty minutes, an old bus appeared, blowing smoke as it came up the hill.

"I've had enough of this." Cataleya started waving it down.

The driver shook his head and was going to drive on until she fired a warning shot. Being in no position to avoid a bullet, he brought the bus to a halt.

"Gracias. Necesitamos usar este bus," she said. There were four locals in the back, asleep until the gunfire. "Relajarse. No te haremos daño."

"What's she saying?" Dan asked.

Rhyll had been quiet since leaving the truck, but with the rest, was more or less her old self. No one really wanted to talk about what she had done. *She* didn't want to talk about what she had done.

"She's thanking the driver, saying she needs to commandeer the bus, and no one will get hurt."

"It's going the wrong way, though," Dan said, pointing out the obvious.

"There's technique we use in Brazil. We call 'turning around'," Felipe said.

Nala punched Dan.

"You do that a lot." Dan rubbed his shoulder.

"Only when you deserve it."

The driver, with a bit of monetary encouragement, agreed to take them back. The passengers chose to get off, preferring the ten-kilometre walk home over the seventy-kilometre trip back to Escoma.

"Everyone, grab a ration pack for them," Cataleya ordered. "It's the least we can do."

Footsteps behind them made them turn, as Benigno shuffled at speed down the hill.

"Miss me?" he asked. "There's no one in sight back for a couple of hundred metres."

They coughed as the dust he'd brought with him enveloped them in the still air. Now was a good time to board the bus. Leaving the farmers as they trudged up the road, the bus completed a multi-point turn on the tight bend and headed back the way it had come.

"We'll see what we can do at Escoma."

Dan fished out his tablet, but there was no signal.

It was an uneventful and uncomfortable ninety-minute ride to Escoma. Even though it was mostly bitumen, the road wasn't well-maintained. They staggered off in relief with their gear, stretching their cramped muscles. The driver left without another word.

It was mid-morning, and the town was bustling with people going about their own business. Their dress here was less traditional-rustic and more modern-urban. Across the road was a small grocery shop and, blissfully, next door was a café.

With no need for encouragement, they traipsed across the road with their gear, settling down at the café, bringing several tables together inside by the window. It was marginally cooler inside, but they could still view the road to the northeast.

"Finally!" Dan exclaimed. "A signal."

Soon the table was full of drinks and hot food, and everyone's mood lifted a great deal. Felipe offered to go shopping to top up their supplies, so they relaxed in comfort. Marco and José went with him.

Rhyll had an appetite, far more than usual, and she was very grateful to Dan and his credchip.

"Got to look after our Incan queen."

Rhyll scowled, biting into a warm bread roll.

"Where to next, big mouth?" Nala kicked him under the table as a warning before he said something else stupid.

"Ahh ... well yes, Escoma." He rubbed his chin. "We're only a few kilometres from the shores of Lake Titicaca, but to get to where we're going ... it's still over two hundred and twenty kilometres to Juli by road."

"Juli?"

"The nearest town to where the gate's located, which is another twelve kilometres past that."

That dampened their spirits somewhat. After their time on

the bus, no one was looking forward to another four-hour drive on these roads.

Cataleya came back from using the shop's phone. "There's no answer back in Manaus. All the lines are dead."

"Blackout?" Dan opened his favourite news broadcast and listened for anything further. "Shouldn't affect phone towers, though."

"Either way, we're on our own, but we expected that. Mind you, we would've been there yesterday under different circumstances. Welcome to Brazil."

Rhyll came back with another plate of fried potatoes and beans. She gazed out the window as she chewed. "Why don't we get a boat?"

They followed her gaze, watching an SUV, trailer in tow, turning into the fuel station up the road .

"Anyone know how to drive a boat?" Cataleya asked.

"I can sail a yacht," Rhyll offered. "But I've only experienced small dinghies."

"More than us, I reckon. We'll be back." Cataleya and Ileana strode outside.

"Rhyll, you better scoff that lot down. I think we'll be leaving shortly," Benigno said. "I'll fetch the others."

"I'm going to the loo." Dan hopped up and disappeared down the back, leaving Nala and Rhyll with the gear.

Rhyll polished off her plate, then helped Nala take them back to the trolley. Back at the table, she kept an eye on the news. When the headlines of Manaus appeared, she turned up the volume so they could both listen.

"The illness that began three days ago has spread marginally, unlike the 'death-wave' sickness sweeping down from the north. Many areas of the city are blacked out due to rioting citizens. Roads from the north are clogged with citizens fleeing south, which now only exacerbates the problem in the city. Manaus Airport is jammed, airlines are putting on extra flights, and the river ports are swamped with passengers looking for ferries and boats.

"The GHO is yet to provide a statement other than they are doing what they can to slow and prevent the sickness."

"That doesn't sound good at all," Nala said. "I hope your mother is alright."

"I'm certain the sickness won't touch her." An uncomfortable feeling came over her. On a whim, she looked outside. "And that doesn't look good either."

A car had stopped across the road. Two burly men wearing sunglasses climbed out, and they definitely didn't look local — both were Caucasians with a military bearing. They looked at the shop, then up and down the road, talking to each other. Coming to a decision, they headed towards the café.

"Shit!" Nala said. "Grab the gear, and we'll head out the back."

Overloaded with all the packs, the girls staggered to the back door. One of the packs' straps caught on a chair, knocking it over with a clatter.

"Perdón." Rhyll apologised to the owner as she passed. "No nos viste." *You didn't see us.*

"What's happening?" Dan met them in the back corridor, confused.

"Trouble coming in the front door." Rhyll shoved a pack into his arms. "Move." She pushed him.

With the bulk of the packs scraping against the narrow wall, they slipped out the rear. Rhyll dropped a pack and caught the door before it banged shut, closing it slowly. She dared a glance inside, seeing the two men walk in.

As they were approaching the counter, one pointed to the table recently vacated and picked up a rectangular object.

Dan's tablet! "Shit, shit, shit!"

"What's wrong?" Dan looked back. "Ah. I see." He picked up the pack on the ground. "I got it." He followed Nala.

They ran awkwardly along the lane behind the shops until they could get to the street, sweating and breathing hard with the exertion.

"Rhyll, you stay here with the packs. They'll spot your hair a mile away. Dan, run across and tell Cat. I'll go into the shop and find Felipe and the others."

Leaving the packs, they split up.

Dan sprinted to the service station just as the SUV, boat still in tow, was pulling out, Ileana driving. Nala was already in the shop and out of sight.

Rhyll watched the café's front door in case the mercenaries came out. There was a split-second warning of impending doom. She instinctively ducked and stepped to the side as one grabbed for her hair from behind.

She regained her balance, moving backwards on the uneven footpath.

"Where are all your troublesome friends, little girl?" he said.

Rhyll didn't answer, but kept moving back. If he wanted to grab her, he'd have to come out onto the street to do so.

He hesitated, looking back along the lane.

Felipe reached around the corner, grabbed the man's hair, and pulled his head into the wall. And again, for good measure. He let the hair go, and the man collapsed over the backpacks.

There was the roar of a motor as Ileana raced across the road, screeching to a halt. "Hop in, quick."

Nala, José, and Marco, standing behind Felipe, all grabbed the packs and tossed them into the boat. Benigno and Felipe then climbed on, readying their rifles as Rhyll and the others found a seat in the car. Cataleya was in front with Ileana. Marco and José climbed into the back so Rhyll and Nala could share the back seat with Dan.

Ileana gunned the motor as the owner raced out onto the street yelling abuse and shaking his fists. The mercenary in the pursuing car didn't try to swerve. The car struck the pedestrian, sending him sprawling to the gutter.

"Which way?" Ileana called back.

"Oh. My tablet's in the packs," Dan answered.

Rhyll told him the bad news. "We left it in the café."

"We have to go back and get it!" he declared.

Cataleya rolled her eyes. "We'll get you another tablet."

"We have to turn back anyway," Nala said. "I saw the map too. There's a bridge over the river behind the town. We'll need to turn around to get there, unless you want a very long drive north."

They looked back at the sounds of gunshots. Benigno and Felipe were firing at the pursuing car.

Ileana braked hard, turning at the next street; the chasing car continued straight ahead, missing the turn. She turned again, now heading back the way they came, paralleling the main road.

"You have to admit," Rhyll spoke to Cataleya and Ileana, "it's my fault we left it behind. Having the tablet has been a great help to us. It provided news updates and helped us get out of Amarete. We wouldn't have known about that mountain trail if Dan didn't have it—"

The car came to a halt. "Hurry up, Daniel, or we'll leave you behind," Ileana warned.

Rhyll only then realised they were near the back of the café already.

Dan almost fell out in his rush and ran to the café's rear entrance, Benigno right behind him. Less than a minute later, they were returning, and Benigno jumped back into the boat.

"They killed the café owner," Dan said as he clambered inside.

"Bastardos!" Cataleya swore.

Dan activated the tablet. Ileana tapped the steering wheel and waited.

"Turn left next street." Dan studied the map. "No, make it right!" he added as he turned the tablet the right way.

All four wheels of the SUV churned gravel as it sped off, sliding around the next corner.

"When we get to the outskirts of town, this road will join another road to take us across the bridge."

"Maybe there's a boat ramp near the bridge?" Marcos suggested.

Dan shook his head. "Nothing here. The nearest access to the lake is Villa Puni … a small town … some farmland."

"Haven't you noticed yet? It's *all* farmland," Nala said.

They saw the main road and the lane joining the two. A quick veering to the left was followed by a bump, and they were on smoother bitumen again.

The bridge was a short way ahead. Once over, the road turned due west and straightened.

Dan continued giving directions. "In about a kilometre, the road will turn right, but I think there's a track going straight. That should then get us onto a dirt lane — a short-cut which heads directly to the lake."

Gunfire made them look back.

"Looks like our friends are back."

There was the distant sound of return gunfire and a few pings as bullets ricocheted off the panels. Rhyll, Nala, and Dan all ducked, knocking their heads.

"Here's that lane coming up. Hang on!" Ileana slowed at the last minute, seeing a large pothole. Even so, they were jarred. "And a gate!" It snapped open, flung to the side.

"Let's not lose the boat, Ileana," Cataleya cautioned.

"Don't lose the boat. Right, boss." She turned sharply right, then left, and the road straightened. The car fishtailed in the gravel, but Ileana managed to regain control. They could see the blue water ahead. "Everybody get ready to climb into the boat. Start passing the packs through the back window."

Marco and José lifted the back window on its gas struts. Felipe and Benigno were nowhere to be seen. José called out.

Felipe picked himself up off the floor, swearing, and looking worse for wear. It took a second for him to register what was happening, before calling his partner.

As Benigno continued to cover him, Felipe lowered his weapon and caught the packs as José tossed them over.

Everyone stopped and ducked when the firing started again. Benigno returned fire until all the packs were stowed. There was so much dust in their wake now, he decided to save their shots for a target they could see.

"Lake ahead. Everyone hang on."

"There's a boat ramp?" Marco asked.

"Of course there is. Why else would there be a road going directly to a lake?" Ileana retorted as she stopped. "Did you want me to slowly back the boat in?"

"No. I'm good."

"Everybody out. Boss, can you unstrap the boat? Don't want it to go down with the car."

Once everyone was inside the boat and the straps were laying on the ground, Ileana drove down the ramp straight into the water. As the water deepened, the SUV lost traction and drifted. The engine died as it slowly submerged, taking the trailer with it.

The boat drifted free, bobbing in the turbulence of the sinking vehicle.

While Rhyll was getting the boat started, Felipe and Benigno waited for their pursuers; everyone else was looking for Ileana.

"Here they come," Felipe warned. "Now would be a good time to start."

"Working on it." Rhyll thought hard. There was no key ... battery on, cooling system ... water pumps ... flick these, press that. In desperation, she touched the ignition with her fingers, and the engine burst to life with a rumble.

"There she is!" Nala pointed as Ileana surfaced, spluttering water.

"I thought safety belts were supposed to save lives," Ileana complained as Marco and José grabbed her arms, lifting her out of the water.

"Rhyll, wait!" Cataleya ordered. She straddled a back seat as she rested her rifle on the headrest and took aim. Felipe and Benigno wisely moved to the sides.

"This is for the café owner and the boat owner." She took into account the gentle rocking of the boat and fired two short bursts.

Both men went down.

"You can go now." She turned, making her weapon safe.

"Hang on, people," Rhyll warned as she slowly accelerated.

The engine roared, and the bow rose. They were away. "How far is it?" she shouted.

"About eighty kilometres!" Dan yelled back.

The group sorted out the packs and seating arrangements, having to share seats or risk bouncing over the sides.

"I hope we have enough fuel."

"Why do you think it took so long? We were waiting for the owner to fill the boat and an extra jerry can," Ileana called out over the noise.

The lake surface was relatively smooth, there being little wind, but even so, the small waves were enough to get the boat bumping rhythmically. Some found it soothing, but half an hour of bouncing over the waters revealed those who didn't.

"This is like Ileana's driving," Benigno joked to Felipe.

Nala was looking squeamish, and no matter what she did or how she lay, she couldn't get over the seasickness. They made sure she was at the rear, nearest to a side and as comfortable as possible.

Dan felt bad for her and was about to go and try to cheer her up.

Benigno shook his head. "Amigo, when you're throwing up, do you like someone sitting by your side and making conversation?"

"Hey, Dan," Rhyll called to him. "Come here and make yourself useful."

When he joined her, she showed him how to steer and use the throttle, then she handed it over to him, watching as he got the feel of it. "Remember, it steers from behind. Never do anything drastic. If you need to stop, pull this back gently; feel for the clicks." Satisfied after a minute of watching him, she climbed over the packs to join Nala, but instead of talking, she put her hands on her back as her friend heaved over the side.

Within a few minutes, Nala stopped throwing up; a short time later, she felt much better.

"I never want to be seasick again. It's awful." She hugged her friend. "Thank you so much."

Rhyll only wished she had rinsed her mouth out first.

There was no signal out on the lake, so Dan couldn't update the map. He pointed to where Juli was situated. "The gateway is about twelve kilometres north — a short distance inland from that cove. All I can remember is that it's on the west side of a main road."

Following his rough directions, Rhyll navigated the boat on a south-westerly course.

She shared the steering with the others, and it was a good distraction for Nala. By late afternoon, they were nearing the shore they hoped was the cove Dan mentioned.

"Head towards that north end of that shoreline. I think that distant rise could be what we're after."

When they got closer, they realised the shore was mostly mudbanks and swamp. Seeing the rooftops of a town, Rhyll throttled back and steered farther north, following the shoreline until they saw vegetation close to the water's edge. Seeing other moored boats was definitely a positive sign. She then navigated slowly towards the beach. When the hull scraped on the bottom, she revved the motor a bit more to ground it firmly before powering down.

The boat listed to one side. The soldiers jumped to the damp bank, and Cataleya and Ileana kept watch while Benigno and Felipe grabbed the packs as they were passed.

"Now we'll see if it's the right place," Dan said.

Feet firmly planted on the ground, Rhyll had her pack and was ready to go. "It is. I can feel it."

CHAPTER NINETEEN

Williams read through the report several times before his boss finally answered the comm.

"An update from our ICON contact, sir."

"I'm all ears," Tyrone replied.

"Firstly, we can confirm there is a leak — that's been rectified — and there are now several groups involved. Not ICON officially, but they're sponsoring their freelance covert operatives.

"Our boys have been in place for most of the day. I believe the pod took damage over the Andes and landed on the western foothills. Some freelancers spotted them, but we've had no updates for several hours now. It's presumed they were taken out."

"Who has this girl got helping her?"

"GHO has aided her and teamed her up with jungle specialists from the Brazilian Army."

"Are they any good? Do we know who they are? Maybe we can get to them through their families?"

"Can't say how good they are, but if they've taken out ICON freelancers, they can't be too bad. Mind you, they're not in the jungle anymore."

"Okay. Now then … our boys … what's happening there?"

"They're positioned overlooking this supposed 'gate' area. We've got eight men — two teams. Some are in the local town keeping an eye out, and the others are keeping watch on the gate itself."

"And the last we heard of the girl and these Brazilians was they were in the foothills of the Andes?"

"Correct, so they'll watch the roads north and south now that flying isn't happening."

The group stumbled through some bracken before a dirt track appeared. Cataleya and Ileana took point with Benigno and Felipe at the rear. After a few minutes, the track angled towards the sun, the town lying directly ahead. There was little on offer in Santiago Mucho, and it was close to sunset by the time they found accommodation in a rundown pensione.

There was the suggestion that they push on to the gate area, but Cataleya decided for them. "We still have dangerous people out looking for us. I'd be much more relaxed having a look at the terrain before wandering up there at night. We'll stay here and go for a look at dawn. Then we can see who else is out."

Dan asked, "Can't you use those night-vision goggles to see if anyone's out there?"

"And what if they have them too and are already in position, waiting for us to appear?"

Dan frowned at the obvious answer, and traipsed up the narrow stairs to the allocated rooms. They had to share, so all the women had one room, with the five guys in the other.

"But there are only four beds," Dan pointed out.

"Not a concern for you." Benigno patted his shoulder. "We'll be rotating watches; there is no telling who saw us come in here."

"You guys are real suspicious types."

"Suspicious? Nah. It's paranoia keeping us alert and you still alive." Felipe dumped his pack in a corner next to Benigno's and settled down to clean his weapon.

Dressed in wrinkled civvies, Cataleya and Ileana joined Nala, Marcos, and José for a stroll to see who was around.

"What about Rhyll and me?" Dan asked.

"Your white skin doesn't blend well — and definitely not Rhyllien's red curls. We, on the other hand, are natives. Few will pay us any attention. We shouldn't be long. I can't see this village having much of a nightlife."

Felipe and Benigno tossed for first watch.

"I'll see you in a couple hours." Benigno slapped Felipe on the shoulder and found a comfortable bed.

Felipe finished cleaning his weapon and checked his pistol and dagger were holstered and ready before he stepped outside. He found a shadowy position on the balcony and got comfortable.

Dan thought it was uncanny how these guys could blend in so well, though perhaps not against others kitted with the ninox goggles. He was now reluctant to step onto the balcony, so instead, he slumped on the ragged lounge and pulled out his tablet.

There was some signal here, but it was very slow to update anything.

Rhyll came through to join him after having a quick wash. "Much happening?"

He showed her the tablet, complaining how slow it was. "That was nice what you did for Nala, stopping her seasickness."

Rhyll shrugged. "I wasn't sick at all, but I did feel her discomfort, so it helped me too."

"Do you still doubt there's something about you? You get premonitions when we're in danger—"

"Not all the time."

"When it counts; you sense when people are unwell. You *heal* injuries for crying out loud. And when your feet touch the ground, hey presto, 'I know where we need to go'."

"I still don't know what I have to do." She flicked through an old magazine on the rickety coffee table, and a tourist brochure fell out. 'Hayu Marca'. Rhyll picked it up to glance through it.

Other than the info she'd heard and read dozens of times, the brochure did have some interesting photos, both from ground level and drone shots. It also listed tour dates.

"What day is it?" Rhyll flicked him the brochure.

"Twenty-sixth of October. Friday. Why?"

"There are tours to Hayu Marca on the weekends, at 10:00am and 2:00pm."

"Sounds very convenient." Dan scanned the pages.

"I'm thinking of cutting my hair," she said out of the blue.

"What? Why?" Dan stopped reading.

"Well, as Cat said, it does kind of stand out." She ran her fingers through her long, curly locks to work out some knots.

"Just a bit. At least, here in Brazil. I reckon it'd be okay in Ireland or somewhere in the UK."

"Which we aren't, and I can't see happening. I still haven't got a passport. I thought Mum had organised one, but the stuff Pacha handed me before we left didn't have one in it."

"You know passports these days are all bio-chips embedded in our hands? The heel of the thumb. Feel this."

"Bio-chips?"

"Biometric chips. Here." He put his right hand out for her, her fingers feeling the hard, square chip embedded in the fleshy heel of his thumb.

"Better check those locker items again. Easy to miss if you didn't know what to look for," Dan suggested. "It's about the size of a SIM or a postage stamp."

Rhyll went off to her room, emerging shortly with a small chip. "Is this it?"

Dan nodded. "Sure is. Looks undamaged."

"Got a knife?"

"What? You're kidding!"

"Isn't it simply slipped under the skin?"

"Sure, I believe so. It's not like it's wet-wired to your brain or anything."

"I can heal it afterwards. Show me yours again." She held his hand, feeling for the chip placement.

"Let's check it online first. You don't want to be putting it in upside down or back to front." Dan sat down again and tapped at the keypad, then waited for it to load.

Eventually, several pages were found. "Look here." He pointed. "See how it's placed? Also recommended to be inserted by a qualified medical practitioner."

Rhyll compared her chip to what she was seeing, turning it around to match. "You sound like a grandmother. It looks straightforward enough." Coming to a decision, she went out onto the balcony to speak to Felipe.

"I have a favour to ask." Then she went on to explain what she wanted.

"I think you should wait for Cat. She will skin me alive if you are hurt."

"You've seen what I can do. You know I'll heal it as soon as it's done." She cajoled and badgered him until he relented. "We might not get another chance."

"You are a strange *chica*, Rhyllien. But before we do this, can you tell me the area is clear?"

Rhyll closed her eyes and concentrated. There was no feeling of impending doom. "There are two stray dogs in the alley across the road, a cat on a roof two houses up on the right, and several people, but they are all in their houses. The others are nowhere near here, so you won't get caught."

"I will get my razor and first-aid kit." He slipped through the door.

In five minutes, they were ready. Rhyll massaged her hand. As there weren't any towels, she had a length of toilet paper by her side. The chip was cleaned with antiseptic.

Dan sat opposite, not daring to say anything but prepared to assist if need be.

"Are you ready?" Felipe asked.

"Are you?" Rhyll nodded, and relaxed her mind.

Felipe got her to rest her hand on the table, then sprayed antiseptic over the area as well as his fingers and the razor. He had watched his own passport being inserted but checked the images on the tablet for the precise area and depth.

Satisfied, he pinched the flesh in a deft but firm action, slicing the heel of the thumb with a precise cut.

Blood flowed freely, and Rhyll inhaled deeply. "All good. Keep going."

With a pair of tweezers, the soldier peeled back the skin and gently placed the chip as depicted on screen, then he folded the skin flap down.

"Done."

Applying pressure, Rhyll put a swab of the paper over the area to soak up the blood until the bleeding stopped. As she did for the others, she relaxed again, breathing deeply and rhythmically. She felt the heat in her hand build before it went numb.

After five minutes, she opened her eyes and removed the damp paper. The skin was slightly red, but there was barely a scar.

"Good job. Thank you, Felipe." Unexpectedly, she gave him a quick hug. "I'll wash my hands." She picked up the remaining sheets of paper and disappeared into the bathroom.

Felipe cleaned his razor and packed his first-aid kit. "We not just shoot people." He gave Dan a wink and was back on watch two minutes later.

Feeling a bit squeamish, Dan removed the web search history for the last half-hour.

When Rhyll returned, she had a plate of whatever she could find to eat. "You know, I should have asked Felipe to cut my hair, too."

"Maybe there's a hairdresser in town?"

"Not an option if Cat wants me to keep a low profile." Rhyll filled her mouth and chewed before continuing. "I think if the girls got their knives out, we could make considerable changes.

It's not as if we're socialites or going out to fancy restaurants. I've seen hairstyles that looked chopped."

"True. But those women paid hundreds of dollars for that look."

"Then I can get it for free. What do you think?"

"Sure. I mean, I like it the way it is, but I guess you're right. Pretty pointless these guys blending into the shadows and doing ninja shit, with you and your high-vis hair."

"I'll ask them when they get back."

"Good idea." Dan was tapping at the tablet. "You going to tell them about the passport?"

"If it comes up in conversation, but Felipe had nothing to do with it. Okay?"

"Fine by me. How's your hand now?"

She wriggled her thumb around with full motion. "It looks the same and feels just like yours."

Dan rubbed his fingers over the area. "I admit I was worried, but that's amazing."

The group returned about thirty minutes later in a good mood. "We found ice cream."

Ileana and Nala had a spare one for each of them, even Felipe.

"We found some brochures, too. Cat has worked out a plan for tomorrow." Nala fished the folded paper from her back pocket.

"Snap." Rhyll showed them her identical brochure. "What's the plan?"

Cataleya knelt on the floor and laid out the brochure for all to see on the rickety table. "Before dawn, while it's still dark, Ileana and the boys will head a bit up the road to the north and approach the gate through here." She pointed at the aerial shot of the Hayu Marca area. The long hill had straight ridges of rock outcroppings, some barely a few metres in height, others much higher, judging from the length of their shadows.

"We saw a couple of upmarket SUVs parked in town — not what you'd expect in this sort of village — so we fully expect the area is being watched. Our people will use the western ridge to cover their approach as they move south. I'm betting they'll find spotters here, here, and possibly here." Cataleya pointed to three locations overlooking the gate. "It's where I'd be to keep an eye on the approaches to the gate. We'll book the 10:00am tour. Marco and José will remain behind here. There is no point putting more in possible danger."

"What about me?" Dan was licking his ice cream. "With my white skin and all?"

"It's for tourists, so you shouldn't raise suspicions in this instance. Just take pictures as you normally do."

"And if they find those people watching?" Rhyll asked.

"Watch and wait. We won't start trouble, but we will be in a position to stop it before it gets out of hand. Having said that, you are our priority. If push comes to shove, we'll take them out. So, myself, Rhyll, Nala, and Dan will be the tourists. After that, we'll need to see how the tour goes before Rhyll can try the disc."

Since everyone was sitting around in the cramped guest lounge, Rhyll took the opportunity to speak to them.

"Firstly, I need to thank you all for risking your lives to do this." She put her hand up to stop them butting in. "I know you're following Pacha's orders, but thanks all the same. Next, why are we here, and what am I doing? I have only a vague idea, to be honest, but I do have something to show you." She put her hand in her pocket. "Are you aware of my parents' work?"

"Weren't they archaeologists?" Ileana offered.

"I heard relic hunters," Benigno answered.

Rhyll nodded and continued. "More or less true, but dedicated and very good at what they did. My father, in particular, had been very interested in ancient cultures predating the Incans by thousands of years — something referred to as a mother culture. Finding it would explain how other cultures on different continents with no way of meeting or communicating could have so many similarities. He found this." Rhyll took the sun-disc out of her pocket and placed it on the low coffee table.

"That's the disc I heard about?" José asked. "I've seen those in tourist traps in the markets".

"I'm sure. However, not this one. This one, current analysis says, is over three thousand years old."

"Surely, it is wrong?" Benigno picked the disc up, flipping it over to study both sides, then passed it to Marco.

"If it's wrong, then so is every other dating analysis on every other artefact this century. We have good reason to believe this disc is the one used by Amaru Muru. Tomorrow," she continued over the excited talk, "when we get to the gate, we'll see if it works or not. If it works ... well, the myth says I'll disappear, but to where I don't know. No one has seen Amaru Muru since; if it fails, this will be all for nothing, and I'll be suitably embarrassed, holding an old piece of metal."

"And we'll probably have a few pissed-off tour guides," Dan added.

"How do we convince whoever else is out there they're wasting their time?" Benigno asked. "Other than shooting them?"

"Easy. They'll see nothing happens and realise it for themselves," Ileana stated.

"I can't say if it will work or not, but we have our duties." Cataleya continued, "You'll all note though, what Rhyll has been able to do these last couple of days has been awesome as well as very unusual. We will follow Major Pachacutec Bocaiúva's orders and give Rhyllien — and her father — the benefit of the doubt."

All agreed wholeheartedly. Ileana handed the sun-disc to Cataleya, who barely looked at it before giving it back to Rhyll. "It doesn't matter what I think of it."

"Thank you." Rhyll wiped her eyes. "Now, who wants to cut my hair?"

They boarded the bus with half a dozen other tourists. A couple were supposed to be pilgrims to the Temple of the Seven Rays, and each was wearing a triangular medallion.

Cataleya couldn't conceal her rifle, so she had to rely on her pistol, knives, and good intel. She made sure her team were in place well before joining the tour. As expected, they reported two pairs of spotters in more or less the positions she'd determined.

"They've got eyes on the road and the approach to the gate area. Nothing will happen without us knowing it first, though. When we get off the bus, stay in the middle of the group and act natural — be amazed at what they say and do. Dan, you'll just nod and take pictures."

"He does that anyway." Rhyll lightened up the group, hiding her nervousness. "Thanks for this spare commlink."

"No problemo, *chica*. Seems pointless my three hogging them when they'll be close to each other. What do you think of your hair now?" She raised her voice over the engine sound as the bus moved off.

"I don't know. I haven't had hair this short since ... well, forever. It'll take time to get used to it."

"Hair and our attitude to it is such a silly thing, really, but it did stand out. I'm glad you asked for it to be cut."

The bus bumped on its way; if there was any suspension on the bus, it needed a severe overhaul. In a couple of hundred metres, they would turn onto the road that passed the pathway to the gate.

"Is that one of the SUVs you saw last night?" Dan pointed.

A short distance south of the turn-off, a dark car was parked to the side of the road.

Cataleya nodded. "Ileana says they both drove off after sunrise. The other one dropped off the four men and then drove around the hill to head north. I reckon they're watching the roads from both directions."

Dan hung on as the bus turned. "We could have walked this!"

As they turned, the tinted windows prevented them from seeing if anyone in the SUV was watching. Now the road was dirt, the bumps really started. Thankfully, it was only for a few hundred metres.

With grinding gears and squealing brakes, the torture trap of a bus pulled up on the side of the road. As per Cataleya's instructions, when the group disembarked, they made sure they weren't first or last out.

The girls could speak the local language and made polite small talk with fellow tourists as if they were all together. They were directed up the ill-kept path, where one could easily roll an ankle if not careful.

After a few strides, there was a dilapidated hut where they sold postcards and cheap knickknacks. Dan was happy to walk past, but the girls were fussing over some of the items.

"Seriously?" he said, coming over.

"We need to buy some incense; it's the done thing, according to those two pilgrims. To appease the gods. It might give us an excuse to get really close to the gate, too."

Dan put his hand out for them to scan his credchip, but they only wanted cash. Muttering under his breath, he dug out a couple of GCees.

"Muchas gracias," the old vendor called.

Soon they were in front of the area known as Gate of the Gods, following directions and overhearing the other conversations.

"We're to sit down here"—Rhyll pointed—"and the ceremony will start in a couple of minutes. After it's finished, around a quarter of an hour later, we take turns lighting the incense by the flame they'll be using for their ritual, and then we take it to that niche, the doorway. We can pray if we want."

"And that will be your cue to try the disc, I gather?" Dan asked quietly.

"Couldn't have asked for an easier opportunity." She made herself comfortable, or tried to, on the slabs of rock laid in the area, fending off thoughts that they were being watched by armed men. Nala sat on one side and Cataleya the other, leaving Dan to wander around and take photos.

Shortly after, the ritual began.

Though he'd be the first to admit he needed rugged equipment for some of his trips, his camera was his pride and joy, and it was top-of-the-line. The built-in telephoto capability was something he had found very useful more than once.

In his meandering around the group, he endeavoured to focus on the areas Cataleya indicated would be lookout areas; he'd be across the ritual looking north, on his knees, pretending to film the priest's actions, but he'd be zooming in on the heads just above the rocks. Even so, it was still too far to get much detail.

He'd come back and sit, and they'd go through the photos like tourists, but really they would be checking their enemy. At the very least, it did prove they were there and armed.

When the panpipes started, one of the two pilgrims got up to start the incense burning. They wafted the incense within the alcove while praying, getting on their knees and putting their forehead to the ground. The next person then rose, making a coughing noise to move them on. They took the hint, noticing the line-up.

Soon it was Rhyll's turn. All three of them stood, lit their sticks, and wandered closer in reverence. Again flanked by Nala and Cataleya, Rhyll put her hand in her pocket and pulled out the disc, keeping her fingers wrapped around it.

The irregularly cut door was just over her head, the sides slightly angled. Part of the natural rock curved up to the base of the door, and quite clearly there was a depression where the myth said the disc went. The most impressive thing about the whole doorway was the ten-metre-square flat surface sheared off the original rock formation to create the wall for the door.

Rhyll climbed up the steep lip and now stood in front of the alcove. She heard Nala and Cataleya behind her, and the clicking of Dan's camera to her left. Slowly fanning the incense with one hand, she moved her other hand to place the disc in the depression.

She heard a faint metallic sound. She waited, but nothing happened. In her disappointed panic, she dropped the disc, making a loud clang. Quickly, she picked it up, deciding to try again but inserting the other side. She heard a call behind her; the guide was enquiring what she was doing.

There was a bright blue light, and everything around her slowed and expanded like in one of those trick movie scenes.

"Fu—" Cat's voice faded to nothing. All sound stopped as she sensed herself floating away, up and back towards the lake. In her hand, the disc glowed.

Below her now, she saw everyone staring at the alcove where she had been moments before. It was now vacant. Looking north, she saw the watchers — some were standing and pointing, and some had their weapons raised.

"Cat?" She remembered the comm, but it didn't work. *Dead.*

The road, then the town, passed below her to the north. With the mere thought, she was now facing the lake, heading directly east into the sun. Over the water, at a height of what must be two hundred metres, she thought she saw their boat, still beached. Her speed increased.

In the far distance, the Andes reared up with a touch of snow on the highest peaks, though most of it was the grey-brown of millennia-weathered rock. Directly ahead was the Isla del Sol — Island of the Sun. One of her father's notes quoted the myth that the ruins there were the birthplace of the Incans and where the *Templo del Sol* — Temple of the Sun — was situated.

Stands to reason, she thought, *considering the namesake of the island.*

As her form flew closer to the island, she began to descend sharply. At this rate, she'd be in the water soon. Heartbeats later, she plummeted into the icy, cobalt-blue depths of the freshwater lake … and didn't feel a thing.

It was like she was scuba-diving without any gear; she could see the depths clearly, but nothing affected her. She recalled reading about archaeological digs discovering ruins within the lake. These ruins even preceded the Tiwanaku, who were here a thousand years before the Incans.

The lakebed, strewn with megalithic blocks and large paved areas, rose to meet her. She went into and through the ground, emerging into a vast cavern. There were no crystal columns here. Where it wasn't natural rock, the walls were large, carved stone — similar to what they found on the lakebed and a dozen other ancient sites. The cavern roof arched high overhead, covered in glowing moss similar to schistostega, and fungi, in clumps, covered the floor.

Her body slowed and gently landed on an expansive, flat, paved area. The paving was so precise not even a razor could fit between the slabs. Large statues of animals surrounded the perimeter of the paving. Water gushed out of a serpent's head carved directly out of the bedrock, spilling into a trough that flowed through the cavern to the far side.

In the centre, close to where she now stood, was the one crystal formation — a bed similar to the crystal bed on which she'd woken, naked, less than a week ago. The smooth body-shaped depression was there, but there was only one niche for a coloured crystal, about where her navel would be.

This was where the orange diamond should be placed; the sacral chakra. She took off her backpack and searched for the orange diamond. With a deep breath, she placed it in the niche.

Nothing happened. As she had with the disc, she tried moving it around, thinking maybe a different facet might do something. Then she remembered the rune or glyph carved into it. She rotated and slipped it in. Other than the faintest of snicks, little else occurred.

"Maybe it takes a bit of time?" she muttered.

Mesmerised by the magnificence — she was truly the daughter of archaeologists — Rhyll wandered around, exploring and touching everything. It suddenly came upon her that she was corporeal again, feeling the textures of the rock carvings and the mixture of cool, crisp and slightly stale air.

Coming back to the crystal bed, she noticed there appeared to still be no change in its glow. She knew her father's notes made no mention of any of this. Now the excitement of being in this unknown and astounding cavern faded; the next step was obvious. She guessed part of her mind shied away from this step, not wanting a repeat of her thirty-five-year slumber.

Rhyll took off her shoes and clothes, folded them on her pack on the floor, and climbed onto the crystal bed, positioning herself within the contoured depression, fitting perfectly.

Slowly the platform began to glow and gently pulsate. An urge to close her eyes came over her. She fought it, but eventually, her lids slid shut, and she was aware only of a pulsing light beyond them. She did not sleep, but many visions, possibly instructions, flowed through her mind. Time was needed to assimilate all that she had experienced.

EPILOGUE

"Fuck!" Cataleya raced forward, more from instinct — there was no sign of Rhyll at all nor the sun-disc — than from concern about the sudden disappearance of the girl. Wasn't this what they'd been expecting?

Nala cried out in shock. The tour group screamed at the sudden flaring light. The two pilgrims dropped to their knees despite the gravel, starting a tumultuous wailing and chanting.

"Boss, those men are on the move, fast ... Cat?"

"Take them out." Cataleya had no time to respond to the disappearance of Rhyll. Part of her wanted this to happen — to prove there was something to all this — and part of her mind, despite everything she saw the girl do, denied the possibility.

Right now, though, she had armed men moving in on her position, and she still had Nala and Dan to protect.

Gunfire broke her from her thoughts. "You two, with me now!" she called to Nala and Dan.

Too captivated with the suddenly empty gateway, Dan needed to be pushed.

Stumbling over the rough terrain, they made it to the trail and bolted towards the bus, more for cover than anything else.

They heard the growl of a motor; the SUV from the main road was bearing down on them, trailing a huge cloud of dust.

Cataleya saw a window opening, and a gun barrel protruded. "Get behind the hut!"

No sooner did they deviate course than they heard the rat-a-tat of a submachine gun. The ground erupted as it was riddled with bullets ricocheting off rocks and pavers.

Panting hard, they made it to the shelter. Turning at the last instant to avoid smashing his camera, Dan almost dislocated his shoulder when he staggered into the stone wall. Cataleya returned fire with her pistol. Her shots were echoed by other gunfire up the hill. During the intervals between gunfire, she heard the other tourists screaming and crying.

"Stay here!" she ordered. When the car braked, the trailing cloud of dust enveloped the vehicle as she'd hoped it would. She had a few seconds to sprint to the bus before they would have a clear visual of the area.

Cataleya skidded to a halt with the bus as cover and watched to see what the men would do next. From their actions, it didn't look like they had spotted her. It was dim inside the car with its tinting, but the barrel was still out towards the hut.

She was uncertain whether she could sneak up the side of the bus before they realised she was there. She activated her comm. "Progress report."

"We winged one. Got both groups pinned near where they were," she heard Ileana. "How about you?"

"I'm at the bus. I'm thinking of sneaking around to take out the car."

"Wait out."

After a pause, a spray of bullets took out the gun-toting passenger. The car accelerated to move behind the bus for protection.

Cataleya reached around, took aim, and fired, hitting the driver in the chest.

She turned to the hut. "Come on!" she shouted, waving at them to move.

Nala and Dan ran down the path to the roadside. By the time they arrived, Cataleya had dragged the two men onto the opposite roadside. She was going through their pockets: some cash, no ID, spare clips, and the submachine gun might come in handy. Getting their commlink was a boon.

"We'll get in the back," Dan said, noting the blood on the front seat.

Cataleya hopped into the still-warm driver's seat and placed the reloaded sub on the passenger seat. Luckily, the windscreen only had the one bullet hole and hadn't shattered. She sat there for a moment, listening in on their comms. Those up top weren't enjoying themselves; the other car was coming down the back road on the west side of the hill from the north where they'd been watching the first approach.

Muting their link and activating hers, she called in. "Thanks, Il. I've got their car. The other SUV is coming down the west road. I might surprise them. Get down to the west road, but keep an eye out for it, just in case."

"See you in five."

"You two in back. Get down low and hang on tight." She gunned the motor and raced for the next right turn.

As she approached, the other car had started to slow for the bend. Hoping her interior to them was as dim as their interior to her, she powered her window down and reached for the submachine gun.

Taking them completely unaware, she peppered the car with a spray of bullets as they passed. In the mirror, she saw it roll off the road, missing the turn. No brakes were applied as it careened into the field. She was unsure if it was smoke or steam issuing from the engine.

"There they are," Nala called out, pointing to the slope of the hill.

Cataleya slowed and waited, an eye on her three people and one on the rear-view mirror. Felipe was limping, and Benigno had a bleeding face.

"What's up?"

"Felipe jumps like a boy." Ileana helped him into the back seat, while Benigno made his way to the other side. Nala and Dan climbed into the baggage area and squished down among the bags there.

Benigno climbed in next to Felipe. "I took some rock chips."

Ileana grimaced when she had to sit in the blood of the previous passenger.

"The fruits of *your* labour, *chica*." Cataleya laughed, then gave them a rundown on the situation as she sped north. "The other car's out of it, I reckon. We'll collect Marco and José and get out of town."

"Where's Rhyll?" Ileana asked, looking back to Dan and Nala. "Anyone?"

They shook their heads in silence.

The pilots were relieved to see them return. "We heard the gunfire—"

"And you naturally thought we were kicking ass?" Felipe finished for Marco.

"Yeah. Something like that." He nodded with a half-smile.

"Where's the redhead? Rhyllien?"

"Vanished in a flash of blue light."

The pilots stared.

"We shit you not. She's gone." Felipe shrugged.

"Do we wait here for her?" José asked.

All eyes turned to Cataleya. She was listening in on the other's comms. She looked up.

"Shit, no! We've still got at least four shooters out there. They don't sound happy, and this town isn't big enough for the twelve of us — including non-combatants. La Paz is our next stop, three hours away. We got barracks there — not that they're expecting us. Fun as it's been, we can drop José and Marco off and let them do what they do best."

Nala gave Dan a warning look.

What? he mouthed with an innocent smile

"Let's grab our gear." She dragged him away. "You know you were going to say 'crashing pods is what they do best'," she whispered.

Ileana and Benigno came in with the shooters' bags. "Might be something here of use." They dumped the two large duffel bags on the loungeroom floor.

While they rummaged through the bags, each took turns in the sole, pokey bathroom to quickly wash and prepare for the road trip.

Within half an hour of Rhyllien's disappearance, they were piled into the SUV and making tracks south.

Relieved at not being chased, they stopped frequently to stretch, swapping driving duties and generally trying to be as comfortable as they could for the trip.

"Everyone, shut up!" Cataleya was trying to listen on her comms. She bumped up the volume as everyone quietened.

"Rhyllien? Holy shit. Where are you?" She waved them to shut up again as they started asking questions.

"You're where? Copacabana?"

Dan quickly searched his tablet, cursing at the lag.

Ileana used the Nav in the dashboard. "Got it," she said, giving Dan the bird when he looked up, then grinned at him. "Too slow, puta."

Everyone was on edge, hating hearing half a conversation.

She took her headset off. "Our *chica* is on her way to Copacabana by speedboat."

"How the hell did that happen?"

"She'll explain it all to us when we catch up."

Ileana made a U-turn. "The turn-off is about fifteen minutes back up the road. We're only fifty clicks away."

"That's great." Dan beamed, nodding his head. "I've always wanted to go to Copacabana."

"You are an idiot." Nala punched his shoulder. "It isn't *that* Copacabana."

THE END

Continued in Book 2

ACKNOWLEDGMENTS

I'd like to send a huge thank you to both:

Belinda Crawford who created the covers; https://designedbyboots.com , &

Noel Osualdini for his excellent editorial assistance.

I would also like to acknowledge the work of Wayne Herschel from the Hidden Record website who allowed his image of the sun disc to be used for the front cover of RELIC.

The Inca gold disc is the most researched and reconstructed by author
Wayne Herschel of the lost Inti Sun disc that once resided in Coricahcha Cuzco Peru.

My original beta-reader crew: Peter J Aldin, Stephen Kerwin, Aaron Cordy, and a big welcome to Karl Martin, Heather Stone, Doug Switzer and Scott Burnard for all perseverance and politely pointing out my failings.

And finally but most importantly, my wife Morag for putting up with my absent-minded rantings, and all my friends. I'm slowly learning what that glazed stare means.

ABOUT THE AUTHOR

Andre Jones was born in Wollongong, NSW Australia and currently resides in Melbourne with his very understanding Scottish wife, a British Shorthair cat, and more recently, a Jack Russell Terrier pup.

As a child he devoured the works of Enid Blyton, Tolkien, McCAffrey, Asimov, Heinlein and Bradbury just to name a few. As a young adult, he got lost in the many and varied roleplaying games, including MERP, GURPS, Harn, Skyrealms of Jorune, good old D&D *(and its many variants)* and Traveller … and spent far too much time on video games like Skyrim.

He wore many hats including; Security Officer, Police Officer, Park Ranger and finally as a Petty Officer in the Royal Australian Navy for 18 years *(sadly, his role-playing stopped there for too long)*.

As a Navy Veteran, his retirement has provided the opportunity to write, roleplay, draw and potter to his heart's content.

ALSO BY ANDRE JONES

Death Wave Chronicles

RELIC

DRUID

SPHYNX

Seven Portals Series

City of Bridges

Shadow of the Tower

Ripples in Time

Please consider subscribing to my website … I even send out newsletters now and then.

https://www.andrejonesauthor.site